THE FINAL WAVE

The Final Wave

A Terrorism Techno-Thriller

Fred G. Baker

Other Voices Press
Golden, Colorado

Published by Other Voices Press, Golden, Colorado
ISBN 978-1-949336-24-5 paperback
ISBN 978-1-949336-25-2 e-book

Cover design by Nick Zelinger, nz graphics
All rights reserved by Fred G. Baker.

Printed in the United States.

Acknowledgments

I would like to thank the following people for their aid and support in the writing and production of this book:

Dr. Hannah Pavlik, for her support and encouragement.
Jennifer Bisbing, for her editorial assistance.
Donna Zimmerman, for her word processing and interior design contributions.
Nick Zelinger, for the cover design.
My beta readers, who provided helpful comments and ideas.

Prologue

Over two hundred and thirty million people had died from COVID-19 as the world entered its third year of the dreaded pandemic. As economies shattered, people everywhere searched for the means to survive as savings ran out, jobs vanished, and lives descended into misery.

Lockdowns became the rule of most governments as the means to control the virus's spread through different populations. Many governments and companies worked furiously to produce a vaccine that could stop the monster plague. The wily virus seemed nearly contained when new variants appeared that were more easily transmissible and more deadly, making the much-anticipated vaccine largely ineffective. Exhausted scientists tried to create a new vaccine, but the variants required revamping their approach and beginning anew. Estimates predicted that they would have an improved vaccine by mid-2023 and could mass-produce it by late that year.

But no one was confident that it would work.

Politicians stirred up fears that the first vaccine had been rushed and that the new one would be just as ineffective. Fear and chaos rose to the surface as hate-mongers and those who sought to gain power whipped up mobs around the world.

Mob rule took over in many major cities as special-interest groups overwhelmed city and state governments. Even in Europe, until now a relative bastion of calm and order, major cities succumbed to chaos. Anti-government forces rose to occupy city centers as weak leaders dodged their responsibilities and failed to resolve the crisis.

With no clear plan to alleviate any problems that had beset the people, revolution was in the air. Opportunists reigned in open opposition to elected government officials, in some places superseding them and ruling by self-appointed committee or personality or ideology. Islamic caliphates were declared in Turkey, Paris, and Berlin as immigrants overwhelmed the cities.

And many nation-states that had waited for an opportunity seized the chance to take what they had always craved: land, resources, and power. Russia annexed Belarus on their western border and invaded the Baltics—Estonia, Latvia, and Lithuania—weakened neighbors that Vladimir Putin had always desired. Iran expanded its proxy wars and essentially annexed Syria and Lebanon to their sphere. Having broken all agreements and trust, China brought Hong Kong to heel in 2020 and annexed much of the South China Sea to its homeland waters. Then overbearing China began an aerial attack on Taiwan as it prepared for invasion to bring the wayward island into their web of Communism with Chinese characteristics and settle an old score against the nationalists. The power of the red Communist star was rising as other countries were enmeshed in economic crises and social disorder. No nation stood in China's path to world domination.

In America, where government had failed, the people had begun to rise up and reclaim their neighborhoods from the roving gangs that were marauding their lives and stole their peace. No city was more torn by violence than Chicago, Illinois—the Second City, a commercial hub of the heartland and a place where men still had the will to fight back against the darkness that had swept the land.

Chapter 1

Monday, March 13, 2023

On the Atlantic Ocean, Just East of Washington, DC

The ship rolled rudely from side to side in the rough Atlantic waters, waves slapping against the bow, throwing spray across the deck of the freighter in the darkness. Each time the shower of salty seawater shot over the railing, Muhammed pulled the hood of his windbreaker forward to deflect the flow from his face. The timing was such that his face was inundated about every fourth time the ship rolled. He couldn't prevent the spray from shooting down his neck with his hands primarily occupied with holding the cable under tension.

"Pull harder, you fool, or this will take all night," Captain Khadem of the Iranian Quds Force snarled in Arabic instead of his native Farsi. He torqued the long wrench. "There . . . maybe that is done. Praise be to Allah." He used the wrench to tighten the cable that held the forty-foot-long sea container in place on the surging deck.

"Good. We can go inside out of this hellish weather. I'm soaked through to my undergarments." Muhammed released his grip on the cable and stood fully upright just as an enormous volume of water shot over the bow. The force nearly knocked him off his feet.

"No, my friend," the captain said. "Now we must check that the other cables are tight. We cannot have our precious cargo shift on these rough waves. It could lead to trouble tomorrow when we arrive."

Muhammed tried to wring seawater from the sleeve of his sweatshirt. "Allah is asking much of us to endure this weather as we carry out his will. I would rather ride a camel across the desert for ten days with no food than fight this devilish sea."

He wiped water from his dark face and beard as he followed Khadem to the next tie-down of the container. Cold and wet, he wished they would finish so he could go below deck and have some tea to calm his stomach. Suddenly, bile rose in his mouth, and he bent over to purge himself again on the water-washed deck.

Khadem turned toward him and laughed. "Allah is testing us in many ways on this voyage of destiny. Not only must we endure this unrelenting sea, but we must work closely with this damn cargo that makes us ill." He placed a hand on Muhammed's shoulder as the man pitifully wretched pink foam onto the deck. "Come, we must finish while we have the strength."

They scuttled to the next cable and found it tight, holding the container securely. They moved to the final cable, and Khadem applied the wrench to turn the buckle for a quarter-turn as Muhammed struggled to tighten the line.

"There. I think we're done for tonight. Tomorrow, we will have to check these lines again before we begin our action. By then, our other men will be healthier and can do the manual labor. Hopefully, their sickness will abate after a good night's rest."

Muhammed wiped his mouth. "I will not complain tomorrow. And now I understand why you insisted that the container be lodged on the deck of the ship in this unobstructed location. Our messenger of Allah will fly freely once we remove the top of the container." He looked toward the black, western sky. "It will be a glorious sight, will it not? Our masters in Tehran will be pleased."

"Indeed." Khadem smiled broadly as he spoke. "And tomorrow morning, we see the place where our falcon of death will bring misery on the infidels of the Great Satan."

Muhammed directed his gaze to the north, even though the ocean spray and the darkness prevented him from seeing beyond the ship's railing. "May Allah protect our brothers out there in the storm. Tomorrow, we will join them in Paradise."

"Yes, it shall be so. The Prophet has foretold it."

Chapter 2

US Navy Lieutenant Commander Logan Gordon, supposedly retired, watched through the night-vision binoculars at the happenings in Millennium Park near the Lake Michigan shore. A crisp breeze blew off the lake on the clear, star-studded night, causing the twenty-one-foot Bayliner 215 Deck Boat to slowly drift toward shore.

At the controls of the boat, Jasper Reynolds kept the throttle low so he could keep the boat from drifting too close. He sought to keep the bow oriented so that Logan, who sat cross-legged on the foredeck, could keep his eyes on the park. In the meantime, Cal Barker ran the controls of the stealth quadcopter drone they were flying over the park, recording the ghoulish festivities that were taking place. The low-light camera was working well except for when one of the revelers on the ground periodically shined a flashlight up in the air to see what was making the buzzing noise above them.

"They're bringing in hostages from the far side of the park. They are blindfolded and have their hands tied behind their backs," Logan said in a quiet voice. "I hope this isn't what it looks like." He shifted his gaze to a tall, dark, wooden structure on a raised stage. It appeared to be a homemade guillotine, with a bench on one side that was oriented perpendicular to the raised tower that held the blade above a one-foot-diameter hole in the frame.

"I can see the hostages coming through the crowd. And there is a small stage area on the south side," Cal whispered. "They are herding them to the stage."

Logan climbed back to the cockpit area of the boat to see the camera display on a laptop screen. Together, the three men watched the first of the hostages be pushed up onto the stage, tripping as he blindly stepped forward to the bench at the rear of the medieval-looking device that had been placed at the stage's front edge. Two men dressed in black with black ski masks pushed him onto his knees, held him down on the bench, and shoved his head through the hole in the tower. They tied him to the bench with his head protruding through the hole, facing the crowd. Even though the sound was poor in quality, they heard the onlookers cheering and the muffled screams of the hostage as he struggled to get free.

"Oh shit!" Cal yelled. "They're going to chop off his head."

"Shh," Logan commanded. "You'll give us away." He scanned the shoreline to see if there was any response to Cal's outburst. "Looks like they're too excited to hear anything from us," he said quietly. "My God, they are going to do beheadings now like the Caliphate guys. This is becoming gothic."

As they watched silently, a man with a sword stood up and waved the weapon over his head at the crowd, receiving a loud and merciless cheer. Then the man stepped up to the guillotine and took hold of a rope that dangled from the tower. He set his feet and looked out at the crowd for their signal. Many of the onlookers held their hands up with their thumbs down as they cheered.

"I think that's Chief Simon, the new executioner," Jasper said. "He must have upped the theatrics of these gory sessions for some more digital coverage. There are several cameramen just in front of the stage to livestream the events."

Simon shouted something like a war cry and jerked the rope downward, releasing the heavy blade that fell down the tower and onto the neck of the sacrificial human. Apparently, the blade had not fallen far enough to achieve the needed momentum to slice the neck through, and the hostage's body thrashed around with his head half-detached.

Simon jumped back, and the people in the front of the crowd did the same as blood spurted from the victim onto the stage. Simon and an assistant struggled to raise the blade again, apparently to a higher level this time. Simon tugged the rope to trip the blade to fall again and chop harder to finish the job. *Thunk*. The head fell free and bounced on the stage before rolling off the edge to the crowd's feet. Someone grabbed the head and held it up by the hair for all to see. He danced around with it to the delight of the morbid spectators.

"Jesus Christ," Cal said quietly. "They're just savages, aren't they?"

"They have to keep up with the Caliphate and their level of cruelty," Logan whispered. "That is how they attract followers, just like ISIS did a few years ago. 'Come join us, and you can pursue whatever depravity you can imagine.'"

They watched as another hostage, an overweight woman this time, was led onto the stage and the body of the first victim was tossed aside. Simon dispatched this sacrifice with a single drop of the guillotine's blade. The crowd cheered in approval. Bloodlust bubbled up in the onlookers as a third victim was pulled forward for execution.

Cal was upset as he tried to keep the camera stabilized above the crowd. "Geez, man. There are forty or more hostages. Do you think they'll kill them all? I can't believe this can happen in *Chicago.*"

"Well, the Caliphate began their formal executions," Logan said softly. "Up till now, Simon and the Antifa-slash-BLMX gangs just lined their enemies up and shot them in the back of the head. Now it's show biz and YouTube ratings."

"Well, they have a big enough crowd tonight. Maybe two thousand sycophants," Jasper said with disgust.

"It's like a scene from *Caligula,* or what's the name of that horrific movie Mel Gibson made about the Aztecs?" Cal asked.

"Mayans . . . *Apocalypto,*" Logan replied. "Yeah, gruesome."

They watched as two more poor souls were executed to the cheers of manic believers. Then Cal stared at the battery indicator for the drone. "Hey, if we want to check on the Caliphate boys, we better do it soon or I'll run out of juice to fly over there."

"Yeah, you're right," Logan agreed.

"We should drift their way and see what they are up to in Grant Park," Cal added.

Logan shifted his attention south along the lakeshore to focus on the Buckingham Fountain in Grant Park some three hundred yards south of the Art Institute of Chicago. The fountain was where the Central Caliphate conducted their executions. They had to provide entertainment for their followers, and execution of infidels of all types was their blood sport, much as it had been for the ISIS worshippers. They had staked out Grant Park for their showgrounds two months before and had publicly executed over three thousand luckless Christians and Jews in that time.

Monday evenings were the chosen days for executions on both sides. He wondered how long this state of affairs could go on.

Jasper turned the boat southward, and they cruised quietly to a position just offshore near the fountain. A huge crowd was gathered around it as a tall man dressed in a red robe and a white kaffiyeh headdress shouted at the gathering over a public address system. He had the people whipped into a frenzy and was shaking his fist in the air over his head. Logan couldn't see more than that with his binoculars, so he turned to watch the drone's camera feed on the laptop screen.

A long line of future victims—all white, by Logan's first impression—were positioned in a row on their knees with their hands tied behind their backs and either blindfolded or with hoods over their heads. A man dressed all in black with a ski mask pulled over his face marched back and forth behind the prisoners. He brandished a large, shiny scimitar, an Arabic sword designed for slashing from horseback. This one was unusually large and designed for a single purpose: chopping off heads. The man wielding the device was apparently the executioner for the night.

The drone slipped into a moderately low orbit that let the men see the activity on the ground without being so low that the agitated crowd would notice it. Cal let the drone hover once he found a good angle to watch the proceedings. "They are going to kill a bunch of people tonight, by the looks of it," he said. "Maybe eighty souls."

"You would think they would run out of victims after so much of this killing," Logan whispered. "I heard they sentence people to die for insulting Allah and then confiscate their property for the cause—the Caliphate, usually."

"Sometimes Sarkohan reserves the stolen goods for himself," Cal said. "At least, that's what I've heard."

Suddenly, a bullet whizzed past them, making a zip sound, followed by the crack of a rifle.

Logan turned around sharply and said, "We're under fire, guys. Get down."

They all huddled in the cockpit of the Bayliner, and Jasper shoved the throttle forward to the max. The boat leaped forward, and he brought it into a wide, right turn, creating a foamy wake that was visible in the dim light of the park lights. Logan was already on the rail of the boat with his M4A Carbine, ready to shoot back at their attackers. He scanned the area south of them and saw a powerboat with its running lights on, racing their way. A man was standing unsteadily on the boat's deck and pointing a rifle at them.

"Let me get the drone back before we get out of range. I don't want to lose this thing," Cal said loudly over the roar of the engine. "I need about a minute to at least get it on our course, let alone land the damn thing."

More bullets zipped around them, and a few hit the boat, taking out chunks of the fiberglass hull. Logan lined up for a shot as the Bayliner briefly cruised in a straight line before Jasper began to swerve back and forth to make them a harder target to hit. Cal was preoccupied with the drone's controls and practically laid down on the deck to focus on saving it.

Logan fired single shots at their attackers, who were still two hundred yards away and closing fast. He saw his shots land on the windscreen of the other boat. He tried to shoot the man steering the boat, who was hunkered down low.

"Make a hard turn left, Jasper," Logan said. "I think I can hit him when he has to bank this way."

Jasper looked worried. In making the turn, he would have to bank into it too, exposing them to the enemy's fire as well. But if they weren't prepared for the turn, Logan figured he could strafe the boat and hit a few of the men on board. He switched to fully automatic on his rifle.

Jasper cut left, and the boat responded as nicely as it would in competition water skiing, banking into the turn. Logan watched as the other boat followed suit. He aimed as well as he could in the dim light and opened fire. He could see that he hit the boat's pilot and two armed men right away. The other men didn't respond quickly, so Logan dropped the empty magazine and replaced it with another. He strafed the other boat again, hitting two more men and shooting chunks of plastic from the console. The boat went dead in the water.

"I think we got them!" he cried. "Pull up next to them, and let's see who they were."

Jasper jerked the wheel to continue the turn and swung the Bayliner around to draw parallel with the other boat. When they were next to their pursuers and could tie up to the derelict, he cut the power. They drifted to a halt.

The first thing they noticed was that all aboard were dead. They also noted that the men were dressed in black clothing and black boat shoes. Two wore ski masks, and one had a kaffiyeh on his head. The pilot wore a Chicago Cubs baseball cap.

"Do you recognize any of these guys?" Logan asked. "I think they're just guys out on patrol. No big fish."

"Yeah," Jasper said.

"There we go," Cal said as he landed the drone on the foredeck of the Bayliner. "We can go now, if you like. I got my toy back."

"Let me check them out for any papers or phones that might be useful. I'll hand you their weapons too," Logan said. "Just a sec."

Logan grabbed the rail of the other boat and hopped over into it. He searched each of the bodies quickly and collected the weapons and ammunition on the deck. After about two minutes, he hopped back on the Bayliner with four cell phones in his pockets.

"We may have some useful info on these, and I found one written order we can read back at base," he said. "I guess we'll have to leave the boat here and let it drift. Maybe they'll think Antifa shot up their patrol." He turned to look his men over for wounds. "You guys OK? No hits?"

"No hits, sir. Let's boogie," Cal said with a grin.

Logan turned to Jasper. "OK, Jasper. Let's get the hell out of here."

Jasper complied, and they raced north along the lakeshore in the dark, heading for safe waters near Uptown.

Chapter 3

Monday, March 13, 2023

Chicago, Illinois

Logan radioed ahead to the harbormaster at Montrose Harbor to let him know that a matte-black boat would arrive shortly at the entrance. *No sense being shot up by a nervous guard who might be drowsy by this time of night,* he thought.

The harbor was one of several small shelters for watercraft along the north shore of the city. It was the farthest south of the ones used by the Chicago North Force, or the CNF, a collection of militias that held this part of the city from inundation by the terrorist scourge. Last year, the US Department of Homeland Security had added Antifa and the Central Caliphate to their list of domestic terror organizations.

Jasper turned on their running lights and approached the harbor at a moderate speed. A guard waved from the end of the breakwater and held his rifle downward in a nonthreatening manner. Jasper entered the harbor via the simple barriers erected to keep suicide boats from ramming their way inside and brought them to their slip.

Logan jumped out of the boat and onto the wooden pier. He tied the front line up to a bollard and helped unload the arms they had taken with them and the captured weapons. He scanned the dock to see if anyone would meet them. Seeing no one, he led Jasper and Cal along the pier and up to a small parking lot on the shore. Their Jeep Wagoneer was parked where he had left it two hours before.

"Let's drive up to General Jorgensen's office and tell him what we saw. He'll be interested in Antifa's new *activities*," Logan said as they all threw the weapons into the rear of the vehicle. "We can see how he thinks this changes things."

Cal gently placed the drone's storage box and laptop on the back seat next to him. "I can play back part of the beheadings if he wants to see. Not that it's very entertaining."

They drove directly to the general's office via Montrose Avenue and then North Ashland Avenue to an office building on the corner of North Ravenswood Avenue and West Winona Street. It was formerly a gas station that now served as the logistics base for the CNF, even though it wasn't a very impressive headquarters. Everything in the CNF was decentralized for good reason. Besides, there weren't many good staging areas in that part of town unless they occupied a building near the lakeshore. They were still sorting out how to organize the several existing militias into one army. Full integration did not seem like it would happen soon, given the suspicious nature of the groups and the personalities involved.

Logan parked the jeep and walked across the street to another building that had once been a thriving restaurant but now was blocked out into offices and a large conference room. Cal carried the laptop, and Jasper unloaded the captured weapons into the gas station building for a staffer to deal with.

Logan stopped in the small bathroom along the corridor to freshen up after the evening's harrowing adventure. He walked to the sink and threw water on his face to wash off the lake water and grime that had splashed upon him during the unexpected chase. He touched up his longish, light-brown hair that he always parted on the right; he had let it grow out from the short-cropped look he had kept while on active duty. His brown eyes looked tired and his entire face grim. He tried a smile in the mirror, and that helped him look more like his usual self. He had started a beard and mustache, which were dark and scruffy, but he knew from previous experience they would grow in thick within a month. He straightened his clothing and decided he passed muster for the meeting.

He exited the bathroom and met Jasper and Cal waiting in the hallway. They found the general's office door open and marched right in to see him.

General Carl Jorgensen was an affable, middle-aged man of average height with short, graying hair; a mustache of the same color; and a friendly face. He was of Norwegian descent and had features that betrayed that heritage. He had served in the US Army and, upon retirement, had joined the local militia in Evanston, Illinois. He was a no-nonsense leader who had brought needed discipline to the men he now led. He didn't subscribe to the belief that a militia was just a bunch of guys who liked to go out and shoot up beer cans on the weekend. He had instituted formal firearms training and classes in tactics and methods, and he had told the men that the militia was intended to be an integral part of any war-fighting mission that could help the republic and supplement their police and military brothers.

"Logan, you're back. Good," Jorgensen said matter-of-factly. "What did you find out?"

"Antifa now decapitates prisoners like the Caliphate do, but they are using a homemade guillotine. They had about forty prisoners lined up for execution," Logan replied, nearly growling the last few words. "They seem to be competing with the Caliphate, possibly for recruitment purposes."

Jorgensen was generally mild-mannered in his personal relationships, enough so that he would have a beer with his men, but he was tough as nails when he needed to be. Now his face turned red as he contemplated this news.

Logan continued. "We encountered a Caliphate patrol boat and had a short firefight with them. Killed five and captured their phones and a page of written orders that I will leave with you for your intel officer."

"Good work. No casualties on your crew?"

"None, sir. But we found the beheadings to be a major escalation."

"Yes, it is troubling. They have fallen even further into anarchy and mass control. It's reminiscent of the worst part of the French Revolution, the Reign of Terror." The general sat down and motioned for the others to also do so.

"We have other information that I only received tonight," he said with exhaustion in his voice. "Antifa has invaded homes throughout the West Side, particularly the area around Garfield Park. They are stealing anything of value, then eliminating the residents." He stopped and looked at each of the men. "They take the stolen goods back to the Loop and kidnap some women as hostages. Sometimes, they take men if they can get a ransom for them. They have been doing this for some time in the West Loop, but they seem to have completed their rampaging through that area. They are housing their new recruits in houses and apartments that remain standing in the West Loop after their people move through and destroy the neighborhoods."

Cal said, "Antifa has gotten more violent and bold since they split from the old Black Lives Matter. Now BLMX is the radical version of the movement. Word is they merged with Antifa here in our city. It seems the former BLM members who joined with the Caliphate were moderates compared with BLMX."

"They want to expand north into Cabrini-Green. We will have to hold them back there and keep them from crossing Chicago Avenue. That's the only defensive line out there," Jasper said.

"That is the issue we must discuss at our strategy meeting in the morning. That will be all for tonight," Jorgensen said. "Logan, I need you to stay behind for a moment."

Everyone stood, and Cal and Jasper left the room. Logan stepped closer to the general and asked, "Did you need me for something, sir?"

"Yes, Logan. I have a surprise for you. Your old commanding officer, Captain Cotes, is in town to talk to you. I assume it's important because he came here directly from O'Hare this evening. He said you two had a lot of catching up to do."

"Yes, I haven't seen him in a couple of years. Last I heard, he was assigned to the Domestic Terrorism Task Force in November. He is supposed to come up with a plan to support states and cities that are overrun by Antifa and the like."

"Well, he is waiting at the Humboldt Grill. He asked me to send you over there as soon as you were free." Jorgensen smiled. "We can pick up your report on what you saw in the Loop tomorrow." They shook hands and parted ways.

The restaurant was only a block away, so Logan walked briskly to see his old commander and sometime friend. He thought about the times he had worked with Captain Charles Cotes, commander of Alpha Sixteen, the covert ops organization. Cotes had led field operations in the Middle East, where they had encountered faulty information that had led to complications during missions. Some of it had been caused by Cotes's tight control of information—sometimes so tight that he had failed to supply Logan with crucial intel that, on two occasions, had led to mission failure or unnecessary injury to his men. Cotes secrecy had led to the deaths of two of Logan's team members on one mission in Libya four years before. Logan had argued with Cotes about these problems, and they seemed to have worked them out by the time Logan had left Cotes's command. But it still bothered him that Cotes was too much of a control freak to work with.

He put on his surgical mask as he approached the bar. When he pulled open the wooden front door, two of the patrons whom he worked with in the militia greeted him. The grill was the principal hangout for members of the CNF when off duty. He often stopped at the bar at the end of his days to loosen up and share jokes with his fellow warriors over beers. In this day and age of anti-terrorist fighting, all the men needed a place to let off steam and consider the absurdity of their daily lives in dealing with events in their hometown. Fighting terrorists was commonplace now, but here, as in other cities, the terrorists were mostly fellow Americans—Marxist Americans, anarchist Americans, misguided Americans, but still terrorists.

He searched the many faces for Cotes. He walked toward the back of the long bar, where there were a few booths that would provide a certain level of privacy. Sure enough, Cotes was ensconced in one with a bottle of Guinness Extra Stout and a bottle of Bass Pale Ale, the key components of a black and tan, Cotes's favorite drink when he was in a good mood. Shots of Jameson Irish Whiskey were a sure sign that things were *not* going his way, and the slightest cause could unleash his temper.

"Hey, Cotes," Logan called out as he approached the booth. "How the hell have you been?"

Cotes looked up at the greeting and smiled vaguely. Stress showed in the pinched skin above his eyebrows as he raised his glass in salute. Logan slid into the bench opposite him and noticed that no hand was offered. Something was wrong for that to happen.

Logan flagged down a passing server and ordered a Beck's Pilsner before sitting back a moment to scan his companion. Cotes was only six years older than Logan, but today, he appeared to have aged another decade since they had last met. Lines arced around Cotes's eyes and mouth, but the close-cut hair was the same, if somewhat grayer than before. He had lost a good deal of weight from his six-foot frame. His dark-brown eyes told the story: too much worry and not enough sleep were taking their toll on the man. He seemed exhausted and animated at the same time. He stared back at Logan as if he were evaluating whether he was sure what to say. That was unlike him and warned Logan that his old boss had something heavy to tell him.

Suddenly, Cotes grinned, and his face lit up as he reached across the table to shake hands. "Sorry, Logan. I've had a long day and been out of sorts lately. Too much work and bad news. You know how it goes."

He still had a firm grip, and Logan relaxed a little as his beer arrived.

"How have you been, Captain? You seem beat up. They got you working too hard back in DC?" Logan wondered what was weighing him down. This was going to be a serious discussion.

"Yeah, you could say that. I just got promoted to take charge of a new operations group that I can't talk about tonight. Promoted to rear admiral so I can manage the group. I have a lot to cover with you in a short time." He raised his eyes from his beer to gaze directly at Logan's face. "But before I get into that, why don't you fill me in on the situation here in Chicago? Who are the players, and how did things get so fucked up so quickly?"

Logan was surprised at this turn of events. He wasn't prepared to make a formal situation report to an admiral after the long day he had put in. But if Cotes needed a sitrep, he would provide one.

A server stopped at the table and asked if they would be having dinner. After a few seconds and not even a glance down at the menu, they both ordered the grill's famous bacon cheeseburger and fries.

"Well, sir, where do I start?" Logan said as he gathered his thoughts after the server left. "It all began with the riots of 2020, like in many other cities. Some say it was worse here in Chicago because of the tension between the mayor and Antifa and, later, Black Lives Matter."

"Like in New York and LA and a dozen other places," Cotes said.

Logan continued. "Then the presidential election happened, and you know about that mess. Rioters claimed that they were protesting the results of the elections that were still in contention until January 2021."

"That whole election issue was a clusterfuck that caused much more tension when the results finally came out," Cotes added. "Biden won by such a small margin amid so many claims of fraud that no one trusted the results. Many people thought the election was illegitimate, so many took to the streets even though Biden officially won."

"Here in Chicago, I thought Antifa and BLM would be happy with the result, but they wanted more, and the mayor was too compliant. They wanted self-rule in the urban center that they had occupied—like the Loop, our downtown here. An autonomous zone."

"A travesty in all the cities that caved in," Cotes said as he sipped his black and tan. "Then we had the second wave of the original virus as the new UK, Brazilian, Indian, and South African variants emerged to plague us."

"The mayor and city council caved into the demands of the mob in the summer and rapidly cut back on the police force in hopes that the rioters would be pacified. But that left the city unprotected, and the riots intensified as Antifa declared the center of the city to be a new nation called Paradise. They occupied the Loop in the center of the city and were left alone by the mayor, who fired the last of the police force that protected the citizens. She was promised that she could continue running the day-to-day functions of the city. That did not last."

"Giving into these extremists is never the right thing to do. I don't know why our leaders keep making the same blunders."

Logan nodded. "Well, that situation lasted into the autumn, and then we all had to deal with the third wave of new variants of the virus. As you know, that hit Europe hard because they had a lot of trouble getting their vaccination program up and running. Hell, most of the world hadn't even begun vaccinations yet. Several vaccines came out but didn't work very well on the new variants."

The admiral straightened up from his slouch and said, "That caught us by surprise after all the scientific work. Damn virus mutated enough that the vaccine only had a thirty percent success rate. You know the story. There were fourth and fifth waves, depending on where in the world you were counting. Then all hell broke loose, all over the world. And COVID type 2 broke out last year—the seventh or eighth wave—even more viciously than the first COVID wave." He paused as he recalled those grim days. "Lost a lot of good men to disease and war, damn it."

"It's been going on for so long that it's hard to find hope for an end to this misery. I've seen too many people taken by the scourge, even with the improved treatments. We need a new vaccine now, or Chicago will never be the same," Logan murmured angrily.

"They *are* working on a new vaccine, but still, it will be a while before anyone trusts it," Cotes said quietly as he slouched back in the booth again. "The economy has gone to hell under the repeated lockdowns."

"Tell me about it. Anyway, I came back here to help settle things down, but it's just gotten worse every week."

They sat there quietly contemplating the events that had unfolded around them, now slugging their beers more aggressively. Logan thought the whole situation was unnerving, especially the national and international changes that were undermining democratic governments and people. It had to stop. He had his hands full trying to keep Chicago from falling into something unrecognizable.

After the server approached with their burgers, Cotes straightened up again and looked Logan in the eye. "That is all very interesting, but I have something else to discuss with you." He leaned forward and whispered, "I have the honor of recalling you to naval service, effective immediately. I have a secret mission that requires someone out of the normal chain of command. Officially, you will report to me, even though you'll not show up on any government roster. It's top-secret, eyes-only stuff."

Logan didn't think he had heard the admiral correctly. Maybe it was the beer cutting into his comprehension after such a long day.

"What did you say?"

"You heard me. You're back in special operations, and only three of us know about it: you, me, and another person who shall not be named, but whom you used to serve under."

"I don't believe it. You're joking."

"I thought you'd say something like that, so I brought proof." Cotes tapped at the screen of his secure, government-issued cell phone and held it up for Logan to read the brief letter on the screen. The letter verified what Cotes had said. "Look at who signed off on it."

Logan scanned down to the signature. "Admiral Smithton Shumwalt, head of naval intelligence operations. I thought he retired a few years ago."

"No. He just migrated to a new intelligence entity code-named Jackal. You are now full Commander Logan Gordon and are part of it. You may need the rank to do the new job and command multiple units of an operation. But don't let it go to your head."

"And I have to accept this arrangement exactly why?" Logan asked.

"Because your nation needs you and it's the right thing to do." Cotes sat back and considered Logan's question as they ate their dinners. Then he said, "Hell, you have every right to know." He leaned forward again as they both sipped their brews. "I can tell you this, Logan: I chose you personally for this mission because you are a patriot, because you're one of the best at the undercover game, and because I know you won't fail. I need someone with those abilities to make this work." He stared at Logan as he drank his black and tan.

"Well, I'm not sure I want to accept this assignment. The last two missions you talked me into nearly got me killed. I recall a lot of bad intel from the CIA boys. I hope you're not relying on them for this deal." Logan sipped his beer and watched Cotes squirm a little at the mention of past failures. "Where exactly are we going, anyway, and will I have to kill people?"

"San Diego to start, and yes, probably."

"Great. You have a real touch with recruitment skills."

"I'm not hiring you as an assassin. But just so you know, this job is so important that if anyone learns of our mission, we will most definitely be in harm's way."

Logan finished his beer and stood up. "I have to give you an answer in the morning, Admiral," he said. "I need to sleep on it. And by then, you will have to be a little more specific about the task."

"Yes, and fair enough. I'll see you back at the general's office in the morning—08:00?"

"Sounds good."

They shook hands, and Logan walked toward the door while Cotes ordered another round.

Logan felt that there was something not quite right about this setup, and he needed time to think about it. He wasn't sure he could just drop what he was doing in Chicago to go off on a secret mission, whatever it was. He had commitments here that he planned to keep.

He walked to his car and started the engine. He sat there for a while and wondered what the mission might entail. He would have to find out in the morning. Right now, he needed to get some much-needed sleep.

He pulled out of the parking lot and headed for his issued motel room nearby.

He arrived at the seedy, partially trashed building within fifteen minutes and parked his car as close to his room as possible so he could hear if anyone tried to break into it during the night. A thief would have to be crazy to try anything because twenty-five armed militiamen were housed there.

Logan wearily climbed the stairs to his second-floor room and inserted the key in the lock. He carefully pushed the door open with his hand on his sidearm, just in case. Nothing happened and he relaxed. He checked the room to see if anything had been disturbed since he had left earlier in the day. No problems or signs of mischief.

He dropped his briefcase on the small writing table and sat down to remove his boots. His feet had gotten soaked during the water chase, and he had to dry his socks by morning. He quietly padded over to the bathroom to wring them out and then swish them around in the sink with dishwashing detergent in a meager attempt to wash them. Finally, he hung them on the towel rack to dry.

He filled a plastic bottle with water and made his way over to the small stool next to the window, where he watered his sole roommate, a geranium plant with red flowers. It had recently perked up, despite his routine neglect, and bloomed for him. It added life to his dull abode.

He grabbed a Pabst Blue Ribbon from his half fridge and popped the top as he sat on the edge of the bed, enjoying the muted color of the flower in the dim light. The plant wasn't demanding and tolerated his irregular comings and goings well. It was the one thing he could look forward to at the end of the day, and it cheered him up.

He finished his beer as he pulled off his uniform and slid under the blankets on the sagging mattress. He thought about his meeting with Cotes and how the man still withheld information, even about a mission that he wanted Logan to join. Maybe some people never changed. He wondered what the mission was about. It had to be extremely important for Cotes to show up unannounced like that. Something urgent.

Logan turned out the light over his bed and stared at the silhouette of the geranium against the window shade. The backlight only provided an outline of the flower, much as Cotes had only provided a vague sketch of the mission ahead. Maybe he would feel more motivated to help Cotes in the morning. One never knew what could shake things up.

Chapter 4

Tuesday, March 14, 2023

Chicago, Illinois

The following day, Logan rolled out of bed at 7:00 a.m., having slept in for a change. He showered and dressed in his usual khakis and deck shoes before heading for the door. He was disturbed to see that someone had scratched the left front fender of his car, an old Toyota Camry with high mileage.

He drove slowly over to CNF headquarters while listening to a CD of the Bob Dylan album *Rough and Rowdy Ways*. He felt in good spirits, despite a fitful sleep that came from worrying about the sudden appearance of his old boss.

When he arrived at headquarters, he noticed that two troopers he knew were running out of the office to a car nearby. Then he saw two men carrying M4A rifles come out of the building and take up positions by the doors, something that the CNF hadn't needed to do for several weeks. He wondered if they were in a new state of alert this morning because of some incident that had occurred overnight. He picked up his pace and stepped to the door.

"Sorry, sir," the guard said as he approached the door. "I need to see your ID."

Logan pulled out his ID card and flashed it at the guard, who knew him from a past assignment. "What's going on, Jerry? Did something happen last night?"

"You haven't heard, sir?" Jerry was grim and excited at the same time. "It's about New York. Something is happening to our communications with the city. They dropped off the air."

"What? How can that be?"

"We don't know, sir. It's like the power went off for the whole city. Even the TV stations have lost connection."

Logan took his ID back and saluted Jerry as he stepped through the doorway. He hurried into the conference room, where several people, including Cotes and Jorgensen, were sitting around a TV set watching the local FOX News channel—the only station still broadcasting locally after the riots. An orange banner flashed on the screen, and a female announcer was speaking rapidly in an excited tone.

"We're still waiting for confirmation that all electronic communications with New York City have somehow been lost only moments ago. At 8:03 a.m., our station was broadcasting our usual morning news program when the satellite signal just broke off. For some reason, we can't reestablish contact with our parent broadcast. We apologize for this interruption in our programming and will now go to . . ."

The woman's eyes suddenly widened, and her face blanched. She pressed her fingers to her ear like her earpiece was faulty and intently listened to someone speaking. She stared into the camera with her mouth open, then said, "Really? . . . I mean, I can't just say that, can I?"

"What the hell is going on, General?" Logan asked.

"It appears there has been a complete breakdown in communications with New York City. I can't raise anyone on the radio there either. Luanne ran down to the comm center to find out what's happening."

"Is it a power outage of some kind? Those usually happen at night," Logan asked.

"My satellite phone isn't getting through to anyone there either," Jorgensen said. "I wonder if the North Koreans have disabled our power grid. Those bastards would do something like this."

A woman in khaki uniform burst into the room with a wild look on her face. "Sir, it's gone. New York. It's just gone."

They all jumped to their feet. Jorgensen asked, "What the hell do you mean, Luanne? What's gone?"

"The city, sir," she said breathlessly. "There was an explosion in Manhattan. It was a bomb."

The general's face flushed. "You're not making sense."

The news announcer spoke again in an uncertain voice. "I have just been told that a bomb has struck New York City and destroyed all of lower Manhattan. It was believed to be a nuclear device. Video has just arrived in the studio showing the blast as it occurred."

The screen was filled with a clip showing a fairly common view of Manhattan from Liberty State Park in Jersey City, New Jersey, showing the city's skyline framed by blue water and clear sky. Suddenly, a white light appeared just above the skyscrapers and instantly covered the screen with a white glare before the camera went dead and the signal was lost.

"Jesus!" Jorgensen shouted. "It's an air burst. It was a nuke, all right."

Cotes was on his satellite phone. He lifted his gaze up from his conversation to look at the TV and then held up one figure in the air to gain everyone's attention. "I'm on with Sec Nav's office. We are under attack. A nuke hit DC at the same time. It's a coordinated attack."

The TV played the blinding flash footage over and over again. Then a new video came on, taken from farther to the west. It appeared to be the feed from a camera somewhere else in New Jersey, perhaps one used to display weather conditions in Newark. It showed a portion of Manhattan in the distance. Then there was a sudden flash. The camera went to a white screen, then recovered to show a huge fireball that grew into a dark-orange cloud that nearly filled the view. Within seconds, the cloud formed a giant mushroom that roiled upward to tower over the city. It looked like the classic A-bomb clouds shown on the History channel of the old nuclear tests from the 1950s.

A shock wave flew across the sky, throwing up dust and debris as it came directly at the camera. The view shook violently and was obscured by dust for several minutes before clearing and showing a changed landscape from a slightly different orientation, the result of the shock wave. The familiar skyline of Manhattan had been largely erased by the explosion, with only a few buildings remaining on the north end of the island. Finally, the mushroom cloud appeared again, much taller and broader after the intervening minutes.

The room was silent except for Cotes speaking frantically on the phone. Everyone was frozen, staring at the cloud rising on the TV screen. Cotes hung up and began to tap his phone's screen.

"Holy shit," Logan said quietly. "We're at war."

Cotes shouted to be heard over the many conversations that filled the room, "I'm getting a secure text message. It reads: 'All stations to DEFCON one immediately this date March 14, 2023. US under attack by foreign powers. Two nuclear bombs detonated on NYC and WDC at 09:00 EDT this date. Source unknown. Stand by for update.'

"All right, gentlemen," Cotes said, then added, "Ma'am." His face was a mask of calm, but Logan knew that the admiral was holding back his emotions. His eyes seemed glazed. "Washington is completely out of action. The blast was centered somewhere on the National Mall, close to the Capitol. There was no warning, so it is assumed that casualties will be enormous because no one had time to get to a shelter. It will take time to assess the number of victims. There is no communication from the president or anyone else from the White House—or from Congress. The president was conducting his morning cabinet meeting that started at 09:00. Congress was in session, but we have no idea how many congressmen or senators were in the Capitol at the time. Right now, it is assumed that the president is dead, or at least injured."

"What about the Pentagon? Was it damaged?" Logan asked.

"Reports say it was directly struck by the shock wave and suffered considerable damage. We don't know how extensive casualties are yet. Emergency procedures have begun in response to the emergency plan developed for nuclear war. People around Washington should begin dispersing to secondary command locations in case there is another strike. Search and rescue teams are mobilizing to search the area of the strike to find the president and key survivors, as well as assess the damage."

"If the president was killed, who will be in charge, sir?" Luanne asked.

"Per the Constitution, assuming both Biden and Vice President Harris were killed, Pelosi, the speaker of the House, would be next in line," Jorgensen responded. "But with Congress in session, she may have also been killed, so it falls to the president pro tempore of the Senate, which is now ... I don't know who that is, but then you go through the cabinet until there is a survivor."

"So we have no idea who is in charge right now," Luanne said. "The whole cabinet could have been wiped out."

Everyone was quiet. Logan knew they were all thinking about people they knew in those two cities, people who may have been killed. They were also thinking about the losses to the government and the nation. No one knew what would come next. Would Chicago be a target?

This event caused Logan to make up his mind about the mission. If Cotes was in charge, the mission had to be of national importance. He walked around the table to stand next to the admiral, who was dialing a number on his phone to no effect. He said, "I'm in."

Cotes nodded his head. "Good, Logan. Good to know." He caught Logan's eye, but had no expression on his face. "I can't get through to anyone now. I hope to God that my team survived. We're located in Falls Church."

"That's pretty far away. But communications take a big hit when a nuke goes off. A lot of stuff gets fried by the EMP," Logan said.

"What's the EMP?" Luanne asked. "I haven't heard of that before."

"Electromagnetic pulse. When a nuke goes off, it throws out a ton of electrical energy that overloads most electronic devices within miles—. You know, radios, TVs, cell phone towers. Everything is affected ... computers ... the internet. That's probably why we aren't hearing anything from the affected areas."

"I never thought I would need to know something about what this pulse did," she replied, sounding disheartened.

Cotes's phone beeped as a text arrived on the screen. "Another message: 'NYC and WDC hit by cruise missiles launched from freighter ships offshore. Large, dirty warheads. Air and naval resources dispatched to intercept hostiles. No additional strikes recorded' ... Freighters?" Cotes said quietly. "That sounds like it could be terrorists, not the Russians or the Chinese."

Several CNF soldiers entered the conference room in a solemn manner. One of the men asked the general, "Is it true? Is the president dead?"

"We don't know that yet, men. A search and rescue team is going into the White House and Congress to look for survivors." Jorgensen surveyed the room of a dozen people and said, "I believe that we should divide our forces into two stand-alone divisions in case there's an attack on Chicago. We need to hold our lines here in the city and move as many men as possible out of harm's way."

"Sounds prudent, sir," Cotes said. "But as I mentioned yesterday, I'm drafting one of your men to assist me on a special project that is of high priority."

Miffed, Jorgensen said, "I hate losing Lieutenant Commander Gordon. We're at war here in Chicago, let alone what just happened." He motioned to the TV like it wasn't really true yet.

"We need him. I will try to have him back to you in a few weeks, if our project goes well."

"In that case," Jorgensen said, "I have to get my troops into staging positions." He shook hands with Logan and Cotes. "Come on, men," he called over his shoulder as he walked out of the room.

"Sir, is our mission still a go?" Logan asked hesitantly. "I mean, conditions have completely changed since yesterday."

"Absolutely, Logan," Cotes responded. "And you can drop the 'sir' stuff. We're going off the books as soon as we leave this room."

"Where are we going?"

"I'm assuming we are a go until I receive orders otherwise," Cotes said as he pocketed his phone. "First, we have to get your travel gear. Pack everything you would take to a war zone. Then we're off to O'Hare Airport."

Chapter 5

Logan and Cotes were wheels up by 11:30 a.m. on board the admiral's Gulfstream G280 jet, a nimble and luxurious plane that was at his disposal for the mission. It came stocked with top-shelf liquor and a kitchen. Cotes didn't have a steward or server of any kind, so they had to pour their own Scotch while the pilot, Captain Robert Williams, flew the craft.

"I wouldn't usually imbibe this early, but today, I need a stiff one to deal with reality," Cotes murmured.

"So it's true? The president is dead?" Logan asked. "I heard it on the news but couldn't believe it. And the cabinet?"

"I heard the morning news, same as you. There's a great deal of speculation about what happened. Could the president and his staff have made it into the White House bunker in time to survive? They had about a two-minute warning, but that was pretty damn short."

"But the bunker is right underneath the White House, so maybe they made it."

"That was the hope at first—that they made it inside, but were unable to communicate after the blast." Cotes wiped his hand over his face as if it would clear his mind. "I got an update from my HQ. The rescue team worked mightily to get to the White House and look for survivors. It was challenging and dangerous, to say the least, given the size of the blast. Everything was torn up or blasted to smithereens. Roads were blocked by fallen buildings and rubble. And radiation levels were deadly high. They of course had to go in wearing hazmat suits and other protective gear, which slowed them down. The early estimates are it was a three-megaton bomb and that the White House could have been vaporized. But that's all speculation."

"Did they get there yet? Or are they still looking through the wreckage?"

"The last I heard this morning was that they made it to the White House and found the building largely blown away, as if a category-five hurricane had struck," Cotes said. "It would have been right at the beginning of the blast radius. Only the bases of the fireplaces were left in place. If they were above ground, everyone would likely have been swept away in the high winds created by the bomb."

"They didn't find anyone alive?" Logan asked as he shook his head. "Did they get into the bunker yet to see if anyone is there?"

"They found the entrance to the bunker elevator at the basement level, but it was unclear if it had been used before the bomb went off. They could have made it there if they left the cabinet room immediately and ran down the staircase that leads to the lower-level basement. It's not clear if they had time to make it that far, but no bodies were found down there. The team was trying to get into the elevator to check the bunker three hundred feet deeper in the earth."

"Have you yourself ever been down there?"

"No, I didn't have that level of security clearance when I visited the place a few years ago. But it's deep. If they made it down there, they could all survive for two weeks, if necessary." The admiral seemed overwhelmed by this news. He dropped his head and wiped his eyes with his shirt sleeve, then muttered, "It appears that the elevator was never activated. They broke into the elevator shaft and found the cage sitting at the basement level. No one rode it down below."

"So they are likely gone." Logan felt as though he couldn't breathe for a few moments. They were both silent for a full minute as they gathered their wits.

"They are still trying, thinking that maybe a few made it down to the bunker and that they sent the cage back up for a second group of passengers. We will hear back this morning on that."

"Who's in charge of the government right now, sir?"

"According to the communications we had from just before the meeting, the VP and all the cabinet secretaries were in the meeting. Only one person in the chain of command is known to have survived so far: Secretary of Agriculture Mary Callahan, who was in meetings in Des Moines this morning. She was whisked away to a secure location as soon as the Secret Service found out she was alive." Cotes added sadly, "She may be our president now because everyone else in the chain of succession is either dead or unaccounted for."

"Even Pelosi was killed?" Logan asked, dumbfounded.

"The Capitol building itself was scraped away in the explosion. No survivors have been located there either."

"Jeeesus!" Logan said loudly. "They're all dead?"

"I received a call from the Pentagon on the way over to O'Hare that they managed to survive the worst of the explosion and are getting back to business—at least some of the military is operational. More will come online in a few days, they say."

"I read on my phone just now that New York is in complete ruin. A lot of Manhattan is just gone—vaporized," Logan said. "At least, that's what they said on TV."

Cotes straightened up in his seat and held up his glass. "Let's toast to the brave souls who perished and those who have survived so far."

They toasted quietly and glumly sipped their drinks.

"That's why I poured us whisky this early. We must acknowledge our dead. All of them." He finished his drink and then closed his eyes for a few moments.

"To brave Americans," Logan said as he finished his drink.

They were silent again and avoided each other's gaze. Logan knew they were both wrapped in personal thoughts of the horror of what had happened.

"Now," Cotes said, "let's get down to business, shall we? We still have a mission to accomplish, and my orders have not changed. We will carry on."

"Yes, sir. We must go ahead." Logan stared at him. "So now you can fill me in."

"First, let me give you your cover for this mission and an ID." Cotes handed Logan a badge and an ID card in a thin wallet.

"There are credit cards and other cards to support the legend. You are Logan Willis, and I am Victor Martz, both out of the DC office of the US Marshals Service. For most people we encounter, we're marshals working on a smuggling case that we can't talk about. As marshals, we have permits to carry weapons on aircraft and just about anywhere else, so that should explain most of what we're doing. But I would keep your handgun under wraps unless you need it." He stopped and scanned the weapon on Logan's hip. "You still carrying a Springfield XD .45?"

"Good to have a reason to carry one," Logan replied, then pointed to his handgun. "No. I shoot a Glock model G21 now in .45 caliber. Nice weapon—thirteen rounds in the magazine."

"Right," Cotes said calmly. "We are flying to Mankato, Minnesota, to meet with Dr. Hamilton Grimley, who is one of the nation's top virologists. Our mission is to get him and several biological samples to the Naval Air Station in San Diego as soon as possible."

"What kind of samples are we talking about?"

"Dr. Grimley and his team have developed a new vaccine to protect against the latest wave of the coronavirus. We must get it and him to San Diego, where a vaccine manufacturing plant is standing by to produce millions of doses. No one knows that we have the vaccine yet, but word will leak out soon, if it hasn't already."

"Why the secrecy?"

"There are people who don't want to see a successful vaccine distributed throughout America. Some are foreign actors, and some are domestic terrorists who want to prevent any stabilization of the current chaos that has flooded our nation. We have to protect the doctor and the samples while we transport them to safety."

Captain Williams's voice came to them over the intercom. "We are on approach to Mankato Regional Airport now, Admiral. Touchdown in twelve minutes. A vehicle is waiting for us."

Cotes pushed a button on the intercom and responded, "Sounds good, Captain. Proceed."

"Why Mankato?" Logan asked as he peeked out the window at the agricultural landscape below.

"This is where one of the best virology labs in the country is located. It was placed here partially due to when there was a scare in the eighties about domestic terrorism using biological agents. It's also here because the Mayo Clinic is close by, and Dr. Grimley is officially listed on their staff as part of his cover. He runs one wing of the lab that specializes in bioweapon countermeasures. That part of the lab is secret and not known to any of the locals. Otherwise, there could be a lot of misunderstanding."

"I thought our only bioweapons lab was at Fort Detrick in Maryland," Logan said as he scanned Cotes's face.

"That is the public face of our biowarfare unit. They handle publicly acknowledged projects or inquiries," Cotes said. "But this is different. Our guys here are set up for biosafety level-four and the newest level-five containment facilities, so they volunteered to work on the COVID project too."

The plane banked left, and the captain lowered the flaps as he made his approach. The plane came in at a steep angle, and the ground seemed to rapidly rise up to meet them. Within two minutes, the wheels touched down with some force, and the plane rushed along the runway. After several seconds and the application of some braking, the plane turned left again and came to an abrupt stop.

"Did I mention that Williams was a crack carrier pilot before he worked for me? He knows how to deal with a short runway," Cotes said, chuckling as he saw Logan's face. "Leave the big stuff here, and it will be delivered to our motel for us. We'll go meet Grimley now and grab some lunch."

Logan laughed as they picked up their briefcases to deplane. He followed Cotes to the front of the fuselage, where Williams was lowering the staircase. They all shook hands, and Cotes asked Williams to bring the bags with him to the motel after refueling and seeing to the plane's safe parking.

As planned, a car was waiting for them from a car rental agency. Cotes drove out the front gate of the commercial portion of the small airport and turned north on a two-lane, asphalt road. After a few turns and several minutes, he pulled off onto a road with a sign that was marked PRIVATE ROAD—NO PUBLIC ACCESS. He continued along the road that threaded its way through a coniferous forest to a steel gate. A small guardhouse at one end of the gate was manned by two men who wore olive-colored uniforms that had no identification on them. The men acted like they had military training as they thoroughly searched the car, including using a mirror to search under the chassis.

All Cotes said was, "Marshal Martz. We're expected." He handed over his ID card to one man, who took it inside the small building and returned later with two ID badges on lanyards labeled *V. Martz* and *L. Willis*. A knock on the roof of the car told them they were cleared, and Cotes drove forward as the steel gate lifted.

They proceeded to the front of a large, metal building that must have been some sort of warehouse facility and parked the car in a parking space marked with a VISITOR sign. They put on their surgical face masks, part of the daily ritual nowadays, and walked to a manway that was the sole entry into the building.

Inside, a young woman in a drab, olive uniform and blue, surgical mask met them and courteously led them into a small meeting room, where she pointed out the obvious coffee pot and cups for their use. After a few words, she left them, promising that the doctor would be right with them.

"I thought we would meet the doctor at his lab right away," Logan said. He scanned the nearly bare walls of the room, adorned only with a calendar and a bulletin board with memos tacked to it.

"The warehouse is a functional part of the national strategic stockpile of medical equipment and supplies. You could only see part of it as we drove up, but it has millions of face masks, gowns, shields, operating equipment, beds—you name it that may be needed for this and upcoming epidemics and pandemics. The government has been hard at work for nearly three years to rebuild our stockpiles after COVID caught us flat-footed. This is one that was expanded last year and is used as the support facility for the lab.

"The medical wing of the lab was built into it on the ground surface and below ground. They have everything they need for this to be a fully functioning hospital if it's needed during the next wave of the pandemic. The warehouse has a lot of traffic coming and going as they transfer supplies in and out to other parts of the country."

"Sounds impressive."

"Well, that's not the half of it. There is also a secret lab built underground here. That's where Dr. Grimley works—in the deep underground levels." Cotes glared at Logan. "By the way, that's classified information at the secret level."

Someone knocked on the door, and an elderly man with long, white hair and wire-rimmed glasses over piercing blue eyes entered. He wore a white lab coat, a face mask that he removed, and Hush Puppies-style shoes. He smiled and walked directly up to Cotes to shake hands.

"It's good to see you again, Admiral Cotes," he said warmly. "I didn't think we would meet again for another month or two, but here we are."

"It's pleasant seeing you too, Doctor," Cotes said as he grinned cautiously. "Let me introduce Commander Logan Gordon. He will be accompanying us as we deliver the samples. Logan, this is Doctor Hamilton Grimley."

Logan shook Grimley's hand and felt a strong grip as he sized him up. The doctor was younger than Logan had assumed when he had seen the shock of white hair, maybe only sixty. He had a friendly face and was only an inch shorter than Logan. He thought maybe Grimley was a runner, given that he was light of frame and fit for his age.

"Have you eaten?" the doctor asked. "I thought we might walk down to the cafeteria to have our discussion. Frankly, I'm starved after the long morning we've had here."

"No, we haven't," Cotes answered. "We were wondering where we could eat lunch, so that would be fine."

Grimley led them down a hallway for about twenty yards and took a right turn before entering a double doorway simply marked CAFETERIA. Inside, they found a large venue with a wide selection of delectables and drinks. Twenty or thirty people wearing face masks were already in a slow-moving line past steam tables and coolers, all chatting loudly among themselves as they perused the dining choices.

"We can go over here to the private dining area, where we will be able to speak freely." Grimley pointed to a door marked DINING 2. He led them there, opened the door, and directed them to seat themselves at a wooden meeting table with chairs while he distributed plastic menus from the center of the table.

"We can order our entrées and avoid the long line this way. A server will appear in a minute." He pressed a buzzer and flipped open his menu.

Within a minute, the door opened, and a tall, slender woman with blonde hair and blue eyes entered, wearing a lab coat and surgical mask and carrying a small, padded envelope. She walked up to the table and smiled at Grimley as she removed her mask. She was about to speak when Logan called out.

"I'll have coffee and a roast beef sandwich."

She stared at him without an expression other than a slight hint of arrogance, and he realized by the looks he was getting that she wasn't a waitress. Grimley chuckled at his mistake, and Cotes glared at him.

Cotes stood up and extended his hand to the woman, who graciously shook it. "Hello, Dr. Grimley. It's nice to meet you after talking on the phone several times," he said. "I'd like to introduce Commander Logan Gordon. He has *just* joined our team."

"Hi, Commander. I'm Dr. Kayla Grimley, daughter of the man sitting next to you. I'm a researcher in biomedical science, not a waitress."

"Sorry, I just assumed, given the circumstances . . . ," Logan said, embarrassed by his mistake, and shook her hand.

There was a knock at the door, and the senior Grimley said, "Enter."

A server came into the room, took their lunch orders, and quickly departed. Kayla sat down across the table from Logan between her father and Cotes. She ignored Logan as she spoke with the admiral. "There will be a delay preparing the sample for transport," she said. "One of the transport refrigeration units failed our standards for maintaining the needed ultra-cool temperature and will need to be repaired. Our techs say it needs a new regulator, and they can't seem to find a replacement here in Mankato."

"Did you try to borrow one from Mayo? Maybe they have a spare?" Grimley asked.

"Not yet. The request will have to come from Dr. Franklin, and he wants to check other sources in the Twin Cities first for a regulator." She turned back to Cotes and said, "We are a secret lab, so any request like that goes through Dr. Franklin, who is the administrator of the surface lab. We call it that because it is the publicly known entity, and they have a relationship with all the other medical facilities in the area." She glanced at Logan. "It would be commonplace for them to ask for help on a repair or borrow a piece of equipment. But we down here don't exist as far as the rest of the world is concerned."

Cotes appeared agitated. "How much of a delay are we looking at? Can we still leave in the morning?"

"We must have three identical refrigeration units for transport," Grimley said. "We can fit all the samples in two coolers if we must, but we want to begin the trip with three in case one breaks down in transit. Then we can double up if needed. But if we start with only two, we would lose samples if we had a failure."

They quieted as the server returned with their meals. They all began to eat in continued silence as they considered the dilemma.

Logan asked Kayla, "Dr. Grimley, what is your role in this project? I mean, I know that your father developed the vaccine, but what do you work on?"

She gave him a menacing look, then glanced at her father. "Listen, Commander, why don't you just call me Kayla and call my dad Dr. Grimley? It will save a lot of confusion for us all."

"Oh, OK." Logan smiled. "You can call me Logan, if you like, instead of Commander. It seems more friendly somehow."

She grimaced. "To answer your question, I work with my father on the vaccines we develop here. I also work on new viruses that come into the lab to evaluate their potential as bioweapons."

Logan nearly dropped his sandwich that was halfway to his mouth. "What? You work with bioweapons?"

Cotes quickly jumped in. "I haven't brought the commander up to speed on what you actually do here. He didn't need to know to carry out this particular mission. But since you mentioned it, maybe you can explain what you do."

Grimley turned to Cotes and then to his daughter. He briefly gave her a look of fatherly disapproval, perhaps because she had let slip information that she shouldn't have mentioned or because now he had to speak very carefully about their work.

"We are one of two labs in the United States that works on viruses that can be weaponized by the military. We do not develop weapons, but we evaluate all sorts of viruses that may one day be used for that purpose. We do that for several reasons. One is so that we can keep up with what other countries are doing to develop weapons for their own use. Even though there is an international agreement banning the use of biological warfare agents, several countries have them and are researching them, and some are producing them for testing and possible use. The Russians and the Chinese have extensive programs and are suspected of developing small stockpiles in their arsenals. But so do Pakistan, Iran, North Korea, and others. The list is quite long."

The doctor hesitated, and Kayla took over. "We work exclusively with viruses, our specialty. We evaluate any new viruses sent to us from other countries and those that are secretly stolen from outside labs. We investigate their infective and spreading mechanisms to interpret how they could be weaponized. We also develop vaccines and treatments that can be used to fight these organisms. In short, we know a lot about vaccines."

"I had no idea," Logan said.

"It's all top-secret work, so I suppose that this means you have that level of clearance." She looked at Cotes for confirmation. He nodded his head. "We have been working with COVID for two years and were called in when the original vaccine failed last year. You see, the commercial labs did a great job in producing a vaccine and treatments, but the virus mutated enough to make the vaccine impotent."

"But don't all viruses mutate?" Cotes asked.

"Yes," she continued, "but this time, it affected the site that the vaccine targeted. Usually, there is a small change but not one that directly affects the vaccine. In any case, the SARS-CoV-2 virus had a different infective mechanism that we haven't seen before in nature. It has a unique spike protein with a special affinity for human ACE2 receptors and other changes from bat viruses that likely were caused by genetic manipulation in a lab. You can also create recombinant viruses in a lab, where you piece together parts of two or more components to add special properties from one virus to another that does not have the ability. It is very dangerous stuff, this playing God. This type of work was banned in the United States for several years."

"That is probably all we should say, Kayla," Grimley said cautiously. "They aren't interested in the details of the scientific work that we do here."

"I find it interesting," Logan said. "I didn't know you could create viruses like that."

"Oh yes," she replied, clearly excited about the subject and the fact that someone outside her field was interested. "That is why we knew right away that the novel COVID virus was man-made. It has all the characteristics you would get by manipulating it in a lab."

Chapter 6

Tuesday, March 14, 2023

Mankato, Minnesota

Logan's jaw dropped at the news. "Wait . . . are you saying the COVID 19 virus was man-made?"

"Why, yes. It had to be," Kayla said. "The spike protein differs from anything else we have seen in nature. That's how it invades the human cell structure so well." She saw that this level of detail was losing her audience. "Anyway, it is now generally accepted among researchers that it was made in a lab in Wuhan, China. Some say it was designed as a potential weapon that somehow escaped the lab."

"But we've had any number of scientists on the news saying that it came from an animal market in Wuhan and that it's natural," Logan said.

"Most of the people who claim to know about the virus just don't know what they are saying," Grimley mused. "A few are using the bat theory to cover up what we already knew shortly after the virus left China. There is mostly misinformation out there that obfuscates what actually happened."

"Why would anyone want to hide information about the virus's origin?" Logan asked.

"Because some want to hide the fact that it was part of a bioweapon program in China. Many companies would lose money if people in America knew the Chinese made it in a lab and didn't control it," Kayla said. "And if it got out that it was a weapon, it would cause a worldwide panic."

"That's why the president and the CDC downplayed the danger from the virus at first. To avoid a panic," Logan said incredulously.

"We knew it was a weapon all along, but couldn't say so, or it would create terror and might lead some people to demand retaliation," Cotes said grimly. "Possibly war with China."

"So you knew about this?" Logan asked Cotes. "You knew the Chinese made it as a weapon?"

"Yes, we had to assume it was a weapon that they had released on the world for economic gain. The fact that the Chinese contained the virus to Wuhan, but then it escaped to everywhere else in the world, was very suspicious. At first, we assumed it was the Chinese playing another of their asymmetrical warfare strategies. They are masters at that. They do something nefarious that they can potentially deny while causing us a lot of damage without them getting caught—like building islands in the South China Sea and claiming land and ocean they don't possess. They just do things to create facts that they then defend. It's not enough to go to war over, but it's clearly aggression."

Logan couldn't believe what he was hearing. "And now?"

"We think the Chinese were going to release COVID-19 at a future date, but it slipped out of the lab before they had their plan in place. When the release happened, their military saw it as an opportunity to move the plan forward anyway. They would just pretend they were surprised. That's why they came up with the Wuhan seafood market explanation as the starting point for the pandemic. It was all part of an ad hoc coverup supported by some in the World Health Organization and other allies of China. They contained the virus in Wuhan, where nearly two million died, but sent infected people all over the world to spread it. They knew exactly what they were doing. It was asymmetrical warfare that would cause most of the world to shut down while their economy grew dramatically."

"So they planned it all along?" Logan asked. "It seems so brazen and inhumane. And they really lost two million people?"

"That's the best estimate, but you won't hear that on the news. Remember that Mao Zedong said that China could lose millions of people in a nuclear war and the country would still go on," Cotes said. "They have just substituted viruses for bombs in this scenario."

They all sat at the table, eating their sandwiches in silence. It took a little while for this new information to sink into their beings. Logan thought it was outrageous that the Chinese Communist Party, or the CCP, who controlled that country could be so callous. They had killed nearly seventy million people worldwide so far with the pandemic just because of greed and desire for power.

Cotes was the first to break the silence. "I had hoped to fly out of here first thing tomorrow, assuming the samples were ready. Can we still do that?"

Kayla stood up from the table with her food tray in hand. "I have to go check on the cooler situation before I can answer that. I think we can still leave as scheduled, but I had better make sure." She walked to the side bar and set her tray down for collection. "I'll catch up with you on level two, where we are prepping the samples." She took long strides, hurrying out of the room.

The others finished their lunch, and Grimley led them out of the room. They walked down a corridor to an elevator that

Grimley activated using a security card. They all entered the elevator car and waited for it to reach the targeted floor.

Grimley explained, "Our lab was constructed almost entirely underground. That was done for security as well as for containment. We do administrative work on the ground floor and then have our lab stratified according to its biohazard containment level. Sublevel one is containment level one, our least-secure level. Sublevel two, where we're going, is biohazard level two, and so on. Our deepest level is where the newest and most restrictive biohazard work is done, and only a few people have access to it due to the risk of infection and protocols . . . and level of secrecy."

The elevator door opened on level two, and they stepped out into a secure corridor. Grimley said, "We go down here. It's the area where we prepare shipments and containers for other levels and labs. It's not in the biohazard containment area, so you only need to put on masks and lab coats for entry."

He led them through a door, then handed Cotes and Logan white lab coats with ID tags and monitoring badges on them. "The badge acts as a virus detector. If there is an undue level of contamination present, it will beep as a warning. No worries where we're headed.

"On official tours, I take people down to level three so they can see some of the containment areas. It looks like what you see in the movies: people in full PPE, glove boxes, and all that. They got it about right in the movie *Outbreak*, but our level four is much more dramatic, and level five—well, it's otherworldly. There you must be on a separate air supply and have three layers of PPE, all pressurized separately. It is extremely difficult to work under those conditions until you get used to it."

They entered a cold room, where two men were working on boxes the size of compact home freezers. They had one unit partially torn apart and were intently manipulating a small, electrical circuit inside the unit. Grimley asked about their progress.

"We're sure it's the sensor that's causing the problem, sir. If we can get a replacement for that or for the whole circuit, we'll be back in business," one of the men said.

Just then, Kayla entered the room with a sour look on her face. "Mayo doesn't have a spare refrigeration unit, but they have the part in one of the other clinics in Wisconsin. They're having someone drive it over this afternoon. It will take three or four hours, but at least we'll be able to make the repairs."

"That's good news," Grimley said, then turned to the technicians. "Can you men finish the repair if the part gets here by, say, five o'clock?"

"Yes, sir. It will be on overtime, but we should have it repaired by seven or so. Will that be OK?"

Everyone nodded their heads. Then Kayla pointed to one of the other identical cooling units. She walked over to it and lifted the lid as they gathered around.

"This is the Opex 12 stand-alone transport, ultra-low refrigeration unit," Kayla said. "It holds up to twenty liters of specimens and keeps them at a constant temperature between minus eighty and minus one hundred degrees Centigrade for eight days at a time on a fully charged battery. It weighs three hundred pounds. One-third of that is the battery."

"It certainly appears to be built to last," Logan said.

"It's the model designed for military use. It's rugged and has shielding on the electronics in case of an electrical attack." She looked up. "I hope we don't need to worry about that on this trip."

"Oh," Logan said, "are you going with us too? Cotes didn't say anything about it."

"Yes," she said. "I work with Dad on the vaccines and will need to go along so the lab can ramp up production quickly. I can handle the questions about the supporting medium, stabilizers, preservatives, and other components that go into the vaccine."

"Oh, that's great." Logan evaluated the others in the room. "So we're done here for now?"

Grimley turned to his daughter. "I think we're done. Maybe Kayla can give you the nickel tour of level four, and I can finish a couple of tasks I need to wrap up before I leave." He raised his eyebrows as he looked at her.

"Sure, I can do that, but I have to do more to prep the samples for shipment too. It will have to be quick," she said as her father left the room. "Follow me this way." Her eyes sparkled with eagerness as she walked to the elevator.

They rode the elevator down two levels and stepped out into a corridor with a pressurized door on the opposite side. They walked through it as purified air that smelled like disinfectant blew all around them. Once through the door, Kayla walked them up to a viewing window that revealed an enormous room that served as the first of a series of decontamination chambers. They saw several people in blue, Tyvek jumpsuits, with fully enclosed headgear and air supply lines attached. Some of them were entering the controlled rooms through additional pressurized doorways with intervening decontamination stations.

Some scientists stood inside control rooms working with slides and samples at sterilized workbenches.

"There isn't much to see except how many glass-walled rooms are all separated inside of the lab. Every doorway has a negative pressure seal on it, and to get into the individual labs, you must pass through a series of decon steps, each of a higher biohazard safety level, until you reach level four. It's quite tedious to go through all the steps you need to perform to get in and out of the high-level workspaces, so you have to be sure you plan all your work and have your ducks in a row before you commit the time for it. Level-five work is even more time-consuming, but it's super safe and can handle just about any pathogen we have ever discovered."

"I didn't realize how much time is involved just getting into the high-level areas. It looks claustrophobic to me," Cotes said. "It's like when you do deep diving. I tried one of the suits for a three-hundred-foot dive for an hour, but I couldn't wait to get out of the suit even as I sat in the decompression room waiting for my blood to regain its normal oxygen content."

"That's one reason we use glass everywhere—to keep people from feeling oppressed. It takes nerve to do this work every day," Kayla said with a frown. "I can't do it for more than a few days in a row, or it affects my sleep. I dream I'm underwater and wake up in a panic." She tried to smile and shake it off.

Logan sympathized with her. How could she do her work if she wasn't comfortable with the confined-space aspect of the biohazard rooms? Or the safety concerns? He wondered how she could deal with it if she felt claustrophobic. He didn't think he could handle doing it every day. He didn't get along well with confined spaces.

They left the fourth level and returned to the surface lab. She showed them into an examination room, where a technician handed her a metal tray with two small, plastic syringes. "I'm going to give you each a shot of the vaccine so you'll be protected against the virus. Might as well start now." She had each of them roll up a shirt sleeve and then injected them with the clear liquid. It was over in a minute, and they stepped back out into the hallway.

While saying their goodbyes, they arranged to meet for dinner at 7:00 p.m. at the Bar-TX Steakhouse close to the motel where the men were staying. Logan and Cotes retreated to there and checked in before making phone calls and dealing with the New York City and Washington, DC, catastrophe. Logan made three calls to men in his company to ensure they understood he had been called away for a few days. He wanted to check on the planned defense of the Cabrini-Green neighborhood from Antifa. It was all under control, and he felt better about leaving so precipitously.

He turned on the TV just in time to see the evening news broadcast. A large red banner on the screen declared *Breaking News*. A demure woman on the local station read her lines in a stoic manner, her eyes red like she had been crying. Makeup could do only so much to cover up tragedy.

"Our sources tell us that US Navy helicopters responded rapidly after the bombing this morning of Washington, DC, and New York City. The team from New York discovered the location at sea where a freighter ship was sinking at the time of their arrival some twenty-two miles off the coast of New York. There were no survivors to be seen either in the water or in any lifeboat. A US Coast Guard cutter arrived at the scene thirty minutes later and marked the location with a buoy while they searched for survivors."

Poor-quality video appeared on screen, showing a cluster of ships encircling another commercial freighter that was floating low in the water. Waves splashed against the half-sunken hull of the freighter. The news reader stared into the camera and appeared distressed, but continued reading.

"The helicopter that responded to the attack on Washington arrived thirty minutes after the bomb went off there. The searchers found a freighter-type ship foundering in the water with several men working on its deck. The men fired on the helicopter, and it returned fire, stopping the shooting. Our sources say that the men were apparently trying to scuttle their ship. An Arleigh Burke-class navy destroyer arrived immediately and began a boarding operation of the disabled craft. Apparently, the seamen on the freighter fought the sailors but were overcome, and a few of the crew were captured. Additional naval vessels have reached the stricken ship, and they are trying to stabilize it to keep it from sinking." She stopped again and read from the teleprompter. "Our own reporter, Michael Thompson, said the ship is needed as evidence for investigating the attack on Washington, DC. We will have more after this commercial break."

The TV went to a commercial at the same time that there was a pounding on Logan's door. He heard Cotes yelling for him to open up, so he rushed to the door and let him into the room.

"It was the Iranians working with Hezbollah. Damn those people." Logan assumed his commanding officer was talking about the attacks. "They launched Iranian Scud missiles from the decks of two freighter ships. The one our people captured had the launch frame for a Shahab-2 on it. They also caught an Iranian officer, probably from the Quds Force, and another man who may be Syrian. I heard that a thunderstorm last night must have given them cover as they approached the East Coast. Coastal surveillance didn't spot them until after the attacks."

"How about the warhead?" Logan asked. "I didn't think the Iranians had an A-bomb yet."

"Initial analysis of the Washington debris is that the uranium is from one of the old Ukrainian warheads that went missing when Ukraine gave up their arsenal. I knew back then that we should never have let the Russians have the damn things. Half of them disappeared on the black market and wound up all over the Middle East and wherever there was money to be had. We suspected that Iran was in the market to buy a few of them."

"It was a onetime attack on two cities. Why now?"

"I don't know."

"Did you get this information from the Pentagon?" Logan asked.

"Yes, from Admiral Shumwalt," Cotes said. "He thinks there won't be another such attack now. Hezbollah could pull off this sort of surprise only once. We have already shut down ship movements within three hundred miles of our shores. It's a real can of worms."

"But it's another example of asymmetrical warfare. A small, enemy attack through proxies on a major objective that we will have a hard time proving came from Iran. If we weren't so careful and law-abiding, we could just react, but obtaining proof will take time, and they will laugh their asses off watching our country tear itself apart over how to respond."

"And the initial estimates of casualties are coming in. Officially, we are looking at as many as two million dead and twice that in serious injuries. The damage to buildings and infrastructure was enormous, but an accounting will take time."

"What happened to the president? Is Mary Callahan the new one? We need to have someone in charge soon, assuming that Biden is dead."

"The latest that I heard is that she will be sworn in this evening so we don't go overnight without a president. But some people want the ceremony to be during prime-time TV to make it public, or it may be delayed until the morning. We'll have to see what happens."

"And I heard from the general that the center of government is moving to Raven Rock bunker in Western Pennsylvania for now and will eventually move to Denver per our national emergency plan," Logan added.

"Yes," Cotes responded. "That may affect us because the FAA has declared all aircraft grounded for twenty-four hours and may extend that. They are worried about another terrorist attack, possibly via airplane. It means we will probably have to get special clearance and veer far away from Denver because they will lock down air traffic there."

"I don't know about you, but I could use a beer about now. Should we go to the restaurant early for a cold one?" Logan stood up. "We can see if Williams wants to join us."

They picked up Williams at his room as they traversed the two hundred feet to Bar-TX. It was an old-style steakhouse, a ranch-style one-story building with a pair of longhorns above the doorway. They entered and found a long, straight bar along the right side of the room, divided from the dining room by a tall, wooden barrier that looked like a rail fence. They picked out three stools along the bar, took off their masks, and sat down.

A bartender came right over. "What will you have, gentlemen? Just in time for happy hour. All beers and well drinks are two for one until six."

Logan perused the taps behind the bar and selected a Coors Banquet while the other two men ordered Budweiser. There was considerably less choice in beers since the COVID lockdowns now that foreign beers were harder to find and many small breweries had gone bankrupt.

The barman returned with their brews. "Are you fellas here for dinner too? Should I run a tab?" He scanned the nearly empty room. "Looks like you're our only guests tonight because of the bombing. Most people went home to be with their families."

"We're meeting some folks for dinner at seven." Logan surveyed the others. "I think a tab sounds good."

The three of them scanned the bar and made small talk about the elaborate choice of tequilas the bar had stocked. They decided that Williams had drunk more of the brands than Logan and Cotes combined. They talked around the day's disturbing news to keep it from making their bar visit glum, but it was hard to avoid the topic.

But they couldn't put it out of their minds. Logan said, " I just can't wrap my mind around this whole attack." He looked grim and stared at Cotes. "I never thought this would happen in my lifetime." He tried to maintain his composure, even as a sense of dread seeped into his mind.

"I can't talk about it," Williams said. "It is too real and it hasn't sunk in yet. Too overwhelming to deal with up front." He looked away and rubbed his face with his hand. Then he lifted his glass and turned away from the others for privacy.

The barman returned, clicked on the TV over the bar, and selected the local news channel. An eager, young reporter was doing a segment on the reaction of local people to the bombings on the East Coast in a man-on-the-street format. One woman was crying while saying that she hadn't heard from her daughter in New York. "I can't call her. The phone is dead. Just a beeping signal." She broke down, and the reporter took the microphone away. Another woman—apparently her friend—put an arm around her shoulders as the mother shook from violent sobs.

The broadcast was interrupted by a *Breaking News* banner, which caught everyone's attention after this morning's events. A startled-looking news anchor stared at the screen, obviously listening to what his producer was saying into his ear. He swallowed twice and then stared into the camera.

"We've just been told that North Korea has launched missiles a few minutes ago that are headed for mainland US... They appear to be the new Hwasong-15 model . . . I don't know what that is . . . The missiles are heading for our West Coast right now." The newsman jumped to his feet and shouted at someone behind the camera. "Is this real? Are we under attack?" He threw the papers in his hand on the desk in front of him. "What the fuck is going on? Is this real?" The microphone went dead, and the man stomped off the stage with the camera still rolling.

"What the hell?" Logan nearly shouted. He stood up and stared at the TV screen, shock on his face.

"Jesus H Christ!" Williams said loudly as he jumped up from his bar stool. "Now what's going on? More terrorists?"

"I don't know, but I'll find out," Cotes, visibly shaken and angry, said as he stood up and walked outside with his satellite phone to his ear.

Logan tried calling Jorgensen in Chicago, and Williams stared at the TV screen, listening to more news coverage. Then he pulled out his iPhone and dialed a number.

Logan couldn't get through to Jorgensen and left him a message to call him back. He didn't know whom else to call who would have inside information on any imminent attack. He took a sip of beer and walked outside to see what Cotes had learned.

He found the admiral pacing back and forth in the potholed parking lot.

When Cotes saw Logan, he put his hand over his phone receiver and said, "Our observers offshore of NK registered that seven of their largest missiles launched about twenty minutes ago. We should know what the targets are in ten to twenty minutes if they get through." He directed his attention back to the phone and listened intently. "Four got through? Oh shit! How about secondary defenses? How about the GMD from Vandenberg? . . . OK, I'll hold."

"What's happening?"

"Seven NK missiles launched, but we knocked three down over the Pacific. Hang on." Cotes walked away, listening to the phone. "OK, call me back." He turned to Logan. "He's checking on the Ground-based Midcourse Defense system hits from Vandenberg."

The sun was getting low on the cloudy horizon, the light occasionally cutting through the clouds at a low angle as evening progressed. Suddenly, a flash of white light lit up the western horizon for a second or two, and then the sunlight returned to normal, like a flickering lamp.

"What the hell?" Logan said. "Did you see that flash on the horizon?"

Cotes's phone beeped, and he started speaking again. "OK, OK . . . Jesus!" Then he was quiet as he listened. "OK, thanks." He pushed the End Call button and just stared at the phone for several moments.

Suddenly, Williams ran over to the two men. "Did they hit Seattle?" he shouted. "I was talking with my ex-wife out there, and the call just went dead. Do you think they were hit?" Williams, who usually seemed cool as a cucumber, was agitated. His face was flushed, and his eyes were wild.

"Two missiles got through and did space bursts above Tacoma, Washington, and Oakland, California," Cotes said. "They were intended as EMP bombs and detonated about two hundred and fifty miles above the ground for maximum electrical impact. The immediate damage is that they shut down communications on much of the West Coast. We'll know more in a few minutes."

"Holy shit!" Logan said. "At least they weren't full-on nuke strikes this time, so we won't have that kind of destruction."

"Then my ex might be OK? She wasn't blown up?"

"No," Cotes said. "She's probably fine. Most likely, all the cell phone towers and power lines were shorted out in Tacoma and Seattle. The EMP creates huge electrical voltages like lightning striking everywhere at once. It causes voltage spikes in nearly all electrical devices unless they are shielded from it. There should be minor surface damage. It still can lead to carnage for an airplane in the sky or cars on the road. Some cars will get their electronics fried. Hell, nearly all electronics will be damaged to some extent."

"Well, that's good to know. The part about her probably being OK, I mean," Williams said softly. "I mean, we're divorced, but I still love her most of the time." He looked from Logan to Cotes. "It's complicated." He grinned sheepishly. Then his face took on a concerned look. "How does this impact our mission, sir?"

"I'm not sure. Let me call Dr. Grimley and see if they got that cooler fixed." Cotes stepped away to make the call.

"I'm going to call the airport and make sure we had no ill effects from the blasts," Williams said quietly. "We can't be too careful under these conditions. Maybe I'll see if we can get security to put a guard on our plane now that it's getting dark."

"What do you mean, Williams?" Logan asked.

"Well, sir," he replied, "I think this means we're at war with at least North Korea. Things get weird fast during a war. People think of how they can take advantage. Like maybe steal an airplane that isn't damaged yet by the EMP."

"Good point. We should plan for that sort of crime, as well as terrorists and spies. Just what we need," Logan murmured as he thought of their mission and the possible complications this news implied. "See if we can hire security for the plane if they don't have anyone on-site, OK? That will keep with our cover story that we're here on a simple Marshals Service trip."

"Sure."

By that time, Cotes had walked back over. He said, "They received the component they needed and will have the cooler ready by about eight. The doctors are coming over now, so we can talk over dinner and make final plans."

Logan relayed what Williams was doing regarding the aircraft. Cotes nodded his approval and led the other men inside the restaurant. Their drinks were still sitting on the bar, getting warm. They reassembled on their barstools and slugged down their brews.

Cotes ordered another round, saying, "We might as well enjoy our evening. I think we may not be able to imbibe like this for several days."

The TV had an update on what was happening in Seattle. A fresh and noticeably older newscaster was speaking about how the power was out all over Seattle and Tacoma and little information was coming in from the West Coast. A local scientist speculated that the city had been attacked by a nuclear EMP bomb and explained what it was and how it worked. The newscaster was hanging on every word and asking questions to clarify the information for his audience. He wasn't panicked and seemed to have experience covering news that was happening in real time.

"At least someone with a brain is speaking. A man on the radio said it was an alien attack," the bartender commented.

Cotes's phone beeped, and he stepped outside to answer just as the Grimleys entered the restaurant. They saw Logan at the bar and walked over.

"We heard some kind of electronic bombs hit the West Coast. Is that true?" Kayla asked with uncertainty in her voice. "We heard it on the radio on the way over here." Her face was tight with concern.

"Apparently, it's true. Admiral Cotes is getting more information on the phone now, I think," Logan said. "Why don't we get a table? He can fill us in when he finishes his call."

The hostess led them to a table near the rear of the establishment and passed out plastic menus, her hands shaking. By the time Cotes joined them, they had ordered drinks, and he called out his preference to the server who was tending their table. They all waited expectantly for him to say something.

"Well, we were hit by the North Koreans, and the electronic damage is considerable as far south as Silicon Valley." He spoke softly so that only those at their table could hear him. "There is no mistake that NK attacked us. We will probably counterstrike as soon as we designate a new president. But there is concern that we may be attacked again if we don't respond right away. Some people are saying that the Koreans took advantage of the fact that we didn't respond to this morning's attack, showing that we were in disarray and weak."

"What can we do?" Grimley asked as he stared at the table in a grim manner. His hands gripped the edge of the table as if he needed to hold onto something for support. "We have to do something, or it may happen again. Maybe more Korean mischief?" He lifted his eyes to look at his daughter and appeared overwhelmed by the current turn of events.

"That's a good question," Logan said. He wasn't sure what to say next. He was angry about these attacks and yet he felt he had to keep his emotions under control so he wouldn't upset the doctors any more than they already were. "They don't have many more missiles that could reach the continental US, but other people might be tempted."

"Like the Iranians or Russians?" Kayla asked nervously. Biting her lip, her pale face showed a great deal of tension. She reached over and squeezed her father's hand.

Cotes's satellite phone beeped, and he looked at it with dread. He answered, then suddenly winced and slapped his free hand on the table. "Is this confirmed?" he asked. "I'll be damned." He punched the End Call button.

Everyone around the table again stared at him in silence, waiting. He wiped sweat off his brow and stared at the table for several seconds. Finally, he turned to Logan and spoke slowly.

"According to standard procedure and following the current STRATCOM plan, we have begun NOKO2017." He stopped and saw that Logan understood. Then he explained to the others, "We have had a retaliatory strike planned for any NK nuclear attack. It's a plan that requires us to automatically launch a number of nuclear and nonnuclear weapons at the Hermit Kingdom. The response is hardwired because there is usually no time to decide whether to respond. Only the president can intervene to stop it. Since we have no president at this time, the launch orders were sent out."

"We launched missiles at the Koreans?" Williams asked, incredulous.

"It calls for no less than eighty weapons striking all aspects of the North Korea military and industrial infrastructure and the largest military targets. Some of the missiles are to be launched from ships off their coast, so they will be striking any time now. Because of their tendency to place important command-and-control sites within populated areas, there will be enormous casualties. In fact, within a half hour, North Korea will cease to exist."

Cotes, who seemed to be losing his otherwise stoic demeaner, emptied his whisky glass and waved over the server, who seemed to pick up on the fact that something intense was happening and scurried away to get the drinks with a fearful look on her face.

"So who gave the command?" Logan asked, surprised that the plan had been put into operation. He knew there were protocols to deal with many possible scenarios that might arise, but with the national chain of command broken, it left many questions. Still the enormity of such a counterstike was mindboggling. It would change the world.

Cotes said, "I don't know for sure. If the secretary of defense is dead, then the authority passes down the chain of command at the Department of Defense."

"Well, it had to happen. We couldn't have that nut in North Korea continuing his missile strategy," Grimley said as he sadly gazed at his daughter. "I knew he'd try something nefarious sooner or later. And he has had the Chinese to back him up the whole time."

Kayla covered her face to hide her tears. "This is terrible. We're at war, just like that. No warning. No hint of a choice." She began to sob quietly and her father tried to comfort her, even though he looked extremely pale and upset.

"Let's eat quickly so I can get back to the airport," Williams said. "I'm concerned about the safety of the plane even more now, and I have to find out if we can even fly to the coast if half the air traffic control network has been fried."

They waved the server over and ordered dinners and a bottle of wine to share. Cotes announced that they would have to be airborne by 8:00 a.m. tomorrow, if at all possible. The food was good, but dinner was hurried and there was little conversation as they all worked through the idea of being at war. When they finished, they all headed off to carry out whatever tasks they had to finish by the time they left. After Logan, Williams, and Cotes walked back to the motel, Logan made a call to Jorgensen.

"I can confirm the strike against NK," the general said. "North Korea as a nation ceases to exist. But there is something else to worry about: The People's Republic of China has raised their defense readiness to the equivalent of our DEFCON one. They are preparing for an all-out war."

Logan just ended the call and lay on the bed with his clothes on as he worked through all the changes that had occurred in the last fifteen hours. His mind raced as he wondered what it meant for them all.

Chapter 7

The next morning, there was a problem getting the self-contained refrigeration units loaded onto the Gulfstream. All three of them did not fit nicely into the cargo hold within the belly of the plane, so some creative modification of the hold was required. Takeoff was delayed until nearly 9:00 a.m.

By the time they had taken off, Williams had told several airport personnel about their destination for the day—St. Louis, Missouri. Williams had filed a flight plan for that destination, and they initially flew on that standard track from southern Minnesota. But after a half hour, Williams made a gradual turn to the southwest and headed for Omaha, Nebraska. He set the autopilot and stepped back to the cabin to let his passengers know what was happening.

"As you all know, I filed a flight plan to St. Louis to throw anyone following us off our trail—at least temporarily," he said as he poured a cup of the coffee Logan had just made in the small kitchen area at the rear of the plane. "We are now going to skim west of Omaha and fly diagonally across Kansas to Amarillo, Texas. That's the last airport where we can safely land and refuel, based on what we know this morning. That'll take about three more hours if I keep us at a low altitude most of the way."

"Do you really think that anyone might come after us to steal the vaccine, Admiral?" Grimley asked from his seat near the plane's rear. "I didn't think it would be such a problem. We had no trouble when we moved the last cooler of samples to another manufacturer in Chippewa Falls two weeks ago."

"I may be assuming the worst, but this shipment is much too valuable to lose—even more so than the other one," Cotes said calmly. "There have been indications that we may have at least one party interested in this cargo."

"That's right," Logan added. "Two men were surveilling the airport last night. They tried to get close to our plane, but our hired guards challenged them, and they disappeared."

"Why Amarillo?"

"It's a smaller airport that we can slip into with little notice and where we can evaluate the next leg of our journey," Cotes said. "You see, because of the East Coast attack and the EMP burst, many aircraft have been completely grounded, and many that are still flying have been forced onto more southerly routes like us."

"And we know people there who may be able to help us," Logan added.

"I know you explained your strategy this morning, but why can't we just fly straight to San Diego?" Kayla asked.

Williams explained, "We received information from Cotes' HQ that someone is tracking our flight. We don't know how they know about our cargo, but we have disconnected our aircraft tracking beacon in case that's being used against us. That's part of why we started out for St. Louis. Anyway, we may have to ditch the plane if someone has placed a secret tracker on board."

"We couldn't tell you about our suspicions until we were airborne," Cotes added. "There may also be a risk of a second attack from NK or even China at this point because NK is their client state. In that case, we don't want to be in the air."

They settled in for the nearly three hours of additional flight time. Williams first skirted Omaha air traffic and Offutt Air Force Base airspace, then headed straight south across the center of Kansas. He flew at a relatively low airspeed and altitude to avoid other air traffic on standard IFR flight corridors. It kept them more or less off the radar of air traffic controllers and, hopefully, anyone who might try to track them electronically.

Logan and Cotes conferred with Williams in the cockpit, where he was in frequent contact with air traffic control personnel from Amarillo. They advised him that air travel west from that city was problematic. Airplanes flying over parts of New Mexico and Arizona had been fired upon by unknown parties on the fringes of some airports. Shoulder-launched antiaircraft projectiles like the US Army Stinger missiles had been used, knocking several planes out of the sky. The big unknown was which terrorists were responsible. Also, the air traffic control tower at Los Angeles International Airport had been occupied by the local Antifa group of terrorists. All were advised to avoid LA and their neighboring airports because the normal staff had been replaced by "unreliable persons." There had been two airplane crashes on approach to LAX the same day. Local police had not yet reoccupied the control tower.

Logan was assigned to contact local resources that could be relied upon to help them safely travel the rest of the way to San Diego. He started by contacting Jorgensen to see what contacts he had in the militias in western Texas and New Mexico. He was on the phone with various potential allies for the rest of the trip.

Meanwhile, the doctors were engaged in discussions with the people in San Diego to whom they would deliver the vaccine samples. For security purposes, they would deliver them to the naval air base on Coronado Island. From there, the samples would be handed over to the US Marine Corps for final dispersal to the lab.

Kayla also monitored the coolers via a short-range remote device that gave her a readout on temperatures, battery levels, and other vital information about the coolers' performance. All parameters were nominal so far, with all batteries reporting having about 96 percent capacity left.

At 1:07 p.m., Williams began his approach to the Tradewind Airport located three miles southeast of downtown Amarillo. It was a privately operated facility that had the sort of security they needed. They had arranged to park the aircraft in an available hangar that was near the far end of the airfield, where they would have some privacy while they evaluated what to do next.

Despite the short runway, the landing was smooth, and the plane rolled right down to the hangar, where a ground crew helped Williams maneuver the craft inside. The crew closed the hangar doors, and the travelers disembarked. Each of them stretched and walked around a little to loosen up their stiff legs. Kayla asked to open the plane's cargo doors to verify one more time that the coolers were operating well.

"I just received a call that another midair collision occurred near LAX," Williams announced, his cell phone in hand. "This one was over San Bernardino and involved a commercial jet and a private craft. Someone seems to have hacked the air traffic control system and is sending out false information."

"What does that mean for us?" Cotes asked. "How will that change our plans?"

"I hate to say it, but it means that, considering our cargo and its importance, we shouldn't fly any farther," Williams said. "I think we have to leave the jet here and proceed by highway."

The admiral stiffened up, and a scowl formed on his face as he turned away from the others. He lifted his satellite phone to his ear and spoke in low tones to someone.

Logan thought he knew what Cotes was doing. He was likely calling his contact at San Diego to say they would miss the delivery deadline. There was little they could do about the loss of air travel, but they would have to adapt and find another option to travel to California, some one thousand miles away.

As he thought about their predicament, his phone vibrated with the arrival of a voice message from a New Mexico area code.

A voice said gruffly, "Call back in five."

He scanned the phone number and recognized it as one of his contacts whom he had recently called. It was a contact simply named Kreuger, someone that Jorgensen knew through military channels. Jorgensen had said he was a problem solver and had resources that Logan would need. He wondered what resources the general had been referring to. He made a note of the time.

Cotes walked slowly back to the group with a beaten look on his face. "I called San Diego and said we would have to travel by land now. I said it might take us a few days to get to the base to deliver the goods."

Dr. Grimley looked at him and said, "Our coolers are good for up to seven days. We can top up the batteries to add about a day to that, but how will we proceed, Admiral?"

"We have some calls out for help. We have to see who can lend us a hand to travel through three states that are largely outside the law."

"It's not that bad, sir," Williams said with a smile. "Only parts of those states are completely lawless, and most of those areas are the cities. We just need vehicles, manpower, and guns to get through."

"I guess that's like most of the country," Logan said. "While Antifa and other gangs, which comprise less than one percent of the country, are creating chaos, the rest of the people are just trying to survive. Most have their hands full holding down a job if they still have one, finding food and necessities for their family, and avoiding getting sick."

"And another one-half of a percent is trying to fight off the crazies that are wreaking havoc, mainly in the larger cities," Williams added. "That's our police, national guard, and military."

"And organized militias like the CNF," Logan said. "We support our police where they still exist." He paused to glance at the others. "Chicago, like many major cities, had our police force reduced for political reasons, and then we lost many cops when the shit hit the fan. We don't have an organized police force in Chicago anymore."

"How about in the suburbs?" Kayla asked.

"Well, a lot of the smaller cities and towns have survived with their local police and government intact. Like Evanston and some of the city's northern suburbs. Life is close to normal there, except for the pandemic and lockdowns."

"That sounds like Mankato," she said. "People there are busy enough just getting by, even though we aren't occupied by a gang. COVID has changed everything. With all this disruption, food and gas shortages are common. But at least we can go to the store and buy some things."

"Think of it as a war, like World War II in Europe," Cotes chimed in. "There, the population just moved around to escape the major battles and most survived—under terrible circumstances—and eventually returned home."

"But those were organized armies fighting in Europe. There was some semblance of order and regard for the civilians," Grimley muttered. "Except for the Nazis. They went out of their way to kill Jews and other minorities."

Logan threw up his hands. "Well, Antifa follows no rules. People have learned that you must flee their troops, or you will be killed or raped or robbed. They show no mercy."

The conversation stopped on that grim note. Five minutes had crept by, so Logan stepped aside to make his phone call.

"This is Kreuger," was how his contact responded.

"This is Logan Gordon. We have a mutual friend in Chicago."

"Ah yes, we do." The gravelly voice paused. "I understand you are marooned in that outpost called Amarillo in the great state of Texas."

"You are well informed. There are five of us and some cargo to transport." Logan tried to stay vague. "We could use some assistance that I hear you may be able to provide. Is that right?"

"I might be persuaded. Why would I do such a thing? What's in it for me and my men?"

"There may be some remuneration for your help, and you would have the comfort of knowing you did something to help your fellow citizens." Logan waited to see if this was convincing. "And our mutual friend would owe you one. So would I, of course."

"I don't know you, Logan. But our friend speaks highly of you. Said you were helping fight the good fight back in Chicagoland."

"That's true. But I have a task I must finish before I can return to fight in the trenches there."

"And what is this task that is so important?"

"I can't tell you over the phone, but lives depend on it."

"I see. Our friend said you were doing important work for the cause. I believe him." There was a pause as Kreuger cleared his throat. "What kind of help do you need?"

He decided he had to ask directly before the conversation ran off track. "I need transport to San Diego for me and my friends."

"How would I be paid?"

Logan hesitated. He didn't want to promise something that he couldn't deliver. "I would have to know your price before I could answer that."

"And when must you decide on your path forward?" Kreuger asked earnestly.

"As soon as possible."

"What kind of cargo? Is it heavy or bulky?"

"Three packages, each about the size of a pallet and weighing three hundred pounds each."

"Substantial, but manageable. My price would be a half-million US dollars or their equivalent in gold. Twice that if we expect to have special trouble en route. Do we expect trouble?"

"Probably." Logan wondered where he would get that kind of money on such short notice.

"I'll call you back in one hour with arrangements." The phone went dead.

Logan was in shock. Could he really trust this man? Could he really get himself and the rest of the group through the mountains and desert landscape patrolled by militias and roving gangs of thugs? He had to trust Jorgensen on this and hoped that the general knew Kreuger well.

He walked over to the admiral to inform him of the potential good news and ask him if he had the wherewithal to come up with $1 million in cash on short notice. He found Cotes in discussion with one of the airport security guards whom they had hired for the day. He overheard the tail end of the conversation. Apparently, the airport wanted a small fortune for the plane to stay in the hangar for twenty-four hours. In this time of unrest, prices were whatever a person could demand based on the situation. It was wartime inflation, opportunity, and greed rolled into one package.

"These jackals want ten thousand a night to use the hangar and provide us protection," Cotes said. "It's outrageous."

"Wait until you hear what our friend in New Mexico wants for our transport," he said. "We don't have a million in cash, do we?"

Cotes nearly choked at the price, but he settled down quickly. "I guess in these troubled times, that's what we have to expect. No one will take a risk without a reward attached." He paused and scanned their aircraft. "Follow me, Logan."

Cotes marched directly to the jet and climbed up the stairs to enter the fuselage. He checked that they were alone inside and pulled up the stairs for privacy. He then hurried to the rear of the plane and pulled down one of the two duffel bags he had brought with him. He unzipped the bag and held open the flaps for Logan to see its contents. Inside were many bundles of hundred-dollar bills. His eyes lit up when Logan pawed through the money and then looked at him.

"I'm like any good Boy Scout—I came prepared. I anticipated trouble and brought three mil, just in case we had difficulties." He grinned rakishly. "Tell me what you learned."

Logan filled him in on his conversation with Kreuger and told him that Jorgensen had recommended him. Cotes seemed to accept that they would have to do business with outlandish characters and nodded his consent.

"Where is this Kreuger located? Is he nearby, or will we have to hold out here for a few days until he can show up? I need to know so I can placate our hosts," Cotes asked.

"I will find that out when he calls back in . . . forty minutes. What did you learn from the marines?" Logan asked.

"They will meet us once we enter California—maybe at Twentynine Palms in the desert. They can escort us to the base from there. They said we should be prepared to fight our way across New Mexico and Arizona, especially if word gets out that we have secret cargo."

"Great." Logan rolled his eyes. "We have to be careful what we say and do here in Amarillo. Word could get out that we're a good target for a hijacking. That's all we need."

Chapter 8

The travelers, minus Williams, borrowed a car from one of the guards and drove off the airport property to a small Mexican restaurant nearby for a quick dinner. They promised to bring back a chicken chimichanga for Williams, who felt compelled to stay with the airplane to supervise its safety. Anticipating the possible need to defend the jet, Cotes had brought several weapons with them. Williams set himself up in a folding chair at the base of the plane's stairs with an M4A Carbine across his lap. He sipped coffee that he had made in the Gulfstream's kitchen.

They wound up at El Tequila Paraíso near the Tradewind, a family-operated joint with an impressive collection of tequilas along the backbar and a full menu of good, southwestern food. They were seated at a table near the back wall at Cotes's request and ordered their meals. The doctors had margaritas while Cotes and Logan had a single Dos Equis beer each. They settled into quiet conversation as they nibbled at chips and salsa and savored their beverages.

"I heard back from Kreuger just before we came here," Logan said. "He can meet us here with his convoy—that's his term, not mine—at 10:00 a.m. tomorrow. He wants to load up our cargo and be on the road by noon at the latest. We can discuss the route we'll take while the cargo is being stowed. He said he wouldn't talk about it on the phone for security purposes." Logan stared each of the others in the eye to see their reaction. "He said our routes are limited, and he will explain in the morning. He doesn't even want his men to know where we're going."

"Sounds like he's had some troubles before," Cotes snickered. "We'll have to see what he has to say. Playing it close to the chest is the same as I'd do it."

"He'll call just before he gets to town to ask exactly where we want him to pull up for loading." Logan grinned. "Again, saying nothing on the phone until the last minute. He sounds paranoid enough to keep us safe."

They moved on to small talk over the meal. Logan learned that Hamilton Grimley had been born and raised near Dayton, Ohio, the son of a grocer. He had done well in school and earned a scholarship to attend Ohio State University for a premed program. He graduated with honors and completed medical school at the same university.

"To make a long story short," Grimley mused, "I bounced around to several hospitals for my residency, and I ended up staying at the University of Minnesota. The offer was too good to leave. Then I settled in and married a wonderful woman named Mary Haskins."

Kayla picked up the story. "My mom died six years ago of brain cancer, having survived long enough to see me graduate from medical school and later obtain a PhD in microbiology." Her expression became melancholy. "Anyway, I've worked with my dad at the Mankato lab ever since."

When asked, the admiral briefly summarized his career as having been bitten by the idea of military service and having spent his life in the blue-water navy. He had seen much of the world from the deck of a ship. When the Twin Towers had fallen, he had heeded the call to duty to fight terrorists in the Middle East and other troubled parts of the world.

"I've been fighting terrorists ever since," Cotes said with fury in his voice. "It seems that no matter how many of them we neutralize, more pop up to create havoc all over the world. I'm sick of these criminals." In fact, he had met Logan when they had both served in the same counterterrorism unit. He told the Grimleys he couldn't tell them more about it than that. "I can tell you that I just hate terrorists—these cowards that kill innocent people just to get attention for some hateful cause. They keep on coming. We've got to kill every one of them."

The table settled into silence as they all ate and thought about the horrors that had befallen the both coasts. Their expressions ranged from hate for Cotes to anger for Logan and bewilderment for Grimley. Kayla seemed on the edge of tears.

"I know several people in DC," she whispered. "I hope they're OK. One of them works at the Smithsonian. She would have been at work at 8:00 a.m." She pulled out a Kleenex to cover her mouth and excused herself from the table.

Logan stood as she walked away. He thought about how many of his friends might have been lost in the bombings. Both he and Cotes had the ability to push troubling thoughts aside while they focused on tasks at hand. It was part of their training that kept them going, even when terrible losses and grief threatened to crush them with emotion. He knew that the true impact of the recent events would come out as wild emotions later when he could release his rage and sadness. They usually emerged when he lay down to sleep. Then all the fear and loathing would surface as weird dreams and nightmares. He would cope with it as he always did: alcohol and revenge were his usual outlets for pent-up feelings of loss and angst.

The three men talked about how sudden the attacks had been and how they weren't prepared for yet another catastrophe to enter their lives. After a few minutes, Kayla returned to the table, a look of misery on her face. It occurred to Logan that they needed to change the subject. He hadn't listened to the news since they had left Minnesota and had most likely missed out on some important information. "Say, has anyone heard whether we have a new president yet?"

Kayla put down her fork and replied, "Yes, Mary Callahan was sworn in today."

They finished their meal, and Logan said they should return to the hangar with the chimichanga for the starving Williams. By doing so, he dodged Kayla's questions about his own background. He smiled at her as he rose from the table, and she commented on how clever he was to avoid saying anything about his life.

They returned to the hangar at about 9:00 p.m. Williams wolfed down his meal with a beer and reported that nothing unusual had happened in their absence. Grimley sat with him as he ate dinner to keep him company while Logan showed Kayla where she and her father would sleep.

"The plane is set up with the two sofa areas in the back that can be pulled out farther to form narrow beds. You and your dad can stretch out on those. That way, you have access to the head during the night." He walked her to the back of the fuselage for her to see the layout. "The admiral and I will sleep in these comfy seats that lay back into a lounger, so we'll be all set."

"Will you need the bathroom during the night? You could come through and not bother us," she said.

"Oh, no problem there," he responded. "We can use the head in the hangar. One of us will probably be on patrol anyway, along with Williams, that is. We'll have to keep an eye on the guards too."

"You don't trust them?"

"Yes, but you never know. One of them might take a nap or head out for a beer in the middle of the night. We haven't worked with them before, so we can't be too careful."

"What's the story with Mr. Williams? He seems very protective of the plane," she inquired curiously.

"I don't know him very well. He's been working with the admiral for several years, so he must be reliable. Cotes would demand it." He grinned. "But he used to be a carrier pilot, so he must be one hell of a flyer."

"I guess so," she agreed. "I guess I'll call it a day. Goodnight, Logan."

She walked back as Logan pulled a cloth curtain across the aisle to create some privacy for her. Then he walked back to the stairs and climbed down to the hangar floor. Cotes and Grimley were discussing what would happen tomorrow. Logan joined them and picked up an M4A rifle to supplement his sidearm.

"The plan then is that we'll rise early and get ready for a midmorning departure. We will have the coolers ready to unload and all checked out for the trip," Grimley said. Then he said good night and climbed the stairs to the aircraft.

"I'll take the first shift, if you like," Logan said. "How about three-hour stints? That means I'll wake you at 12:30, Admiral."

"Sounds good to me," Cotes said. "We were just saying that we may not want to unload the cargo until Kreuger actually gets here in case there is a delay or we have to depart during the night." He watched Logan to see if he concurred. "We need a forklift for that, and I don't want anyone to see the coolers until we're ready to transfer them to a ground vehicle."

"I think I can find what we need," Logan said, grinning.

"You'll have to make a fresh pot of coffee," Williams said. "I'm going to crash now. Call me when it's my shift. I'll be in the front seat, dreaming of my girlfriend back home." He grinned and climbed onto the plane.

Logan and Cotes climbed the stairs after him, and Cotes settled into one of the recliner seats next to Williams. He was sleeping like a baby by the time Logan had finished making coffee and left the plane.

Logan walked around to talk to each of the guards who patrolled the hangar's exterior to make sure they were properly positioned to cover all entrances. Then he returned to the plane and stretched out in the folding chair as well as he could without being so comfortable that he would fall asleep. He decided he would have to stand up or walk around every few minutes to stay alert in the quiet hangar.

At 11:00 p.m., he made the rounds to check on the guards again. All appeared to be going well, so he returned to the chair he had positioned at the bottom of the staircase. He waited with his rifle lying across his lap.

Everything was calm during the night. He could hear an occasional, noisy vehicle driving past the airport on the asphalt road that edged the grounds. Near the terminal, he could hear the sounds of maintenance workers moving around to collect trash and complete other routine maintenance often performed after an airport shut down active operations. Every now and then, the guards coughed from their positions, and they checked in with one another over the handheld radios they all carried, including Logan. He didn't expect any trouble on their first night at this airport because they had been careful to keep their location secret.

Then he heard movement within the jet that soon resulted in Kayla tiptoeing barefoot down the steps onto the hangar floor. She wore a rumpled T-shirt and a pair of yoga pants. She grinned at Logan as she stepped up next to him.

"I couldn't sleep. Guess I'm too worked up," she said as she looked around for a place to sit.

"Well, that isn't my problem. I was just starting to doze a little. You can help keep me awake, if you like," he replied. "Here, take my seat. I'll get another chair." He walked to the hangar office and brought back another of the folding seats.

Without protest, she settled into his former chair, and he pulled up close to her.

Kayla said, "I keep thinking about how we're going to get all the way to the coast, given the current state of affairs." She gazed at him for a moment. "And you never did tell us how you got into this mission. Or anything about your background. I'd like to know more about you, if you don't mind saying. I mean, we got off to a bad start back in Mankato. I'm just trying to be friendly."

Logan smiled and decided he would have to say something, or she would wonder what he was holding back. "OK, well, first of all, I'm on this mission because the admiral personally chose me to help out. We've worked together before on a number of operations, and we work well together."

"You served in his clandestine unit, I gather?" she asked with a grin.

"Yes. Maybe you know more about that than I thought. If so, I don't have to say too much that might be confidential." He scanned her features to see if she was satisfied with his answer. "As for my background, there isn't much to tell. I grew up in Evanston, just north of Chicago, and joined the navy to see the world. That was more than I expected, but I did spend a lot of time on ships of different types for years. Then 9/11 hit us, and I got sucked into fighting terrorists like a lot of other folks in the services. I seemed to be good at it, so I received specialized training that brought me to Cotes's door. And the rest is history." He grinned in relief to have the story over with.

"But you like what you do, don't you?"

"Yes, I suppose—to a point. I wish I didn't have to fight jihadists so much, but that's the job I have. I feel good that I've stopped some bad things from happening and have made a few really nasty people pay for their misdeeds." He stopped and stared at the floor. "I like the navy and being at sea—well, for a few weeks at a time. It gets monotonous."

"I bet. I don't like cruises because I feel confined, even though we stop in a port almost every day. It must be nice to visit lots of exotic places."

"Some of them aren't very exotic, just dirty port towns and dusty desert. But some are nice enough, and they always have friendly people."

He watched her as she sat quietly and ran her fingers through her hair. She was a pleasant person and someone he might be interested in if they weren't working together. She smiled a lot, and he found that attractive.

"You spent a lot of time in Chicago, then, while growing up?"

"When I could drink and drive, I would go to the jazz and blues clubs downtown to listen to music with the guys. It's sad to see that most of the great clubs have been destroyed in the rioting over the last few years. A lot of downtown has been occupied and trashed by one gang or another."

"Yeah, I know what you mean," she said as she frowned. "Minneapolis has suffered from the riots and occupation too. I wish our city officials would do something about it instead of just giving in to the gang demands. It's not safe in the city anymore."

"When was the last time you ventured into town?"

"It's been over a year now. Some friends and I drove in to see what was left of old places we used to visit, and our car was chased by people in black masks. One of them shot at us. We got the hell out of there and never went back."

"How are things in Mankato? Is it safe?" Logan asked as he shook his head. He was saddened by the poor state of affairs in Chicago, a city he loved and missed now that it had changed so much.

"Oh, it's OK. There isn't much of a nightlife, though, so I don't go out there either. We have a good police force. They keep the looters and rioters out ... Well, they try. They have shootouts with them sometimes." She turned to Logan to see if he understood. "You see, we don't have much to steal in Mankato. No wealthy neighborhoods, like in Minneapolis. Nobody is going to get rich by attacking us."

"Well, in Chicago, they break in and rob everyone. Sort of equal-opportunity robbers," he said quietly.

She grinned. "Regular Robin Hoods."

Logan nodded his head at that. What they had seen play out over the years was that Antifa and Black Lives Matter were both after power, which came along with the need to steal other people's money or to at least destroy what others had. There were other violent gangs too. Many were just street gangs that had learned that the city governments weren't going to stop them from larceny and mayhem. Once the violence and crime had gotten started, it was hard to put it back in the bottle. Most mayors and city councils had just given in to the demands of the criminals. It was easier, and the gangs promised to lay off the wealthier neighborhoods if they got their way. That had led to bad deals for the rest of the residents of the cities and suburbs. And everyone had to contend with the food shortages and the pandemic on top of all the crime.

But there were a few exceptions to the rule. San Diego, for instance, was relatively crime-free because the local government had stood up to the gangs. That was probably why the factory that would make the vaccine was still intact. It was protected within the city's confines and defended by the city and federal government forces in the area. Read local police primarily, with the navy and marines in support.

Logan stood up and stretched. He noticed that Kayla was beginning to fade. "We have to start early tomorrow. You probably ought to catch some sleep while you can." He grinned at her sleepy face.

"Oh gosh. You're right. I think I can crash now." She stood up and stretched before shuffling toward the stairs. "Nice talking with you, Logan."

He intently watched her as she ascended the steps and disappeared into the plane. Logan made the rounds and watched the clock for the next hour, waiting for his shift to end. He mulled over the details of tomorrow, hoping everything would work out. If not, they would have to find a new way to travel west. Even with Kreuger's help, he felt that it was going to be an adventure that he would have been thrilled about if he didn't have to protect such sensitive cargo.

Chapter 9

At 7:00 a.m., they were awakened by the sound of gunfire inside the hangar. Logan and Williams grabbed their rifles and hurried down the aircraft stairs, pausing to determine where the shooting was taking place.

The gunfire stopped, but they heard a scuffle next to one of the manway doors of the building on the side closest to the street. They ran over and found Cotes and a guard named Paul wrestling with a man dressed in black. The man was putting up a hell of a fight, kicking and biting to get free from their holds.

Logan rushed up beside Cotes and hit the man on the head with the butt of his rifle, but not so hard as to kill him. The man slumped in Cotes's arms, and they all threw him onto the floor, face down. Paul secured him with handcuffs on his wrists behind his back and on his ankles.

Cotes had a bloody nose and was enraged. Paul had a cut above his right eye, which was bleeding at a slow trickle. They both stood up and tried to catch their breaths.

"What the hell happened?" Logan asked as he searched the intruder for weapons and any identifying papers. "This guy doesn't have much of use on him. No credit cards, but he has a few bucks and a driver's license. Says his name is Lee Guo." He rolled the man over so they could see his face clearly. His features were similar to that of the actor Jet Li.

"I caught him coming through the door," Paul said. "It was locked, but he must have picked it to get in. I was standing here and just had enough time to react. He knocked my rifle away with a kung fu kick. I had a hell of a time with him."

"I heard the ruckus and came over to help. He's a great fighter. Tough and uses mixed martial arts." Cotes leaned his head back, reducing the bleeding from his nose. "Thanks for the help. He's stronger than you'd think for his size."

"Hell, he may be a Chinese agent, from the looks of him," Logan said.

The intruder began to move slightly, and they sat him up against the wall so they could examine him. That was when Logan noticed the bullet wound in his leg. Blood was flowing slowly from Guo's left thigh. "He's been shot."

"Yeah, I shot him with my Glock when I saw him beating up Paul here," Cotes said as he held a Kleenex to his nose. The bleeding was slowing down. "Then I grabbed him too, and we got into it."

Paul defended his honor. "I had him under control, except for that damn kicking."

Kayla called out from the stairs of the plane. "What happened? Are you OK, Admiral?"

After they nodded yes, she reappeared a short time later, holding a first-aid kit. She stared at the assailant and seemed to realize the severity of the fight that had taken place. This was no short scuffle, but had been a near deadly exchange. Her face blanched, and her eyes narrowed. She looked like she would turn away when she realized the intruder had been shot. She seemed to struggle to contain her fear as she pulled Paul aside to place a gauze patch on his forehead to stop the bleeding.

Cotes took a couple of cotton balls from the first-aid kit and stuffed them up his nostrils. He teetered a little, and Logan reached out to hold him up.

"Watch out! He's getting out of his cuffs!" Williams called out as he jogged over to join them. "He's got his hand in his pocket. He's got something in it." He ran to Guo and grabbed a hand that Guo had placed over his mouth.

The result was nearly instantaneous. The man shuttered for several seconds and then completely stopped moving. His head slumped forward onto his chest.

Williams grabbed Guo's hand and pulled it away from his mouth. The man was dead. "Jeez! He took poison," he said.

Kayla walked over to inspect the body, shock working its way across her features. She took a few deep breaths and put on a pair of blue, surgical gloves from the kit. She opened the dead man's mouth and glanced inside. "It might have been cyanide. Fast-acting, and the inside of his mouth is bright red," she said in a professional manner. Then she seemed uncomfortable and backed away from the body, bumping into Logan.

Logan put his hands on her shoulders to steady her and noticed the look on her face. "You OK, Kayla?"

She averted her eyes from his and stepped away.

Logan asked Cotes loudly, "Do people really use cyanide capsules anymore?"

Cotes knelt next to Guo and sniffed the odor that emanated from his mouth. "Smells like burned almonds, sort of. Maybe it was cyanide, then. He must have been a Chinese agent." He looked up at the others. "Maybe he was here to steal the vaccine. The Chinese government has been very interested in our work in that area."

Logan was assigned to make sure there were no other breaches of security, and he patrolled around the building, checking in with the other guards. They searched for any other signs of attempted entry into the hangar. There was no more evidence of activity.

Meanwhile, the others dressed for the day and packed up their things. They had coffee and granola bars for breakfast as they discussed what to do with the intruder's body. They decided not to report the incident to local law enforcement because that would lead to an investigation and their mission would be imperiled. Cotes invoked national security as the reason the guards shouldn't talk about what had happened. They agreed to keep their mouths shut when Cotes gave each man a personal bonus for their help.

At 9:00 a.m., Logan's phone vibrated with a call from Kreuger. He was inbound, a little early, and wanted them ready to transfer their cargo in fifteen minutes. They hustled to comply. They stashed the Chinese spy on the airplane and wrapped him in a blanket.

Within ten minutes, they heard the rumble of vehicles charging down the road at the airport's perimeter. Logan ran to the door that opened in that direction and was surprised to see a fleet of assorted vehicles approaching along the street at a good clip. The lead vehicle was an H1 Humvee with a large eagle painted on its front doors. The convoy braked to a stop out on the road, and a passenger and the driver stepped out of the Humvee and walked to the chain-link fence that surrounded the airport.

"Are you Logan?" the passenger called from ten yards away. "I'm Kreuger."

Kreuger was a tall, rotund man wearing a flak jacket with muscular arms protruding from a sleeveless denim shirt and a Para-Ordnance .45 semiautomatic handgun on his hip. He also had on a flattened, desert combat hat; camo cargo pants; and camo canvas boots. He had a rounded face with bushy eyebrows and a similarly bushy mustache and beard, all of a reddish tone. His face was sunburned, and his lips were chapped. He gave off the air of being in a hurry and not tolerating any foolishness.

"I'm Logan. Step inside to meet the rest of our team."

He led Krueger to the nearby gate in the fence, which one of the guards unlocked. He then turned and walked back through the manway and into the hangar with Krueger right on his heels. Inside, Logan introduced the others, including Cotes, whom he called US Marshal Martz. He noticed that Krueger was acting nervous—no more than he had expected him to be, considering he was surrounded by strangers. Krueger apparently had trust issues.

Krueger stared at the bright-white jet as he evaluated his new companions. He scanned the rest of the hangar and its contents, and then his eyes settled on Cotes's face. He began to say something and then stopped. He asked, "Where can we talk privately? I mean, just those of you who will be traveling. The other locals need not hear what I have to say."

"OK," Cotes said, indicating the plane. "In there."

They all climbed up the staircase. Cotes pointed to Williams and said, "He won't be coming with us, but he needs to know our route. He'll stay with the plane while we travel."

This was a new plan that Logan had discussed with Cotes last night. They had decided they couldn't just leave the plane unattended for even a few days, so Williams would have to fly it to a secure location: Tinker Air Force Base near Oklahoma City, Oklahoma. He would later meet them at a designated location for their return trip to Chicago.

"I want to tell you the minimum until we're on the road," Kreuger said in a steady voice. "My base is in Roswell, New Mexico. That's where we'll be heading tonight. I know you were probably expecting to travel along the I-40 corridor, but that would take us through Tucumcari and Albuquerque, which are too dangerous to contemplate nowadays. Also, I-40 is patrolled regularly by a couple of biker gangs that claim anything they can find along that road. It's a no-go unless you have an army and a lot of time to fight your way through."

Kreuger pulled out a highway map and pointed to Highway 60 that ran southwest from Amarillo into New Mexico. "Texas has its shit pretty well wired together, but New Mexico has been running wild so far. The southern half of the state is overrun by Mexican gangs that have overwhelmed the border patrol, and the major cities are just like hell on Earth. We need to thread the needle between all these crazies and work our way through Clovis to gain state Highway 70 to Roswell tonight. That's fairly safe and predictable. We'll set out from there tomorrow and go west by the safest route based on some recon I have boys doing right now. Our actual path will depend on what they report back tonight."

"You don't know what our route will be through the rest of New Mexico?" Cotes asked, incredulous. "You're supposed to be the expert to get us through all these badlands. I'm not impressed."

"Well, if you know better, then you pick a route, Marshal. And then we'll see if you can deal with the Comancheros, the Cruces

Vandals, and the Road Hogs armies. Let's see what you do when you encounter three hundred angry rednecks driving armored vehicles and Harleys with machine guns on them. Go too far north, and you run into Los Muertos south of Albuquerque. Go too far south, and you run into the roving Mexican gangs that range north from the border on raids for women and booty."

Logan knew that Cotes wasn't used to this sort of urban and unbridled warfare. He had been inside the government and hadn't seen the collapse of the American fabric that had taken place in the last two years due to too much office time coordinating missions and not much time out on the street. In any case, Logan hoped Cotes would figure it out before he alienated the very people they needed to help them.

"Sir," Logan said quietly, trying not to show his exasperation with Cotes's lack of tact. "I think that the situation down here in the southwest is so fluid that it's hard to predict a route without a good deal of knowledge of the land and the players that we could encounter. Sounds like we need an expert on the region."

Kreuger didn't exactly grin, but he stopped scowling with a sharp furrow across his forehead for a few seconds as he nodded his head toward Logan. "I didn't say it would be easy, gentlemen, lady. And we're going to have to spit some lead at more than a few banditos. That's why you're going to pay me the big bucks." Kreuger nearly fell over laughing at his own joke. He kept laughing for a full minute before he controlled himself. "Sorry. It's the damn tension of the last few days. I lost a few men up by Santa Fe last week. Bushwhacked."

"Sorry to hear that," Logan said. "Listen, we aren't used to the conditions out here. I have seen a lot of chaos in urban areas around Chicago, but not the kind of open country warfare you describe. It sounds like *The Road Warrior* out here."

Kreuger seemed content to hear those words of understanding. He sat up straight and then said, "And there is the subject of my payment."

Cotes nearly had a fit, but tried to control himself when Logan put a hand on his shoulder. Logan knew that Cotes had expected a request for some proof of their ability to pay, but still found it hard to deal with the unstructured environment. He reluctantly stood up and made his way to the rear of the aircraft, where he dug around in his oversize duffel bag. He pulled out a cloth bag and returned to the gaggle of waiting people. He handed the bag to Kreuger, who held it up with his right hand and raised and lowered it a few times.

"Feels light."

"It's only half the money. You'll get the other half when you complete your mission." Cotes had his face made up, ready for an argument. "Don't you want to count it?" He glared at Kreuger.

Kreuger casually searched inside the bag and then cinched it up. "Nope. I trust you, Marshal. I know you just aren't used to the ways of this brave new world we live in, but you will see for yourself what we're up against." He stood up, signaling the meeting was over. "We had better get your cargo, whatever it is, transferred to my truck. We need to hit the road. We have to be in Roswell before dark."

They left the plane, and Kreuger asked Logan to make a way for his truck to drive into the hangar. Then he walked out to the road to shout orders to his men, some of whom had dismounted their vehicles and were standing guard with rifles in their hands, pointing downward.

Logan yelled to Paul to open the gate in the perimeter fence so that a truck could drive into the hangar. While Paul did that, Logan raised the motor vehicle door at the rear of the hangar. He stepped outside and motioned for the driver of a two-ton, flatbed Ford truck to come his way. The driver carefully maneuvered his truck into position next to the side of the airplane by the cargo bay doors. He parked the Ford and stood by while one of the airport guards pulled up in a small, front-end loader.

After Logan unlatched the cargo bay hatch, the guard approached and slid the forks into the compartment. He lifted with caution while Logan guided his forks to reach the first pallet and the cooler that was attached to it. He slid it out and then quickly repositioned the loader to set the pallet on the bed of the truck. Williams and the truck driver reoriented the pallet into position on the truck bed while the guard removed the second pallet and cooler. In ten minutes, they had transferred all the coolers and secured them onto the Ford's bed with a canvas cover.

Williams closed the cargo hatch carefully. He checked the aircraft for any belongings that the passengers might have left behind and to be sure the Chinese spy's body was secure, wrapped in a blanket and propped up in one of the passenger seats. He prepared to leave as soon as the others hit the road. He shook hands with them and then called the airport tower to notify them of his imminent departure.

Cotes opted to ride in the passenger seat of the flatbed truck with the coolers to be sure they were safe. The truck driver handed him a semiautomatic, 12-gauge shotgun, which he laid across his lap. Logan, Kayla, and Grimley, carrying their luggage, walked out the manway door to follow the truck out to the road. Kreuger led them to the lead vehicle of the convoy, the H1 Humvee. He stopped before opening the door and faced Logan.

"Logan, I assumed you would want to ride in the lead with me, so the back seat is yours. Kenny will be driving, and I'll sit next to him up front," Kreuger said. "I assume that the two doctors would be more comfortable in the third vehicle, a Suburban, where we will stash the duffel bags. Does that seem reasonable?"

Logan looked down the line of vehicles and then viewed the Grimleys. "Sound OK to you? The Hummer will be pretty tight and a rough ride."

"Sure, I guess," Kayla said to Logan and then turned to Kreuger. "We can live with that. Is there communication between vehicles?"

"Oh yes, ma'am," Kreuger said with a smile. "You guys can talk back and forth all you want." He handed Logan and Kayla handheld radios. "These are set to a frequency that the crew isn't using. You can switch to channel six if you want to hear what the rest of us are jawing about."

They loaded up in their vehicles and moved out. The convoy consisted of the Humvee, two black Suburban SUVs, then the flatbed truck, and two more Suburbans bringing up the rear. They drove about five car lengths apart and traveled at thirty miles an hour on the two-lane road. They followed Tradewind Street until it crossed Farmers Avenue and turned left onto that. After a mile, they jogged over onto Washington and then encountered Highway 335, which they joined heading westbound. They picked up speed to sixty-five miles per hour on the two-lane asphalt and whizzed past farmhouses and small clusters of homes as they left the city behind.

Within a few miles, they turned onto Interstate 27 south, which ran for a while as both Interstate 27 and Highway 60. Then Highway 60 diverged from the freeway and turned off to the southwest toward the town of Hereford. Just before they left the highway, two dirt bikes and a pair of Jeep Cherokees joined their entourage. Logan wondered how long they would go before they encountered trouble.

"I use the bikes as scouts that run ahead and search for any road jams or other types of trouble," Kreuger said with a look of pride on his face. "The Cherokees carry special equipment. I have a total of twenty well-trained men with us, all loaded for bear. I don't expect any trouble between here and Roswell, but you can never be too careful these days."

Once they left the freeway, all aspects of the suburbs fell behind, and they entered farm country with large, irrigated fields and scattered cattle. They drove through a landscape of ranches and farms, some with center-pivot sprinkler systems for crops and some with dry-land fields. A few feedlots were also present, with herds of black cattle and a few longhorns interspersed along the way. Farmhouses and ranch buildings were clustered here and there, with farmers driving huge tractors with wagons or other implements behind them. It was an industrious part of the country that hadn't been as badly affected as the more urban areas. Law and order still prevailed here.

Two hours passed by without incident, and they crossed the state line into New Mexico at Farwell. They reduced speed to double nickels and continued west.

"We'll cruise over to Clovis and stop for a break there. We can pull over at Leal's Mexican, where they have a big parking lot. We can squeeze in there, and everyone can grab something to eat." Kreuger seemed happy that they had not been delayed so far.

The convoy pulled off the road and parked in sequence behind the restaurant so that they could drive out at a moment's notice. They entered the restaurant four at a time so that most of Kreuger's men could remain on guard. They bought takeout lunches of burritos and tacos and soft drinks and ate them next to their vehicles, using the hoods of the trucks as tabletops. Logan ordered a shredded-beef burrito and a Coke and consumed it with gusto while talking to the Grimleys. Cotes acted worried and stayed close to the SUV with his duffel bag and the rest of his cash in it. "Trust but verify" was his motto.

At 1:00 p.m., they loaded up and headed south on Highway 70, going due south, and then angling southwest toward Roswell. They were still traveling through cattle-ranch country, but there was less water, so the farms were more dry-land style than those across the border in Texas. It wasn't clear at first where their water came from since there was no large river nearby, but Logan figured it out as they drove that most of the farmers used groundwater to irrigate their fields and water their cattle.

They passed through the farm land into dry grasslands for a few miles and then dry desert, with its colorful landscapes of arroyos and bedrock outcrops. The land transformed into red-rock scablands, where little or no vegetation grew. A few people were out driving ATVs around on the bare rocks and tearing up what little soil there was. It looked like fun, but Logan noticed that nearly everyone carried a gun of some sort with them. Apparently, it wasn't the carefree environment it appeared to be, but Logan thought about how nice it would be to come back here when life returned to normal to explore the countryside. The bucolic nature of the landscape attracted him. It certainly was pleasant compared with his current life in Chicago.

They drove through a well field that extracted natural gas and some oil from the widely spaced wells. It was located on a dry, rocky swell of the land just before they crossed the Pecos River. They drove past signs for Bitter Lake and Snow Lake, where there were no lakes at all. Apparently, in some years, there had been enough rainfall for water to pool for a few weeks before it all evaporated in the unrelenting desert sun. A low, rugged mountain range of deformed, red sandstone rose up before them as they drove. It was surreal compared with the restful farmland they had passed that morning.

They crossed Highway 285, which led into Roswell, at about 4:00 p.m. and continued west on Highway 70. That road arced around the town, and they turned off onto a gravel lane that took them more or less westward up into some low hills cut by arroyos trending southeast and downslope. After twenty minutes of slow, cautious driving on gravel and dirt tracks, they pulled into a small, box canyon that contained a ranch house, a few outbuildings, and a grove of cottonwood trees. They passed through a stone wall that was monitored by a man in a guard shack. A desperately narrow stream flowed down from a rocky gorge perched above the steep walls enclosing the rear of the canyon.

The convoy stopped, and the vehicles parked en echelon in the large gravel parking area next to the house. Everyone disembarked and stretched their weary arms and legs after the long drive. Kreuger left the travelers standing next to the Humvee while he shouted out commands for his men about how they were to guard their stations during the night. When he finished, he walked briskly over to his clients.

"We did real good today, folks. We made it here with no problems, so I guess that's a good start," Kreuger said merrily. "We'll spend the night here and continue on in the morning." He turned around and pointed to the house. "You should be comfortable and safe here. We have sentries up on the rocks around here and lookouts down the canyon as well. We keep this place locked up pretty tight because it's our main base of operations."

"Is this safe for our cargo? Shouldn't it be under cover for protection?" Logan asked.

"Well, I was going to suggest that we cloak your cooling units with a steel cover," Kreuger said. "I thought we could move the Ford into the barn over there, where we can encase the coolers with a quarter-inch steel plate that we can weld together, if that seems good to you." He gazed up at the sky and then at Logan. "I didn't know what kind of stuff you had to transport until today. We need it under a bulletproof cover in case we get shot at."

Grimley spoke up. "Yes, a bullet would do a lot of damage to our coolers. But the steel container would have to be vented. The coolers generate a lot of heat and vent some gas."

"Sure. We can accommodate that. Maybe you'd like to supervise the construction work?" Kreuger suggested. "That way we can do whatever you want for their protection."

After more discussion, they agreed that Kayla and Logan would supervise the welding operation while the others hauled their gear into the house for the night. Kreuger had three of his men drive the truck over to the barn and begin the project.

The weather was warm and sunny, a light breeze keeping it comfortable to be outside while the sun was out. It was a clear day, so Logan and Kayla stayed with the steelworkers until they finished. When the work was done, Kayla verified that she could still access the coolers easily to check on their operation. The sun was already low on the horizon by that time, and the temperature began to drop slightly into the sixties.

Dinner was served in the house at 6:30 p.m., and Kreuger, his second-in-command named Charlie Woodson, and the four travelers settled around the table in the dining room. The rest of Kreuger's men ate in the crew quarters in a bunkhouse next door. A man named Kookie made the meal, comprising baked sausage lasagna, and it was delicious.

"Kookie has been with us for about three years," Kreuger said between mouthfuls of cheesy lasagna. "He came from Socorro, where he was a chef at the university. He was in Desert Storm and took some hits there. Left him a little wacky, but he sure can cook up a feast."

"Are these all of your men, then?" Cotes asked as he scanned the table.

"No. I have about three hundred men scattered all over this part of the state," Kreuger replied. "We all have ranches or small businesses to work. But we stay in contact daily, and lots of our guys are like minutemen. They can mobilize quickly if we need them."

"And what exactly do you do here?" Cotes asked delicately.

Kreuger paused between bites of food to respond. "We work with local law enforcement to help keep a lid on things down here in Chaves and Lincoln Counties. The police in Roswell do a great job but lately have needed support a few times. We get more outlaws in the counties just because they abut places where more violence occurs. We are on call, but we only get called out when a big biker gang comes through our part of the state or one of the Mexican cartels moves north of the border. There's a lot of narcotics transport through our little part of the world. You'd be surprised."

Cotes pushed his point. "You're vigilantes, then?"

Kreuger became silent for a few moments. "I take offense at the use of the term 'vigilante.' We're law-abiding citizens who support our local police and sheriff. I'm a deputy sheriff in this county, and my men are authorized to enforce the law around here." He fixed Cotes with his stare and showed his ire. "And I'm not traveling around the country secretly hauling unknown cargo, Marshal." He stopped and snarled at Cotes. "Or should I call you Admiral?"

Cotes reacted like he had gotten an electrical shock, then stared right back at Kreuger. "How'd you know? Did Logan tell you?" He swiveled his head in Logan's direction.

Kreuger grinned at Cotes's discomfort. "No, not him. General Jorgensen. He said you were on some sort of secret mission for the government." He sipped the glass of water he was drinking. "I don't like being lied to, Admiral. Not by you or anyone else. I think it's time for you to tell me what you are up to so I don't arrest you on suspicion of doing something illegal."

Cotes stood up and faced Kreuger, and the big man responded by doing the same. It appeared as if they were going to escalate the confrontation to fisticuffs.

"We're carrying lifesaving vaccine samples to a lab in San Diego so they can bring it into mass production for the general population," Kayla said. "We were going to fly there, but our plane was grounded because of the EMP bombs and other threats. So now we have to travel overland. We weren't prepared for that, so that's why we need your help."

Cotes quickly turned to glare at her, but then his expression softened. "You are not authorized to divulge that information, Dr. Grimley."

"Well, sir," Logan said. "We need to tell Kreuger the facts anyway. His men are putting their lives on the line for us. He deserves to know why this trip is important and why we are worried about our safety."

"That will be enough, Logan," Cotes said, bristling with rage.

"My men deserve to know what they are protecting—that you're not just some fancy drug smugglers. We get enough of those around here." Kreuger sat down again and looked at Logan.

Logan took a sip of water and glanced at Cotes, who also sat down—confrontation over for now. "Admiral, we need to level with this man, so he knows why this mission is important." He looked back at Kreuger. "I didn't tell you everything last night over the phone because of security."

"And now is a good time to tell me how far you want me to take you and if there is a drop-dead date for this travel," Kreuger stated in a firm voice.

Cotes jumped in at that point in the conversation, "We have to meet up with a marine escort at Twentynine Palms in the Mojave Desert in three days—on Monday the twentieth. It's not a lot of time, even in ordinary times."

"You're damn right about that." Kreuger stood up abruptly. "That is all the way across Arizona and right through the reservation, the Yavapai Gap, and the territory of the Needles Cartel, not to mention the river crossing there. Jesus H. Christ! That's a lot to ask of this old cowboy. I have to make some calls." He walked briskly out of the room.

Chapter 10

The convoy pulled out from the ranch house before the sun crested the red soil of New Mexico the next morning, with Logan and the others amped up on caffeine from Kookie's cups of joe. They drove west from Roswell on Highway 70, which merged for a couple of hours with Highway 380 across dry sage and empty, desert terrain. Two-armed motorcycle scouts rode ahead of them to ensure they wouldn't encounter any surprises. Another bike rider had surveilled the road right after dawn to be sure there were no unexpected gangs on that particular roadway.

"We're clear all the way to Socorro as of now," Kreuger said over the radio. "Let's hope it stays that way."

The highway dropped down to follow the Hondo riverbed after forty miles, and their speed fell accordingly. The road arced around to follow the meanders of the canyon the river had carved over millions of years. The canyon walls were stained with red-and-tan banding, remnants of ancient riverbeds etched along the dramatic outcrops like artistic accents on a modern fresco. Meanwhile, cottonwoods and other water-loving trees added their color to the valley bottom along the stream course.

Kayla radioed to Logan, "This landscape is so beautiful, Logan. It's like a scene from a western movie."

"Yeah," he responded. "it's like one of those paintings by Moran or Bierstadt—the ones who first saw these wild lands more than a century ago."

They rose out of the river bottom as the river became a stream, and they passed by abandoned farms along its path. At a small town called Tinnie, the highway joined the old Billy the Kid Trail that wound its way through rough canyon lands and dry arroyos. At Hondo, the highway divided, and Highway 70 ran west as they cut through Billy the Kid's old haunts. They crossed a broad highland south of the Capitan Mountains and descended a wide valley to Carrizozo. They traversed the desolate Valley of Fires soon afterward, where an ancient lava flow filled the valley for miles, forming a flat plane of blackened land with a few hummocks of broken rock thrown up at random.

"I suppose this is what Manhattan looks like now after the bomb," Kayla said grimly into the radio.

They continued west by skirting the northern boundary of the White Sands Missile Range. They reached Socorro just before noon and shortly after crossing the Rio Grande River and drove into the huge parking lot on the south edge of town where the local rodeo was usually held. Parking the truck with the coolers in the center of the lot, they loosely surrounded it with other vehicles, almost like they were circling wagons. Two men walked around and took fast-food orders for lunch, and then one of the Cherokees broke off to drive into town to pick up food for the whole crew. Everyone got out of their vehicles and stretched and walked to shake out their legs from the cramped drive.

Three men set about refilling gas tanks from the fuel containers they had brought with them. Then they drove off to refill the containers at the lone gas station that still had fuel for an outlandish price. The militiamen maintained good relationships with gas station operators, mechanics, and ammo suppliers. All commodities cost an arm and a leg, but could still be had for the right favor or amount of cash.

"We have about forty minutes here before we pick up a few extra vehicles from the local militia," Kreuger said. "They run a tight ship here in Socorro, but the country west of here is overrun with outlaws."

Just as he finished speaking, four Jeep Wranglers pulled into the parking lot. Kreuger walked over to meet the man who jumped out of the lead vehicle. They shook hands and talked in animated fashion for several minutes.

Kreuger returned to the travelers just as the Cherokee returned with food. The driver pulled into the middle of the circle and threw open the rear hatch to dispense lunch like a modern-day chuck wagon. He called out individual orders and handed out bags of food from McDonald's. Grimley seemed surprised that Chicken McNuggets looked like they were stamped out from a cookie cutter and seemed as if McDonald's was not his usual choice for lunch fare.

Logan walked over to talk to Kreuger while he ate his Big Mac. "We came through that leg of the trip pretty well. No encounters with hostiles." He felt like he was referring to Native Americans in an old western movie. "What lies ahead?"

Kreuger waved for Cotes and the Grimleys to join them at the tailgate of the two-ton truck. "Might as well fill you in all together," he said. "We're going west on Highway 60 and will have to cross the Datil Mountains in about an hour and a half. The town of Datil and the pass country west of there is controlled by a gang down from Albuquerque called the Matadors, we think. They have set up shop in town and have an encampment just outside. They are about sixty strong and heavily armed, so we are going to have to fight our way through there."

Logan felt a rush of adrenaline, and the others looked shaken, with their arms crossed and tight expressions on their faces, except for Cotes, who still seemed to have misplaced anger building inside of him.

"Why do we have to fight them?" Cotes asked. "Can't we bypass this town of Datil?"

"We can, but the other routes have similar blockages. This is the most direct route to the town of Eagar across the state line. That's where I want to get to tonight. These boys that drove in just now came across there and think it won't be too bad if we can just blast on through the town. They encountered a barricade, but their Jeep with the battering ram busted it up pretty good an hour ago."

"Come on, I know how the government works. Why haven't the state police cleared these marauders out of there?" Cotes asked incredulously. "Where the hell are they and the national guard for this state?"

"Well, they are occupied elsewhere, that's where," Kreuger said loudly, apparently tired of the admiral's lack of understanding. "Half of them are dead from fighting all these gangs and drug cartels. You know, we've been at this out here for nearly two years with no support from you people in the federal government. We've been muddling along on our own while you bureaucrats have been sticking close to home out east."

Cotes's face turned red, and he seemed about to argue, but Logan cut him off before he got that far. "Why Eagar?" Logan asked.

"These men are with the Eager Militia. They have a fortified camp up there, and Smith, their leader, has invited us to spend the night under their protection." Kreuger smiled. "They, of course, would appreciate any form of consideration for their trouble." He chuckled. "They have to buy gas and ammo too, you know. And those commodities are getting hard to find at any price."

They finished their lunch, and soon, the convoy reformed with the new Wranglers in the lead. The two motorcycles raced after them and soon overtook them to scout ahead as before. Then the Humvee and armed Suburbans followed, with the two-ton next, and the Cherokees bringing up the rear. They headed out on state Highway 60, threading their way through rough mountains west of Socorro and swinging north to go around the Magdalena Mountains.

The landscape opened out into arid plains that extended endlessly, it seemed, through scattered, near-deserted ranch land. They passed the Very Large Array Radio Telescope facility and noted that it was fenced off and protected by Army National Guard troops. They continued on at sixty miles per hour toward the west edge of the plain, where the mountains began to rise up to form a rugged skyline.

Logan held his M4 across his lap with a determined look on his face. He could see that the four Wranglers now bristled with rifles projecting from the windows and that the one with the ram on the front end had shifted into the lead position. Up ahead, he could see that there were several vehicles parked next to the road, and, of all things, a fire truck sat astride the highway. There was no way they could ram through that obstacle.

"The Matadors have the road completely blocked," Kreuger said as he held up the radio. "The Eager fellas think there might be a way around the fire truck. We have to slow down and give them time to find a hole for us to drive through." The Humvee slowed way down to a few miles per hour as a battle began in front of them.

The lead Wrangler with the battering ram lurched off the road to the left and charged a fence that had an old car parked strategically behind it. The Wrangler hit the fence and smashed the wooden structure to smithereens, but it stopped dead when it hit the car. Gunfire erupted from all along the barricade as the Matadors targeted the Wrangler. The supporting Jeeps closed in and began to lay a curtain of lead down across the barricade to stifle the gang's fire. Meanwhile, another Wrangler pulled up behind the first one and began to push it and the car forward. That worked, and they soon had created a gap in the line of vehicles and piles of wooden debris that formed the blockade.

"We have a gap! Come in with guns blazing!" Kreuger shouted over the radio. "We have to get up there and blast through the line before they reinforce."

The Humvee zoomed forward and arrived in time to see all the Wranglers burst through the line ahead. They were taking heavy fire by then and appeared to have fewer men firing out the windows as they rolled ahead. As soon as they cleared the barricade, the Humvee came through and crushed the left side of the opening to make a bigger hole for the truck to pass.

Logan was shooting out the window at Matadors who were firing from behind the blockade. He fired three-round bursts to conserve ammo and managed to hit two defenders, taking them out of the fight. Then in seconds, the Humvee swung right to allow the other vehicles to drive through. This put Logan in a good position to pick off Matadors that were still behind the barricade but were now exposed to gunfire from the rear. A few of those defenders got up and ran away to the north. At the same time, two Suburbans crossed the gap and turned left to fire on Matadors on their side of the gap.

Then the truck raced through the gap with Cotes shooting out the passenger window for all he was worth. The truck followed the Wranglers back up to the road and headed west. The Cherokees followed, and Kreuger's men took up positions to fire out the rear windows at the remaining Matadors. That was when Logan realized that the last one had an M60 machine gun mounted inside the rear window so the gunner could mow down anyone behind the vehicles. The M60 fired 7.62x51mm rounds in fully automatic mode, a great amount of firepower in this sort of fight. The machine gun roared as it spit out lead and chewed up the vehicles in the barrier, not to mention the men, who were nearly sawed in half. The sound was so overwhelming that everyone had to cover their ears if they were not actively shooting at someone else.

The Humvee pulled forward onto the road, following the truck, and the Suburbans followed on the truck's rear. Once they were all on the road, the Humvee and Suburbans took their places in the convoy, and the Cherokees caught up.

"Everyone, call in. What are our casualties?" Kreuger asked calmly.

It turned out that they had been lucky—only three men had been injured, two with arm wounds and one with facial lacerations from shattered glass. One of the guys with a bullet wound was from the Eager crew, and the others were Kreuger's men. Logan was surprised because the fighting had been intense and at close range.

"You have this thing fully armored?" he asked.

"We have armor plate built into the doors of each vehicle," Kreuger said, chuckling. "It weighs us down some, and that reduces speed and maneuverability of the SUVs, but it stops most bullets really well. We armored up the engine compartments too so we don't get an engine shut down when we're trying to drive out of a bad situation."

"You're used to running roadblocks, then," Logan said in admiration.

"Yeah. Plus, it's nice to know that if you must stand and deliver, your vehicle is going to be good cover during a firefight. Without the plates, a rifle bullet will go right through most car bodies these days."

The convoy raced westward on Highway 60 as the men applied first aid to their wounded. Everyone was vigilant for any additional danger, but reports from the motorcycle scouts were favorable. There were no real threats between them and the Arizona state line.

They entered the town of Eagar, Arizona, an hour later. It was a small town of about four thousand souls that had seen better days. Eager had been a well-known haven for outlaws in the 1890s because they could travel safely on either side of the state line as they traveled north from Mexico. Arizona sheriffs had no jurisdiction in New Mexico and vice versa, so outlaws just crossed from state to state, depending on who was chasing them. Somehow, it seemed appropriate for the current travelers as they sought refuge for the night in Arizona.

"The militia has a camp on the far side of town in the Apache National Forest. Seeing as it's nearly six o'clock, we'll spend the night there," Kreuger said as he watched out the windows for any signs of trouble. "I can find out how things stand farther west of here from those guys, and we can confirm our route for tomorrow." He paused. "Sound good to you, Logan?"

"Sure. It's been a long day, and I want to check in with the doctors to see how they're handling this sort of rolling combat." He got on the radio at the selected frequency and talked to Kayla for a few minutes to calm her fears.

The Wranglers led the convoy up a dirt, forest service road to a clearing, where several trailers and recreational vehicles were parked at the margins. There was one large building that appeared like it had been thrown up quickly with rough carpentry skills. They were told that it was the common area, where meals were prepared and members met or hung out for the day. Logan learned that forty-five families considered the clearing home, even though several also had houses in Eager. This was considered the safest place to be when things got tough. That usually correlated with the arrival of a roving motorcycle gang or a Mexican gang moving through the area.

Kreuger had his people pull up their vehicles into a defensive circle on one edge of the clearing within easy walking distance of the common building. His crew then set about refueling and repairing vehicles, washing up after the long day of driving, and preparing a meal on a foldable table set up behind one of the Suburbans. Logan thought that canned beef stew sounded good after the day's excitement.

Logan and Kayla checked out the coolers right away after they parked the truck. There were signs that bullets had struck the steel container, but no damage had been done. They both breathed sighs of relief.

"That was really terrifying back there, Logan," she said. "Our driver told us to just stay down below the windows and we would be OK, but one window was still shot out." She had a look of panic in her eyes. "I thought we were going to die. There were these thuds on the doors when we were shot at and the glass broke, and the wind was blowing wildly. The noise was horrendous from all the shooting and the vehicles gunning their engines."

"It was touch and go, but these guys know what they're doing. They have armor plates in the doors for protection, so your driver was right," Logan said. "They are tending to the wounded over in the common building now. This camp has a doctor who has lots of practice with bullet wounds."

"When I got out, I saw where several bullets had hit the door near me. Thank God they didn't come through, or I'd be dead." Kayla stared at the ground. "I never expected we'd be involved in fighting like this when we left Mankato. I don't know if I can deal with another couple of days of this." Her face mirrored the fear that she felt.

He put a hand on her shoulder, and she leaned into him with her face against his chest. He felt sorry for her fear. She sobbed quietly for a few moments and then pulled away, composing herself and straightening her shoulders.

"Dad was pretty shaken up too. Maybe we should go talk to him."

They walked past a few of Kreuger's vehicles and found Grimley sitting with some men, talking and eating a bowl of stew. The doctor was visibly worn out, with ruffled hair and the muscles around his shoulders and neck tensed up. Kayla hurried over to sit next to him and put an arm around his shoulders.

"Dad, are you OK?" she asked as she gazed carefully at his face. "Logan tells me the doors of our SUV have steel plates in them, so we won't get shot if we stay low."

"I hope there is no next time," her father said. "I don't know if I can handle much more of that sort of shooting." He looked at Logan. "Will we have to do that every day?"

"Maybe not, but it's possible," Logan replied. "It's unpredictable. You never know when someone will want to take a shot at us. Did your driver tell you what was happening? I knew what we planned to do because I was with Kreuger, but I didn't relay everything to you two because it happened so fast. I'll try to do better tomorrow."

"Our driver was good about that, but it was still surreal," Grimley said and took a small bite of stew.

"Well, we made it through OK, even if it was a little touch and go."

"Listen, Logan," Grimley said, "I'm not used to roughing it. I mean, I used to hunt when I was young and did my share of camping, but this traveling and living on the go is beyond my comprehension." He looked around him at the families who were preparing the evening meal and seemed accustomed to rugged living. "I mean, I know we have to do it, but I'm not sure Kayla and I can contribute much. We're spoiled, I guess, having been safely tucked away in our world in Mankato."

"I understand, sir," Logan said. "But these people haven't been as lucky as you in this bizarre state of things. They have been uprooted and forced to flee their homes to keep their families safe and even alive. They have to live the harsh life now, not because they want to, but because it was forced on them by fate."

While they were settling in to eat their stew, Kreuger walked over to join them, holding a bottle of Coors beer in one hand and a sandwich in the other. He was in a hurry.

"The weather is supposed to be dry tonight, so the men will put up tents for us to sleep in. The four of you will be in one over here." He pointed toward a large pine tree. "You can get settled in whenever it's ready." He smiled at the two doctors. "It was pretty bad today, but it sounds like tomorrow might just go well. I have to go up to the commons and talk with the militia leader, a man named Smith, which is surely not his real name. He can tell me the latest intelligence about conditions west of here."

"I'd like to hear that too," Logan said. He stood up. "Will you two be OK here? I see that Cotes is coming this way. Maybe he'll want to be in on any meeting. How about you two?"

"Oh, I think we'll stay here and crawl into the tent as soon as it's ready," Kayla said as she glanced at her father with a worried look on her face. "We could use the rest, I think."

Logan, Cotes, and Kreuger walked up to the large common building, where about twenty people were clustered in small groups around tables while they ate dinner. Kreuger saw Smith at one of the tables, and he walked over to him, with Cotes and Logan following.

"Smith, can we talk about tomorrow?" Kreuger asked as he approached the leader. "My fellow travelers need to know what we may encounter west of here."

"Certainly." The man stood up, revealing how tall he was— maybe six-six or so. He had a full, black beard and long hair. He seemed jovial to Logan, but that may have been the result of drinking a few beers with his dinner.

"I'm Willis, and this is Martz," Logan said. He had decided that this crowd used last names only. "Mr. Smith, we have a few questions."

"Just call me Smith. It's not my real name anyway," he replied, chuckling. "You have to get to California by Monday, I hear."

"Yes," Cotes replied. "First, let me thank you for your help today. You seem to know how to get around this country with all its various factions and all."

Logan looked at Cotes. The "and all" wasn't in his usual vernacular.

"Well," Smith said, "we have a lot of practice living in the wild, so to speak." He genuinely smiled and changed the topic. "Well, if you're trying to get to Needles, you have a pretty good day ahead. You just need to drive below the Rim and stay north of the reservation, and you'll get to I-17 easy enough. Then you can jog up to Flagstaff and cruise on I-40 as far as Kingman. The state has reclaimed that part of the freeway recently, so it's safe."

At this news, Kreuger's eyebrows shot up. "The national guard controls it now? That's great news."

"I thought you'd like that," Smith said with a twinkle in his eye. "It's good news for all of us. It means that Flagstaff is free again. We have some people from that city living here in our compound. They can go back and visit friends and family who survived the gang occupation."

"Who was the gang? Antifa?" Logan asked.

"Oh, hell no! We shot those buggers up a year ago when they got fancy ideas," Smith said. "A Mexican cartel moved north from Phoenix and took it over six months ago. The state has been trying to dislodge them since then. I guess Flagstaff was a bridge too far for the gang to handle." He swigged his beer. "Next will be the big one, Phoenix, then Tucson."

"All Mexican gangs?" Cotes asked.

"Yes, they came up for the distribution channel. It seems Americans have a shortage of cash for food and other items, but not drugs." He grinned at his comment. "I hear you guys came down from Chicago. How is it up there?"

"Our city was overrun by Antifa and Black Lives Matter until last fall," Logan said with a sad voice. "They're both murderous gangs that started out working together, controlling downtown and wrecking everything related to capitalism. They called it Paradise at first. The situation held steady like that until September last year. That was when the Caliphate was formed— a hybrid organization consisting of the New Black Panther Party, Nation of Islam Black Muslims, Black Lives Matter, and Black ISIS, a relatively new organization. They had mostly Black people as members bound together with a neo-Marxist and, in some cases, a warped Muslim ideology. The leadership was constantly in dispute as fortunes and issues changed. Lawrence Sarkohan is in control of the despicable group. They have a common hatred for Jews, gays, white people, Christians, and capitalism."

"Jesus, that's everybody," Smith said. "And we thought we had troubles. But that's different from our Mexican pals down here. They're pure capitalists who just want money and power."

"All the East Coast and Midwest groups seem to have a Marxist ideology behind them. At least, that's the basis to gain control. Later, they become more materialistic and savage to gain more power." Cotes finished his beer and searched around to snag another.

Logan took a swig of beer and continued. "Well, they combined forces in September 2022 after Sarkohan created the first Central Caliphate and declared the southern half of Chicago to be the natural province of their nation. Since that time, thousands of worshippers, Black Muslims, and Black racists have gathered in Chicago to join the movement that was centered on Black supremacy and Islam. They had support and some followers from the original ISIS that lent gravity to the new nation."

"ISIS!" Smith blurted out. "I thought they were destroyed over in Iraq."

"The Antifa crowd didn't accept Sarkohan's requirement that the Caliphate was only for true believers. He threw the infidels out of Paradise when he created the Central Caliphate to exist in its place. That's when Antifa occupied the area north of Grant Park while the Caliphate claimed everything south of the Art Institute of Chicago. That's when BLMX splintered off from BLM and merged with Antifa. They've been at war ever since."

"And your outfit, the CNF, controls everything north of Chicago Avenue up to the Wisconsin state line," Kreuger said. "Is that right?"

"Yes, more or less."

"I am amazed that the Antifa organization has been so successful," Cotes said. "They're anarchists who have masqueraded as antifascist revolutionaries, but in reality, they're just anarchists—anti-government and anti-American. They've pulled the wool over many people's eyes, and that subterfuge allowed them to organize in their decentralized way. Now they're so bold that they're just after power."

"And the same thing has happened in most of our large cities. Hell, there are caliphates in Paris and Berlin now." Kreuger shook his head.

"There's talk that the Detroit area will join the Central Caliphate now that they have annexed Gary, Indiana," Logan said stridently. "It would cover a tristate area if that happens. We must put a stop to this lunacy soon, and only the federal government can do that. I wish the Feds would get off their asses and take charge—get out the national guard and army to do the job."

"Don't get your hopes up," Smith said. "Washington is afraid to make a move unless the governors of the states ask the Feds to mobilize. Antifa has assassinated just about every governor and mayor that even talks about gaining outside help. And without new elections, we aren't about to see any new leaders step forward. Everyone's afraid."

"What happened here that you got the guard out fighting?" Cotes asked.

"Our governor quit, and the head of the Arizona National Guard just took charge. Nobody stopped him, so it's a done deal. He took the matter out of the politicians' hands, so they didn't have to make a decision and set themselves up to be shot by the gang."

"Maybe that's what we need in Illinois," Logan said.

"Well, gentlemen," Smith said, "let's find more beer and then get down to brass tacks, shall we?"

Chapter 11

The next morning, the travelers said farewell to the Eager Militia and headed west with Kreuger's convoy. Smith rode with them as a guide to help negotiate their way through Flagstaff.

They made good progress along Highway 60 across the high tableland that formed the top of the Mogollon Rim—the southern edge of the Colorado Plateau that extend into the northern part of Arizona. South of the Rim, the landscape dropped precipitously through national forests until it fell thousands of feet to the desert floor north of Phoenix.

An easy drive along a two-lane blacktop road for about fifty miles brought them to the quiet town of Show Low. From there, they followed Highway 260 as it descended partway down the long, rugged slope below the Rim and guided them through dry forests of pine trees and scrub oaks. They drove through small towns like Pinedale and Bear Flat as they continued at moderate speed on a never-straight path.

They arrived in Payson at 11:00 a.m. and elected to rest and buy gas since the gas cans were low and the vehicles needed refueling. They had time to buy snacks at the gas station recommended by Smith. Then they moved on through wild country and beautiful forests, gradually climbing back up the escarpment toward the Rim. Along the way, they encountered a few small towns and many vacation homes owned by people from the Phoenix area.

"Many of these summer homes are now occupied by people who fled the city when violence erupted there more than a year

The Final Wave • 125

ago," Smith said. "and some are not the real owners, judging by the looks of the makeshift construction."

After they passed the little hamlet of Strawberry, they rose again into dry-land forest on the Zane Grey Highway, named after the author who had set many of his stories in Northern Arizona. They rose onto the Rim again and meandered through vacant land for countless miles.

After noon, they arrived at the more substantial town of Camp Verde on the Verde River, where they encountered Interstate 17, the north-south highway that connected Phoenix and Flagstaff. They turned their vehicles north and drove at a moderate speed toward the city of Flagstaff.

The national guard had control of Interstate 17 north of Camp Verde. Travel along the freeway was regulated by a series of checkpoints at every major intersection to avoid troublemakers from cruising up from the south. With a convoy of eight vehicles, they drew much attention, especially because they sported New Mexico license plates. They were stopped for twenty minutes at the first checkpoint and a half hour at the second. In each case, Kreuger and Smith had to explain why they were armed to the teeth and where they were going. Smith was finally able to convince the guardsmen that the convoy was part of a transport detail and they were not invading the Flagstaff area. They were directed to bypass Flagstaff altogether and finally made it to Interstate 40 westbound by 2:00 p.m. Still, it was 7:00 p.m. and getting dark by the time they rolled into Kingman.

Fortunately, Smith had called ahead to a pal who had managed to find them motel rooms on the southern edge of town in a somewhat degenerate motel called the Desert View Lodge. They were able to park the entire entourage behind the motel and get rooms at the back of the building so they could keep an eye on the vehicles. Four men stood guard all night in any case. Kayla and Logan checked the coolers to be sure all was well with them.

The men completed the usual refueling and repair tasks on the vehicles, rechecked their weapons, and took advantage of the showers in their rooms. They took turns in groups to walk out to restaurants near the motel to have dinner and were in good spirits by 9:00 p.m. Most of the crew turned in early for the night. Meanwhile, Kreuger, Smith, and the travelers sat in the motel lobby sipping beer and finishing off the last of the burritos they had purchased at the Mexican restaurant next door.

"I haven't set foot in California for at least three years, and I don't regret it," Smith said with a grimace. "Even before the lockdowns and COVID pandemic, the place was a pain to travel through. The powers-that-be were in some hurry to eliminate gas-powered transportation and practically made you take an emissions test just to drive into their Paradise."

"Yeah, I know what you mean," Kreuger said. "But we have to get in there tomorrow and find a place to camp by Twentynine Palms." He looked at Cotes as if he might have some new information. "Now, when we get there, are we just supposed to camp out and wait for your other crew to show up? How is it supposed to work?"

"I'll call tomorrow and get more info on that," Cotes said with a grim look on his face. "I think, being marines, they will be on the spot and on time. I don't think we have to wait right at the town itself."

"But I want to know how we're going to get over the Colorado River and into California," Logan said, a little exasperated. "I don't want to have to fight our way across the river and then fight for another two hundred miles to the meetup."

"That sounds pretty scary to me," Kayla said, watching her father. "I don't think my dad could deal with that either. He has a bad heart, you know."

"Now, Kayla, I can manage," Grimley said defensively. "I do find this all very stressful, though. I can tell you that."

Smith smiled as he surveyed the two doctors. "You may not have to fight your way across the Colorado. My friend says civilian guards will let you pass for cash in hand at the bridge at Bullhead City. I don't know what it's worth to you, but maybe ten K will do the job for your convoy. That's this side of the river. On the other side, they may want the same amount. They have joint custody of the crossing, you see, being Arizona on this side and Nevada on the other."

"Who the hell are these people?" Cotes demanded. "Why do they control the bridge at all?"

"Because they took it, that's why," Smith said, seeming to fume a little at Cotes's attitude. "Now, for ordinary folks, they have reduced rates, but for a big outfit like yours, they're going to want to make a profit. Remember, they're also the same people who prevented the bridge from getting blown up about a year ago, and they defend it every day until our government gets its act together."

"They're a militia of sorts?" Kayla asked.

"Sort of. Just folks who want to keep the bridge open and keep the Mexican gangs from taking it or those Antifa fools from destroying it." Smith smiled at her understanding.

"Well, I'm all for paying the toll instead of shooting it out with someone," Logan said with a grin. "Besides, we're going to have plenty of fighting when we make it into California."

"How about driving down toward the Palms?" Cotes asked. "Any recommendations, Smith?"

"I don't know that area very well. Stay off I-40, for sure. The Mexicans control parts of it," Smith responded. "Maybe you should ask the guys on the far side of the bridge. That's more their country than mine."

"I checked that out before we got started," Kreuger said. "We'll proceed to Highway 95 and then turn west on 66. There's a turnoff that goes through the desert all the way south to the Palms. I don't remember the name offhand, but we can take that through the desert mountains."

"We can ask on both sides of the river for more current info about where we might encounter trouble on the road," Logan said. He looked over at Kayla and said, "I know it's scary, but we'll get through OK."

She smiled wanly back at him and then took her father's hand. "Come on, Dad. We'd better get some sleep and get ready for another long day."

Just then, Cotes's satellite phone beeped, and he looked surprised when he read the number. He stood up and stepped away from the table to talk.

Logan could tell by his face that something bad had just happened. He walked over to stand next to the admiral, waiting for the news. Cotes held his finger up to ward Logan off while he talked. Kayla and the others stood still and exchanged worried glances.

"What do you mean, tomorrow?" I don't think we can move that fast," Cotes said. He talked for several minutes and walked farther from Logan as he did so, out into the parking lot. He raised his voice as he talked, to the point that he nearly shouted a couple of times. When he finished, he nearly threw the phone on the ground, but luckily checked himself before any damage was done. He stood for two or three more minutes, staring at the ground. Then he turned and walked back inside, Logan trailing him. The others came over to hear what had just happened.

"What was that about?" Logan asked.

"We're screwed is what happened," Cotes said acidly. "That was the base in San Diego. They want us to be at Twentynine Palms tomorrow between ten and noon."

"What? That's crazy!" Logan nearly shouted. "How can we do that? It's over two hundred miles, and much of it might be through occupied territory."

"Yeah, tell me about how ridiculous it sounds." Cotes turned to Kreuger. "What do you think? Can we do it?"

Kreuger exhaled so loudly that his cheeks puffed out. He shook his head and ran his hand over his face. He stared at Cotes and replied, "I don't know." He stared at the floor and then ticked a couple of things off on his fingers as he thought about it.

Logan said, "We'd have to leave here before dawn to do that. We'd have to drive in the dark part of the way."

"That doesn't sound safe," Kayla said, looking worried.

Cotes started to swear under his breath and walked away. Logan stared at him and then at Smith. "What do you think, Smith? Can we make it in that kind of time?"

"No, not unless we start tonight—like right now. You could cross the bridge in the dark, I suppose." Smith sounded doubtful and shook his head. "I don't know about the rest of the way."

Kreuger paced back and forth while he thought about it. Soon, all the men were pacing in the small lobby and trying not to interfere with one another's path. Kreuger stopped and said, "Well, the only choice we have is to start right now and get across that bridge. We don't know how long that will take, but it's something we can do tonight while we figure out the rest of the trip."

"And maybe the men at the bridge will have some ideas that will help us." Logan looked at Cotes. "It's worth a try."

"Why did the folks in San Diego change the plans, Admiral?" Grimley asked.

"They said they expect that our route will be cut off farther south if we can't get past Palm Springs by early afternoon," Cotes said. "A Mexican cartel has declared that part of their territory now, and will move in there by tomorrow night." He had a grim look on his face and spoke in a deadpan voice. "It just doesn't seem real, what's happening."

Like many people living during this devastating period of American history, Logan realized that Cotes was having trouble adjusting to the new reality of a world where common assumptions and institutions had been turned upside down. He saw it in the eyes of the many people he met day to day. They had a vacant stare that hadn't been present before the COVID pandemic. *They seem at a loss to deal with all the obstacles that have been thrown in the way of their lives,* he thought. *And they're expected to adapt to them every time.*

He had checked for news on the radio while Cotes was in the shower before dinner. He learned that the new president, Mary Callahan, had placed the entire country under martial law, which allowed federal forces like the marshals and military to perform certain roles they usually could not do. She had also closed all ports of entry to the United States, much as President Trump had done during the early days of the first COVID wave. That was supposed to stop any further terrorists and disease from entering the country. In the current situation, that seemed to Logan like closing the barn door after the horses had all run out. But it also allowed the federal government to provide forces to drive out the Mexican gangs and help mayors and governors take control of their cities and states. Of course, in the worse areas, the leaders had either quit or been assassinated. The resulting breaks in the chain of command in states made everything confused and more difficult to manage.

He also learned that it was chaos in most cities along the West Coast after the EMP attack, and even the ruling Antifa mobs were in disarray. Many social media communications that they relied on had collapsed when the internet servers and cell towers feeding them had been fried. Little information was going into or out of the affected areas.

The only reliable news available was that the EMP had caused many fires to burn uncontrollably in cities and the forests where the power lines had been overloaded and arced into adjacent buildings or dry timber. Firefighters were overwhelmed because their engines would not start due to damage from the EMP, and there was no pressure in most city water systems to fill fire trucks, let alone to fight fires. A lot of the same troubles plagued New York City and Washington, DC. Rampant fires burned out of control in what was left of the cities and close-in suburbs. And that was apart from the effects of the radioactive fallout that drifted across the cities and downwind areas like Long Island, New York; Connecticut; and Maryland.

Logan observed the others standing in the lobby and decided they needed to act immediately. "Hey, look," he said, "we have no choice but to wake everyone up and get moving. At the very least, we can make our way across the bridge and be ready to roll by dawn. Let's just do it and see how it goes."

"I agree," Kreuger said. "The sooner we start, the sooner we'll reach our goal. I'll get my people up and moving. You people should pack up and see if you can line up a few gallons of coffee for the troops. I think we're all going to need as much caffeine as we can drink."

They all set about their tasks with determination. The sudden change in plan caused a lot of bad feelings among Kreuger's men, who had just gone to bed and didn't appreciate losing their well-deserved sleep. But like true professionals, they got their heads in the game and prepared to hit the road again.

Smith walked up to Kreuger as he was about to climb into the Humvee and put out his hand. "I guess this is where I leave you, boys. California is too far from home for this outlaw." They shook hands. "I'll see you here if you get back within three days. After that, I'll head on back home. Hope you make it OK, and we can have another beer in Eager."

"Thank you for your help, Smith. You sure helped us out of a tight spot back there." Kreuger held on to the man's hand a little longer than usual. "I'll be back in a few days, and I assure you, I'll have stories to tell."

They both laughed heartily and then went their separate ways.

The convoy drove out from the motel parking lot at 11:00 p.m. and headed out of town on the Bullhead Parkway that became Highway 163 at the Rio Grande River, which was the state line between Arizona and Nevada. They reached the approach to the bridge abutment and were flagged down by four serious-looking men who were armed to the teeth. A semitrailer truck was parked across the road as a barricade. The men meant business.

Kreuger stopped the Humvee and rolled down his window. A man waved his AR-15 rifle, apparently indicating for him to disembark and disarm. Kreuger did as he was asked, and then an older gentleman slowly walked over from a pickup truck parked at the side of the road. He looked like he had been on duty for quite a while, with bleary eyes and rumpled clothes. He yawned as he approached the convoy.

"I'm General Gomez of the Bullhead Volunteers," he said gruffly. "What the hell kind of outfit is this? Are you the headman?" He eyed Kreuger carefully and waited for an answer as his men anxiously held their rifles at the ready.

"I am General Kreuger of the Chaves and Lincoln Counties Militia in New Mexico. We are on a mission to Twentynine Palms in California. We need permission to cross the bridge immediately so we can reach there by noon tomorrow. As you can see, we're traveling heavy and have already had a few incidents along the way."

Gomez and his men stepped back when Kreuger mentioned the word "incidents." Logan realized they might take that the wrong way. "Look, General, we just want to get across the river and head west. We understand that there may be a toll, which we're willing to pay—if it's reasonable, of course."

At the mention of a toll, Gomez relaxed. He scanned the vehicles in the convoy and smiled for the first time.

"Well, ordinarily, we charge a thousand dollars per vehicle for nonlocals, and that would include folks like yourself. If I counted right, that would come to eight thousand bucks." He grinned to sell the friendly negotiation and asked, "You got that kind of cash?"

Kreuger smiled. Logan knew he had been expecting a higher number and internally breathed a sigh of relief. "If we stretch a little, we can come up with that kind of outrageous sum. But let me ask you this: We hope that we will all be coming back this way and will need to pass over your bridge again. Can we get a discount on the return? We may have a few less vehicles if things don't work out well for us on the other side of the river."

"If you run into one of those Mexican cartels, you might not come back at all," Gomez snorted.

"Just a minute so I can get the cash together, OK? And if you have a few minutes, I'd like to ask you for your advice on what our route should be on the other side."

Gomez smiled and waited as Kreuger dug around in his vehicle for a few minutes. When Kreuger came back with a brown paper bag, the two men walked over to Gomez's pickup truck to talk for several minutes. Finally, Kreuger shuffled back to the Humvee, and Gomez's men pulled the semi off the road so they could pass.

"I'll tell you what I learned when we get past these next guys from Laughlin," Kreuger said when he got back in the Humvee. "They control the west side of the bridge. I'm told they'll take the same payment for our passage."

The Humvee crept slowly across the bridge and stopped short of the next barricade manned by the Laughlin Militia just as the last of the convoy passed the Bullhead barrier. Kreuger motioned to the men on the far side. He was well received by the Laughlin men. The Bullhead boys had radioed ahead that he was all right to deal with.

Logan accompanied Kreuger to make the payment and discuss with these local men what lay ahead. After fifteen minutes, they returned to their vehicle and led the convoy into Nevada. As soon as they had all made it through the barrier, they pulled off at the side of the road so Kreuger could brief everybody on what he had learned.

"Hey, these guys are all right," Kreuger said into the radio. "They said that we're clear to take the current road west to US Highway 95 just about where the Nevada-California state line is. From there, we go south about twenty miles and turn onto a small, blacktop road that will take us across the desert. That lets us avoid the really bad hombres around Needles. Another Mexican cartel there."

Logan added, "It's called Goff's Road and is just a narrow, two-lane deal, but the last they heard, no one had blocked it yet. They said we should be able to drive that OK at night."

"But at the little town of Cadiz," Kreuger continued, "there's a roadblock manned by yet another cartel. The Laughlin guys heard that it was pretty heavy duty, but people have gotten through as recently as a month ago. They said conditions could have changed by now, so we should wait until daylight to try to get through."

"Can we buy our way past that?" Cotes asked.

"They said it was possible, but the Mexicans usually fight and then steal your money," Kreuger said, chortling quietly. "They said not to trust them."

Several questions came in from others in the convoy, and the discussion continued for thirty minutes. There was a lot of back-and-forth about driving at night through "Indian country" and wide-open desert. They agreed to go as far as it seemed safe and then wait for daylight.

The convoy started out again at 1:00 a.m. They drove slowly through vacant land, where it had rained recently. They crossed many arroyos but found only traces of water in the channels. Small, dirt tracks turned off from the road and ran out into the desert for no particular reason that Logan could discern. The road was indeed blacktop but had seen little repair in recent years. They had to keep their speed down to avoid potholes and missing pavement.

It took two hours to reach the intersection with Interstate 40, the major east-west roadway. Fortunately, there was only a sliver of a moon, and they were able to slip under the freeway overpass unnoticed by anyone. A short while later, they came to the town of Essex, a misnomer for a tiny town with in the middle of the desert. The place was deserted.

They drove another mile and pulled off the road to form a defensive circle on desert pavement so their tires didn't sink into the softer sand. They parked the Cherokee with the machine gun facing south along the road toward Cadiz, where they expected trouble to originate. They refueled and rechecked everything in case they had to make a run for it at the next town.

After a brief discussion, half the members of the convoy, including the travelers, took a break for two hours. The militiamen would take turns on guard duty. That assumed, of course, that anyone could sleep under these conditions.

Logan walked back along the row of vehicles to see how the Grimleys were doing and determine if they wanted weapons to use if the worst possible outcome ensued. Kayla said she didn't know how to use a gun, but her father accepted a Colt revolver and nodded to his daughter that it was for the both of them. Logan thought he understood what he meant by the worst case.

"How are you, Logan?" she asked with tears in her eyes. "I know you must be used to this, but everything seems so strange to me. It's not the America I grew up in. It's like the Wild West out here."

"Believe me, this isn't the only place that seems like the Wild West. Some of what's happening in Chicago is like scenes I encountered in Baghdad." He stopped talking and took her hand to comfort her. "But this too shall pass, as it says in the Good Book. I don't know when, but it will change. I intend to help it change in my hometown. I can assure you of that."

She gripped his hand tightly and tried to smile as she looked into his eyes. He felt as though something passed between them at that moment. Something he couldn't define but it made him feel closer to her.

Logan walked back to his vehicle and stretched out for his break. He couldn't sleep, but knew that these could be the last few hours of his life. It was a warm night in the desert, especially for March. He closed his eyes and tried to think pleasant thoughts. The last thing he remembered before falling asleep was the image of Kayla standing in the lab in a white lab coat. Meeting her seemed like the only good thing that had happened to him in the last few days.

Chapter 12

Everyone was awake by dawn and preparing for the upcoming battle. Kayla had helped one of the militiamen make coffee for everyone using a camp stove, which appeared to be her first camping stove experience, but she looked determined to make good coffee. People stood around in small groups talking while they sipped java and ate granola bars and some stale doughnuts. Most of them were really quiet, thinking about all the possible scenarios in store. Some of the men talked about their families back home and how they wished they could be with them soon. What a divided situation the country had everyone in.

Most of the men had bulletproof vests to wear, and Kreuger had brought extra ones for the travelers. Logan helped Kayla and her father suit up in their vests and gave them Kevlar helmets to wear. He could tell the Grimleys were both scared to death, but didn't know what he could say to assuage their fears. His best advice had been to stay below the window level whenever shots were being fired. If their driver told them to get out and run, they should do it while staying low to the ground.

Kreuger had sent his two motorcycle scouts out to survey the route ahead. They had ridden within two miles of Cadiz and were reporting back what they had seen. On the north side of Cadiz, there was a low mountain pass with rock outcrops jutting out to the edge of the asphalt road. The cartel had built a sturdy barricade across the road there of trucks and boulders they had lined up like an ancient fort. One of the riders said it would be impossible to circumvent the barrier because of the strict confines of the pass. They would need to displace a heavy tow truck to get through.

"But there may be another way," he said. "There's another road that runs nearly parallel to this highway, but deviates from it about a mile from here."

"Can we drive that way and get around Cadiz?" Logan asked.

"It's just a desert track. It looks OK from a distance, but we need to drive along part of it to ensure the truck can pass. We can't have it sinking into the sand."

Logan glanced over at Kreuger to see what he thought about this new route.

"Why don't you two ride along it and see what you think?" Kreuger suggested. "See if we can drive it and if Cadiz is as fortified as the pass."

The men roared off and crossed the valley just outside of Essex. Everyone watched them drive away and waited next to their rides while the scouts checked out the new route. Kreuger pulled out his detailed map of the area and searched for the new road.

"I see it," he said. "It's just a dirt track, like they say. It goes through the south end of Cadiz, but there's no good place for a blockade." He was optimistic. "If the ground is hard, we can drive around most barriers."

"We'll have to wait for the report," Logan said, unwilling to get his hopes up.

Nearly a half hour later, they heard gunfire coming from Cadiz. *The scouts ran into trouble,* Logan thought. He rushed over to Kreuger, who was already on his radio.

"Scout One. Come in, Scout One. Bill, this is Ros home. Come in," he said with concern in his voice.

There was no response at first. Then the radio crackled. "Scout Two to Ros. We are under fire and are mobile. Bill is hit. Repeat—Bill is hit."

They heard more gunfire. It seemed to be advancing quickly up the valley. Logan pulled out his binoculars and scanned the landscape for signs of the retreating scouts. He spotted the bikes and then saw one crash to the ground. The bike flipped over, and the rider was thrown free. The first motorcycle stopped and threw a lot of sand as its driver spun around to go back to his companion. He stopped and helped the injured man climb up onto the tail of his bike and then started up the valley again. Logan saw a cloud of dust coming up the valley behind the bike. They were being pursued.

"Everyone to your vehicle!" Kreuger shouted. "We've got company."

Logan gazed at the chase taking place. Two pickup trucks, with several men in each one, were racing after the two scouts now riding on a single bike. They were catching up rapidly and would overtake the bike in a few minutes before it could reach Essex. The men in the back of the trucks were shooting wildly at the bike, but they weren't very accurate due to the jostling of the pickups on the dirt road. When they caught up with the bike, there would be a bloodbath.

"I'm taking the Humvee to cover the scouts. Hold here for my command!" Kreuger shouted. With that, the Humvee lurched forward and crossed the low swale in the middle of the valley. It joined the dirt road headed south.

"Logan, get up in that firing port on top and take the M4!" Kreuger shouted. "Use full auto when we're in range. You know what to do."

They were only a half mile from the motorcycle that was careening in their direction. Kreuger's driver powered along straight down the road, and for a minute, Logan thought they would run headlong into the bike. It veered off the road just in time to avoid contact, and the Humvee shot onward. The pickups pressed straight on but slowed down when they saw the armored vehicle coming at them.

Logan stood up and slid the sunroof-like panel on top of the Humvee aside. He aimed his rifle and fired. The first rounds shattered the windshield of the lead truck and slaughtered the two men riding in the cab. He kept firing at the cab, hoping his rounds would pass right through and hit the men in the truck bed. Sure enough, he emptied his magazine into the cab and windshield, hitting many targets.

As he changed magazines, the first truck ran off the dirt track into the sandy soil next to it and got bogged down. The second truck halted behind the first one, and the men in its bed fired at the Humvee. Logan blasted away on full auto until he ran out of ammo, resulting in every man in the truck being mowed down.

The Humvee rolled to a stop in front of the pickup. Kreuger instructed his driver to test the soil on each side of the dirt track and decided it was safe to drive over it in four-wheel drive. They turned around and returned to Essex to see how badly wounded Bill was.

By that time, Scout Two had regained the road and returned to the convoy. From a distance, Logan saw men lay Bill's body on the hood of one of the SUVs. He was already dead when they arrived.

"God damn it!" Kreuger said as he inspected the dead man, placing one hand on Bill's bloody arm. "He was a damn good man." Then he asked the second scout, "What did you see up there? Is there a barricade?"

"Yes, sir. We saw that they have farm equipment blocking the road and lots of old vehicles arranged on either side." The scout paused to catch his breath. "It would be hard to get through it without dynamite or a really big truck with a ram on the front. There are a lot of gang members, and they're heavily armed."

"Could you see anything beyond the barrier?" Kreuger asked as he rubbed his beard with his hand.

"No, we didn't have time to see anything else. I can say that the dirt road is sound enough for our vehicles and, in a few places, there's soft sand on either side of it."

"Can we drive around with four-wheel drive?" Kreuger persisted.

"Maybe, but our vehicles are pretty heavy. They might bog down."

Kreuger called Logan, Cotes, and his lead men together. They discussed how to proceed based on the new information. The consensus among the New Mexico men was that they should sacrifice one of the Suburbans to crash through the barrier at high speed. To do that, someone would have to drive the SUV and bail out the door just before it hit the barrier. If the collision didn't completely push the barrier out of the way, another vehicle would drive up behind the SUV and push it and the blocking machinery aside to open a path. It wasn't much of a plan, but they didn't have a lot of options.

"Let's get to it," Kreuger said. "First, let's beef up the front end of the number three Suburban. It's the oldest one we have." He paused, then added, "And, believe it or not, we do have some dynamite with us."

Several men set about lashing seven old railroad ties to the front bumper of the SUV with rope to form a battering ram and removing anything of value from the interior. They loaded several boulders into the car to give it more weight and momentum when it was up to speed. Four sticks of dynamite were attached to the front of the SUV with a timer that the driver would start before he bailed out.

By the time they started driving, it was 9:00 a.m., and they were running out of time. They set off with the modified SUV first, followed by the number two Suburban as the pusher. One man named Wilson had volunteered to drive the sacrificial beast. The Humvee was next in line with Logan ready to deliver cover for Wilson once he scrambled out of the vehicle. The Cherokee with the machine gun came next, followed by the rest of the entourage.

They approached the barricade along the dirt road at a steady speed of thirty miles per hour, keeping on the packed surface and avoiding the softer shoulder. They drove all vehicles in four-wheel drive except the Ford truck, which only had two-wheel drive on its dual rear wheels. The truck was at the end of the convoy and would be the last vehicle through the barricade, assuming they could penetrate it.

When they were five hundred yards away, all the vehicles stopped except for the lead SUVs and the Humvee, which increased speed as gunfire erupted from the cartel members who stood behind the barrier. A fusillade of bullets flew past the drivers and into the armored front end of the vehicles as they pushed their trucks to the limit, picking up speed to nearly forty miles per hour just before impact. Wilson threw himself out of the driver's side door and tried to curl into a ball as he rolled on the sand. The second SUV roared past him and touched bumpers with the battering ram. Together they hit the barricade with huge momentum.

And the vehicles stopped dead.

The impact was enormous, and the front end of the lead Suburban crumpled up badly. The second SUV smashed into the first and suffered a lot of damage, losing its grill and bumper as the driver backed away. Then it stalled just as the dynamite on the front of the lead vehicle exploded. The front end of the lead Suburban reared up on its back axle, and a tractor that obstructed it rolled away, leaving a small gap in the barrier. The problem was that the Suburban was now lodged in the gap and on fire.

Logan fired on full auto at the men along the barrier who were shooting at Wilson and the second car. He hit a few before they directed their lead in his direction. Meanwhile, the driver of the second SUV got his car started and reversed toward the Humvee as Wilson ran along the road behind it, using it as cover.

To their shock, a man on the barrier stood up and fired a rocket-propelled grenade at the retreating SUV. The rocket struck the front of the vehicle. It rose up from the road and burst into flames. No one bailed out from the burning wreck.

Wilson ran up to the Humvee and climbed in the rear driver's side door. Logan slapped in his fourth magazine and rattled off shots at another man who stood up with an RPG. Luckily, he hit him, and the rocket flew wide of the Humvee. They waited for a few moments to see signs of motion in the burning car as Logan peppered the barrier with rounds.

The driver of the Humvee backed up to be out of effective range of the RPGs. They waited for the other vehicles to close up behind them and had a brief radio conference on the radio with all members of the convoy participating.

"We don't have time to fight our way through these guys. There's too many of them, and we can't very well flank them," Kreuger said. "We would need to get up on the slope south of them and get around that way. But doing that in broad daylight is suicide."

"We can try to ram through again and knock our SUV out of the way. But we would lose a lot of men doing that. We might get jammed up in there and be sitting ducks," one of the men commented.

"And we need to recover the bodies of our buddies that were killed," another added.

After a moment of silence, Cotes piped up. "Let me try something and see if we can get some help up here."

Logan looked back at the end of the convoy and saw Cotes step out of the truck with this satellite phone in hand. He punched in a number, talked for a while, and then waited. Someone shot at him from the barricade but missed, kicking up sand short of him. Then he hung up. He impatiently looked at his watch, scuffed the ground in front of him with his boot, and then turned back to the truck with a disgusted look on his face. He glanced at the Humvee and shook his head.

Cotes came back on the radio. "No luck there, I guess. I tried my marine contact, but he said he didn't think they could do anything to help us on such short notice. He'll try to get a few trucks with men headed our way, but it may be an hour or more."

"But what do we do?" Kayla asked. "We can't just sit here. Won't the cartel come after us?"

"I don't know," Kreuger said. "We may have to just go for it and hope we get through."

Someone said over the radio, "Hey, they're moving the Suburban out of the way."

Logan turned and saw a huge Caterpillar D9 pushing the wreckage that remained of the battering-ram SUV out of the barrier. It moved the wreck aside and then backed up so that its blade lined up with the rest of the barricade.

"No wonder we couldn't get through if that was behind the tractor," Kreuger said.

Logan felt like this was going nowhere. They were out of options except to somehow outflank the barrier and attack from behind. He had no idea how they could accomplish that before nightfall. The Mexicans would be expecting such an attack, so surprise would not work in their favor.

He looked down the line of vehicles to assess the odds of them crossing the barricade and noticed Cotes again standing next to the truck on the phone. He was animated as he glanced back at the barricade. He then spoke loudly as he waved his arm for someone to come to him. Logan climbed out of the Humvee and ran back to the truck. He halted next to Cotes as the admiral put his hand out in a stop motion.

"Wait one minute, Captain," Cotes spoke into the phone. He turned to Logan and put one hand over the receiver. "We're getting help in about ten minutes. We must be ready to roll as soon as they can clear a path for us. Tell the others." He turned back to the phone and began talking again.

Logan ran back to the Humvee and relayed the message.

"What kind of help?" Kreuger asked.

When Logan shook his head, Kreuger got on the radio. "We are about to see some kind of miracle, my friends. Be ready to roll."

As they sat there, Kreuger told everyone what they were to do when the time came. He assigned the Cherokees to pick up the dead men in the burning SUV. He had them find gloves to use to pull the bodies from the flaming car.

Time passed slowly, and they took occasional fire from the cartel. They backed up their column of vehicles another two hundred yards, and the shooting stopped. Then they saw movement by the Caterpillar. A man climbed into its cab and reversed out of the line of the barricade. Other vehicles appeared in the gap, ready to head in their direction. The cartel was preparing to attack.

Then they heard a faint sound from down valley behind the barrier. Cotes was on the phone again, talking and waving his arms. Logan pulled out his binoculars and scanned the sky south of them. He saw two dark specks flying up the valley just above ground level. He couldn't quite make them out at that range, but recognized the distinctive throb of incoming helicopters. They were some type of attack helo, narrow in cross-section but loaded with weapons, and they came on very fast. At last, he recognized them as marine AH-1Z Viper aircraft, designed for close ground support.

They flew en echelon up the valley, their rotors beating loudly as they cruised low directly over the barrier. They rushed toward the convoy and seemed to look over the vehicles for a moment. Then Logan saw Cotes waving a white handkerchief up in the air for recognition. He stood with the handkerchief in one hand and his other arm extended toward the barrier. The aircraft passed over him and then turned around up valley to begin an attack run.

Everyone got out of their vehicles to watch the show as the helos swept toward the barrier at about a hundred miles an hour. They fired one Hellfire missile each, and the barrier erupted into two fireballs that blew huge gaps in the line of cars and equipment. The bulldozer rose from the ground and did a backflip in the air. Other machinery flew in different directions as the barrier was destroyed.

The helos passed over the barrier and the small town, where they quickly turned and came back with their 20mm Gatling guns raking the barrier from end to end. One helo hovered over the rear of the line and swept it one more time to clear out the vermin hiding behind, shooting up cars, trucks, and a few buildings in about two minutes. Then the helos roared away to deal with the other barricade across the valley on the main highway. Logan watched with anticipation as two Hellfire missiles took out the blockade there just as easily as could be. Then the aircraft raked the entire length of that obstruction and flew back for a little cleanup of the cars and trucks racing away from that barrier.

When the carnage was complete, Kreuger shouted, "Mount up, everyone! Let's go!"

The helos circled close, and one hovered near Cotes, who saluted the crew in the cockpit, and they returned the favor.

After they gave one another the thumbs-up, the helos turned south and headed down the valley.

Cotes climbed into the truck, and the whole column drove forward to the barrier. The Humvee nudged a piece of a pickup truck out of the way to make room for the other vehicles, then passed through the gap. The Humvee led the convoy across the line and then stopped as men climbed out of their vehicles to defend their position. The Cherokees stopped at the remains of the burning Suburban, and men clambered out to recover the bodies. It took a few minutes to get the four charred men out of the flaming vehicle and wrapped in tarpaulins. They carefully placed the bodies inside the rear of one of the Cherokees with great respect, then remounted their Jeeps.

A few of the cartel men who were still hiding behind the barrier returned fire at the militiamen. The New Mexicans soon cut them down in response. After the Cherokees had crossed the remains of the barrier, the convoy reformed and drove on. They were down one motorcycle, two SUVs, and five men. There were a few gunshot wounds and scrapes as well, but they had successfully passed Cadiz.

Cotes' voice boomed over the radio, "Congratulations, everyone. You did great this morning. Millions will live because of what you did here today. Be proud, and let's salute our fallen heroes with a moment of silence."

Everyone was silent for a full minute, and then the radio filled with chatter as everyone celebrated the close call they had just survived.

Logan checked his watch. It was 10:45 a.m. They would just make their deadline.

Chapter 13

They drove through Cadiz to the little town of Amboy, where travel on the gravel road due south proceeded unimpeded. The road carried them through low, craggy mountains and then west directly into the outskirts of Twentynine Palms. They skirted the village itself and followed Adobe Road north of town to the Marine Corps Air Ground Combat Center, where marines trained for desert combat and conducted live-fire exercises.

The convoy arrived at the south gate of the Center at 11:41 a.m. and was met by Major Thomas Reardon, a very squared-away individual who directed them to a parking area near the base hospital facility. He showed Kreuger where he could have his wounded men attended to and where the militiamen could grab some food and clean up. He offered them a place to stay for some rest after their harrowing night on the move. Once that was done, he called Cotes aside to arrange the transfer of his team and the vaccine to another vehicle for the final transport to San Diego.

"Admiral Cotes," Reardon said, "it is an honor to have you with us, even for a few hours, sir," he said as he walked them over to another building, where they could talk freely. "We will need to transfer your gear and the cooling equipment to another vehicle so you can leave here before one o'clock."

"Thank you, Major. And thank the base commander for sending the helos to get us out of a jam," Cotes said appreciatively. "We have three large coolers weighing about three hundred pounds apiece. If you can pull the new transport up to our truck, we can make the transfer quickly. Commander Gordon can supervise the work."

"I can help with that and check out the cooler performance at the same time, Admiral," Kayla said. She and Logan followed the major out to meet the men they would be traveling with.

Within a quarter hour, Kayla had verified that the coolers were working properly, and several men manhandled them onto the back of another two-ton truck. The coolers were secured, and Logan ensured the travelers' personal gear was placed in the back of the SUV that would be their ride for the last leg of the trip. When they were all ready to go, the travelers went to find the brave militiamen who had guarded them for the last three days.

"Kreuger," Cotes said as he extended his hand, "we wanted to thank you for your help and sacrifice bringing us here. Your work is important, and someday, you may know what you have done to save the lives of hundreds of thousands of American citizens."

"Well, sir," Kreuger said, "since learning what you're delivering to San Diego, I'm proud to help. When we first talked, I couldn't figure out what was so important that you'd risk your lives bringing it here and why you would have two of the nation's top virologists along. But I'm glad to have been part of saving our country." The men shook hands.

"And I have new respect for the men in our militias," Cotes said as he surveilled all the men assembled in the room. "You men are patriots, and your names will be listed in my report as the brave soldiers that you are."

"Thank you, sir. It was our honor."

Cotes handed Kreuger a canvas bag full of money. "The rest of our deal, plus something for the damages you sustained and the men you lost. Their families can make use of it, I'm sure."

Kreuger hefted the bag and smiled. "About twice what I expected. We'll use it to compensate the families, as you suggested. We're taking our fallen back with us. The marines have provided us with body bags packed in enough dry ice to get them home in a few days."

"Will you rest up here and drive back tomorrow?" Logan asked.

"We voted to start back now while the roads are clear. We can make it to Bullhead by tonight and spend the night there. We can't wait to get home."

The travelers shook hands with all the militiamen and said their goodbyes. Then they walked outside and climbed into a black, armored Chevy Tahoe in the middle of a convoy of seven vehicles.

They started toward San Diego in the care of the US Marine Corps, passing through Palm Springs within two hours and proceeding without incident to Indio and then around the Salton Sea. From there, it was a long drive west over the mountains to Julian, then down the mountain range to Alpine and El Cajon before completing the more urban drive into San Diego, where they arrived at 6:00 p.m.

They supervised the unloading of the coolers and their gear into a warehouse, where two men stood guard over their goods. They then followed Reardon to an adjoining meeting room off the warehouse floor. He stayed with them since he would also be their host while at the base on Coronado Island. They were provided with coffee and doughnuts while they waited.

As they sat there wearing their surgical masks after eating, Grimley's face took on an odd pallor, and he began to sweat.

"Dad, are you all right?" Kayla asked as she walked over to him. She put a hand on his forehead, and her face registered alarm. "You've got a fever. You're sick, Dad. Why didn't you say anything?"

"I was fine a moment ago, but I'm tired from the long trip," he replied. "I think it's just a cold from being on the road so long."

"You need some rest. Me too," she said. "I hadn't planned for such a long road trip. And the way we were working around the clock to get the samples ready before we left, I'm surprised that I'm not sick as well."

"I know I'm exhausted too," Logan said. "It has been intense the last few days. That wears you out."

"I'll be OK. I just need a little sleep, that's all," Grimley said defensively.

"Dr. Grimley," Cotes said, "We need you well to carry out the mission. I want a doctor to examine you before we continue. I don't want to risk your health."

Grimley stared at Cotes with a sad look on his face. "I won't let you down, Admiral."

"I'm not worried about that. But I want you tested for the new COVID strain, just in case. We can't take any chances," Cotes said. "Major, can we get Grimley to a base doctor and get him a COVID type 2 test?"

"Yes, sir. Let me make a call." Reardon slipped his cell phone from his pocket and stepped away. He explained the problem to whom he had called and then listened for a minute. "Yes, warehouse 106 G, in meeting room D. Thank you."

Reardon walked back to the table where they were sitting. "A doctor is on his way here to check you out, Doctor, and to give you a COVID test. It should only take a few minutes."

They sat there in uncomfortable silence for a minute or two, and then Logan asked, "So when do we take the coolers over to the manufacturing outfit? Will that be today?"

The admiral stared squarely at Logan and said, "Well, I guess now is as good as any time to fill you in, Logan. The rest of us are cleared for it, and I assume the room is secure?" He gazed questioningly at the major. The major nodded.

"What now?" Logan gave the admiral a hard look. "What haven't you told me?"

"Now, Logan, it was need to know, and the others have been read in for a week or so," Cotes said carefully. "I wanted to tell you for the last three days but didn't have the opportunity because we were with the militia fellows."

"What are you talking about?" Logan began to get angry.

"Well, there's more to our mission. More than just getting the vaccine here to San Diego." Seeing Logan's face flush with anger, Cotes hesitated to continue.

Just then, there was a knock on the door, and Reardon answered, "Enter."

A tall, older man exhibiting Middle Eastern features and a friendly smile entered. "Hello, I'm Dr. Abaza," he said. "Who needs my attention?" He glanced around the room and then saw Grimley.

"My father is ill, I think," Kayla said matter-of-factly. "I don't think it's COVID because we have been vaccinated already for types 1 and 2."

"Two? There is no vaccine for 2," Abaza said. "What do you mean?"

Kayla stood up to shake Abaza's hand. "Hi. I'm Dr. Kayla Grimley, and this is my father, Dr. Harrison Grimley. We're the ones who have been developing the new vaccine for type 2. We have both received it as part of the phase-three trials."

"Pleased to meet you, Doctors," Abaza said. "I understand, but let's give him the test for the two strains anyway for protocol's sake. I have the quick test with me now." He turned to Grimley. "May I take a nose swab, sir?"

"Yes, go ahead," Grimley said gruffly. "I don't have the virus, but I think I have a cold."

"Let's hope that is all it is."

Abaza opened a sterile, cotton swab vial and removed the swab. He placed it gently in Grimley's nostril and took a sample. He held it in one hand while he opened a small pouch and removed the test kit, which was the size of a credit card. He tore off a sterile covering, rubbed the swab on a small panel on the card, and checked his watch. Then Abaza gave Grimley a quick examination and asked him a few questions. Grimley explained that they had been doing some strenuous traveling and he felt he was just worn out from that. When they finished talking, Abaza's watch timer pinged. He glanced at the test kit, then at Grimley, and smiled.

"You don't have COVID of any type, and you seem to have a very high count of antibodies in your system. This new vaccine of yours must work wonders." He smiled broadly. "I think you have had a mild heart incident, not a full attack but a precursor to one. I want to give you a few tests to be sure. You can finish your business tonight and come back to see me tomorrow." He waited for a response.

Cotes asked, "Will he be able to travel in close confinement for a few days, Doctor? He's scheduled to leave tomorrow."

Abaza became distressed and looked at Grimley. "Doctor, I wouldn't recommend that you travel until you have had two or three day's rest. At our age, we need to worry about contracting pneumonia and your heart may be compromised. Traveling in this weather could be a bit risky. I wouldn't recommend it."

Grimley protested. Cotes seemed about to say something but held it back. He stood up. "Thank you, Doctor, especially for being so efficient. We have to do some planning now and decide what to do."

The major walked Abaza to the door, thanked him, and shook his hand. He then returned to the table. "Well, Doctor, what do you think?" He stared at Grimley, but Kayla responded.

"Dad, you look awful. I don't think you're up to the trip. I don't want you to risk it." She held his hand and gave him a sympathetic smile. "You haven't been sleeping well at night either. I hear you coughing and tossing and turning. I don't want you to go. What if you get ill on the trip?"

"OK," Logan said to Cotes, "where do you want to go? And why haven't I been told about it?"

Cotes glanced over at Logan and ran his hand over his face as if he wasn't looking forward to this discussion. "Taiwan. We're going tomorrow. It's imperative that we leave on time. The doctor, you, and I will make the trip."

"And you didn't think it was appropriate to inform me about this?" Sarcasm dripped from Logan's voice.

Cotes took a deep breath. "I wanted to tell you earlier, but a lot has been happening, in case you hadn't noticed."

Logan stood up abruptly. He pointed his finger at each person in the room, one at a time. "You people had better get your story straight if you want me to make this trip."

He walked out of the room and into the warehouse, where a base pickup truck had driven inside and parked next to the three coolers. The driver sat in his truck and punched some keys on his cell phone. Two SUVs pulled up inside the hangar door, and four armed marines dismounted and took up defensive positions just inside the large, vehicle doors to defend the warehouse. Their master sergeant eyed Logan as if he were a terrorist.

Logan was angry. In fact, he was getting more pissed off by the minute. Everyone had known what was going on but him. What would have happened if Cotes had been killed during the last few days and he had not informed Logan of the rest of the mission? His excessive secrecy could have led to the failure of the mission because Logan, the second in command, would not have known of the Taiwan portion of their travels.

His mind returned to previous occasions when Cotes had screwed up by withholding information that the men in the field had needed to succeed in their mission. Apparently, his communication skills had not improved over the years.

The meeting room door opened, and Reardon walked over to retrieve him. "The admiral would like you to rejoin us, Commander."

A navy commander outranked a marine major as far as Logan knew, but he didn't push the point. For some reason, Reardon had been informed of the details of this mission and Logan had not.

"Tell me, Major," Logan asked, "how long have you been involved in this operation?"

Reardon stared at the floor and swallowed hard. "For three weeks, sir. At least, I was told of its general nature at that time. I didn't know that you were not informed, sir."

"Neither did I," Logan said. "Let's rejoin the secret meeting, shall we?"

Reardon led the way into the meeting room. The others stared at Logan as he entered, and he realized that they had made some decisions about what would happen next. He scanned their faces and then directed his attention to the admiral.

"So what have you decided? Is there anything I should know?" *As opposed to fumbling along in the dark?* Logan thought. "Is someone going to tell me what our objective is, or am I to guess what we're doing here?" He glared at them all and added, staring at Kayla harshly, "I think your chariot has arrived, Dr. Grimley."

"Admiral Cotes, the security attachment has arrived," Reardon said. "Shall I have them move one cooler to the new transport?"

"Yes," Cotes said, "and perhaps Kayla should show you which one is going to the manufacturing facility. And Dr. Grimley, you should go with them to show them which baggage is yours. Logan will be out shortly."

When Logan and Cotes were alone, Logan said, "Sir, I feel that I'm no longer able to continue in this assignment. I cannot be effective if my commanding officer has no confidence in my ability. And I might say that I cannot work with a man who deliberately withholds information from me that may be important for the success of the mission."

Cotes's face turned beet red, and he appeared about to burst open with angry words. "That will be enough, Commander. I don't need a mutiny on my hands at this moment."

"If you don't come clean and tell me what this is all about, I will not continue." Logan set his jaw, which Cotes had seen before. He meant business.

Cotes threw his hands in the air. "Look, I wasn't keeping it from you on purpose, but you won't believe me about that. I did mean to tell you when we were on the flight from Chicago and we became operational. But I was too preoccupied with the shit that hit the fan on the East Coast." He evaluated Logan to see if what he had said made any difference.

"Not a good excuse."

"Well, that's all I have." Cotes paced back and forth. "We're delivering some of the vaccine to the Republic of China on Taiwan, and then to Japan and South Korea. They are all our allies, and it is imperative that they receive the vaccine ASAP. What we are carrying within each package is the vaccine precursor. It's made from RNA, so the sample is the key ingredient to make the vaccine. Each manufacturer could make their own precursor, but it's faster and more specific to send a standard formula. At least, that's what they tell me. I'm no virologist."

"So that's why we have to deliver the samples. OK, I get that." Logan stared at Cotes intensely. "Why not just tell me in the first place?"

"Well, at the beginning, it wasn't clear if you would travel to Taiwan or not. There are transport limitations on getting there. If you couldn't go, then there was no need to tell you about that part of the operation." Cotes seemed contrite. "Now it looks like you need to go since Dr. Grimley is unable to travel. I was going to have you protect Kayla while she worked with the manufacturer here. Her father will stay here instead to instruct the people at the manufacturing center. And Dr. Grimley will have to remain here to have some tests performed about his heart condition. I found a replacement for the role I needed you for here in San Diego."

"Who's the manufacturer?" Logan asked.

"I can't tell you directly because you don't need to know, but their name begins with a *P*."

"Oh, those guys. Makes sense," Logan said cautiously. "You, me, and Kayla will go to Taiwan. So we're talking about a monthlong trip, then?"

"No, more like two weeks. We're not going to fly but will have rapid transport available," Cotes said. "I can't tell you anything about how we'll travel because I don't know the details myself. Don't ask. It's some special, new ship that's top secret. We'll both find out the rest tomorrow."

"You're kidding me. How come you don't know? We're going into a war zone, and you don't know?"

"Yes, it's a war zone, but it's Top Secret Ultra. Only a few people know about this new device." Cotes was visibly nervous. "All they would tell me is that I'd better not be claustrophobic. We have to repackage the samples we take into smaller coolers. Kayla has to take care of that this evening so we can ship out tomorrow morning." He looked at Logan and stuck out his hand. "I'm sorry. I screwed up, OK?"

Logan reluctantly shook his hand. "Don't hold out on me, Admiral. What else is there?"

"What do you mean?" Cotes still looked anxious. "Look, there is one other detail, but it doesn't affect the mission from an operational standpoint." He hesitated. "I really can't tell you until we reach Taiwan and the samples are delivered. You have to trust me on that."

"It has to do with the vaccine?"

"Yes, it does." Cotes appeared troubled. "I shouldn't tell you this now, but I will so that you don't have any reservations." He paused. "The vaccine we have was designed to prevent the type 2 virus, but it's also a vaccine for the next phase of the virus that our scientists think will develop in the next few months. There will be another wave. A final wave. No one knows that, or there would be a panic in the streets."

"Holy shit!" Logan shouted. "That's awful, sir. People are dying right and left from type 2 in the current wave." He thought a moment. "How can they know there will be another wave?"

"I don't know. Maybe we can ask Kayla later tonight and she can explain it to us."

"Yeah, maybe she can do that. Does anyone else know?" Logan asked.

"I've been told that less than fifty people know about the final wave, so keep it tight. Pray that the virologists are wrong." Cotes checked his watch. "Let's get out there and help her finish whatever she has to do."

"OK. I'm on board again, but keep me informed, will you?"

"Roger that." Cotes started for the door of the warehouse.

Chapter 14

The next morning at 4:00 a.m., Dr. Kayla Grimley looked exhausted and admitted to Logan that she felt miserable. She had been up late the night before finishing the repackaging of the samples. She had broken down the contents of the two coolers into four packages that now fit into two large, Igloo ice chests, each packed with dry ice. She had also said a tearful goodbye to her father.

Logan had been up late helping her repack the samples and checking on news stories about what was happening in the country and the world in general. He hadn't been able to log in to the Internet while they were traveling overland, but he was now able to log on to the secure base network to catch up.

He learned that President Callahan had warned Iran that the United States suspected its involvement in the attack on their cities. She implemented financial punishment against them and had the full support of the United States's European allies. She also declared an embargo against Iran while a detailed investigation was conducted into the attack. She said she would take further action if evidence was found that Iran was, in fact, involved in collaboration with Syria and Hezbollah. Those two entities were also included in the sanctions she implemented against Iran. She stopped short of saber-rattling.

Meanwhile, the remainder of North Korea's forces had launched conventional missiles against South Korea. They had no more long-range missiles left to use in retaliation against the USA. Combined US and South Korean forces were holding back an invasion just south of the demilitarized zone. Fighting was furious, but North Korea had lost most of their military assets in the nuclear attack a few days prior. The tide was shifting in favor of South Korea.

The final bit of news Logan heard was that mainland China had redoubled their efforts to bring Taiwan under their control. The CCP had demanded that Taiwan submit to their rule or be invaded. The mainland Chinese had sunk most of Taiwan's naval vessels and were bombarding the island state with missiles to destroy their air defense system. Taiwan was holding on and being supported by the United States in the form of material and replacement aircraft as quickly as aid could be sent. Members of the US military were demanding that President Callahan send all manner of equipment and naval assets to prevent China from executing an invasion.

Logan had asked around the base as to why there were so few ships in port. He learned from Reardon that most of the US Pacific Fleet had been sent out to sea, partly as a precaution in case of another nuclear attack. Without dispersal of the ships, a direct hit on Coronado Island would destroy much of the navy in the Pacific Region. Everyone remembered Pearl Harbor and the lessons about concentrating the navy in one location.

Reardon also told him that two aircraft carrier strike groups were headed toward Taiwan to help with the situation there, the USS *Ronald Reagan* and the USS *Theodore Roosevelt*. They would arrive while Logan was on the island. Reardon impressed upon Logan that he should prepare for dangerous duty in a war zone.

Now Logan, Cotes, and Kayla were sitting in a staging area inside a building located next to the end of a pier, where smaller ships were tied up to dock. They were informed that their transport to Taiwan would be available shortly. Logan was worried about the travel time. He didn't believe Cotes's story about there being a special ship.

At 5:15 a.m., Reardon entered the waiting room and handed them all clipboards bearing nondisclosure forms for them to sign. This seemed very unusual to Logan.

"What are these, Major?" Logan asked unabashedly, used to the amount of unnecessary bullshit that the navy imposed on its personnel. "Why do we need to sign anything?"

"I can't tell you until you sign the forms. We're dealing with something of the highest level of secrecy, and the brass wants you and your traveling companions to sign off that you will not discuss the means of transport with anyone."

"You've got to be kidding," Logan said. "I have top-secret clearance already, so I don't need this."

"Yes, you do. Even the admiral has to sign off, not to mention the doctor here."

"But I have ultra-clearance, Major," Kayla said. "Isn't that enough?"

"This is specific to the craft you will be traveling on. It requires special eyes-only clearance, Doctor," the major said. "And this also lets you, Logan, have ultra-clearance for the biological materials we will have on board."

"OK." Kayla signed her forms and handed the clipboard back to Reardon. Seeing this, Logan and Cotes signed too.

Reardon collected the clipboards and verified the signatures. He set them down and surveilled the others, taking a deep breath before speaking.

"What I'm about to tell you is known by only about forty people total, aside from the crew," he said. "A number of people have worked on the design and manufacturing of this watercraft that you will travel in. But few of them have seen it once it was complete. As far as most of them are concerned, it was simply a design competition that would never be built. The people who built it only made parts of it, and only a small team actually assembled it. So as far as the navy goes, it does not exist. It represents the coalescence of several new technologies combined into one ship. It is unique, and nine more are being constructed or are in sea trials as we speak. We intend to keep it a closely held secret."

"Is that why we're going to board it in the dark?" Logan asked.

"Yes, exactly," Reardon said. "We don't want anyone to see it at the pier. We will board, and then you will leave immediately. It is a submersible, and you will learn more about its capabilities when you are on board. You will have a full day to discuss it with the captain while en route to Taiwan, where you will dock in twenty-six hours' time."

"Wait," Logan said loudly, "are you saying we will sail over seven thousand miles in a day?"

"That is exactly what I'm saying."

All the travelers were silent as they stared at one another and then at the major. It was a baffling statement.

"You're kidding me," Cotes said.

"No, it's true. Strange as that may seem, Admiral, we have a sub that can move at over three hundred knots underwater." Reardon let that idea settle in for a moment. "Look, I don't have time to tell you more. We need to get you and the samples on board right away. You have to be out of the harbor before first light."

They all stood and grabbed their personal duffels. They followed Reardon out the door and across the wharf to a gangway that led down to a separate pier near the water level. Next to the pier was a flat, black object shaped like a partially submerged salami that was about forty feet long and maybe twelve feet wide. In the dark, it appeared like the back of a whale that was drifting next to the pier. There was no conning tower, but a hatch was open, and a dim glow of red light shone through the hatchway. A ramp extended from the pier to the hatch, and a man in a dark uniform was standing near the hatch.

"This is Captain Alhaadi Ogoro of the *Hydra-X*, your captain for the trip. He is an expert on this craft and will answer any questions you may have. But we don't have time for further introductions, so please climb down the hatchway. You will have plenty of time to talk once inside."

"Welcome aboard," Ogoro said in a baritone voice. "You have a million questions, I am sure. But we must clear the harbor in the next twenty minutes, so please enter."

Ogoro helped each of the travelers start down the ladder to the interior of the ship. Then he climbed in and sealed the hatch. A crewman showed them to their seats in the middle of the craft in a cabin similar to that of a small jet. The room was about twelve feet across and fourteen feet long, containing two rows of four seats each, broken by a central aisle in between. The seats were nearly identical to first-class airline seats, complete with headrest and seat belts. They sat down and buckled up as the crewman placed their duffels in a bin on one side of the cabin.

"Excuse me," Kayla asked, "where are my coolers?"

"They are right here, ma'am," the sailor replied politely. He opened a bin on the other side of the cabin, and the two oversize, Igloo coolers were there, carefully arranged and tied down with nylon straps. "You can check them out now, Doctor, if you're quick. We will be underway in three minutes."

Kayla walked over to examine the coolers and then sat down again. The crewman excused himself and left the cabin via an internal rear hatch.

The three travelers gawked at one another. Logan raised his eyebrows as he observed Kayla for her reaction. She just looked at him in surprise.

"Well, it seems weird to me," Logan said softly. "I've served on many ships, and this is the quietest one I've ever seen. There's usually the sound of people rushing around and clanking metal and engine noise. This ship seems way too quiet to me. It's eerie."

"I agree," Cotes said. "And did you feel the skin of the ship as we climbed down?" He looked over at Logan. "It didn't feel like metal at all."

"And the ladder was like plastic, not metal," Kayla added. "Even the structure of these seats seems like a plastic of some kind. I don't see any metal in here at all."

The ship began to move, but there was no engine noise. It felt like they were being towed by unseen forces. The movement was gentle, but the ship felt like it was backing away from the pier and then slowly turning right, gaining speed. The passengers had no basis for reference, so they couldn't tell what was really happening. They only had their own sense of motion to tell them they were moving at all. They could hear no water slapping against the hull, so Logan guessed that they were already submerged or they would feel the buffeting of waves. Then it felt as though the ship was accelerating based only on the awareness that they were being pressed back in their seats. It was a strange sensation.

"There were rumors a few years ago about a new technology that would revolutionize ship propulsion," the admiral murmured. "I wonder if we're experiencing it right now."

They sat at attention for about twenty minutes, sensing through their bodies the small course corrections as the ship worked its way out of the harbor and to the open sea. It was uncanny, like being in a spaceship where they had no perception of movement—no land to see passing by, no indication of where they were or where they were going. They gaped at one another in awe.

"I think we're accelerating," Logan said.

The hatch at the rear of the cabin opened, and Ogoro entered the compartment. He appeared happy to be underway.

"We are now at sea and on course for Taiwan with a few deviations from a straight line due to obstacles in the sea and other dangers. We will be up to three hundred knots shortly. I hope you are comfortable. Some people who suffer from motion sickness find it difficult to ride in this boat. That's why we maneuver very carefully in the harbor. It is a strange feeling for sailors in particular."

"Why is it so quiet?" Logan asked. "I can't hear the engines or even sense water moving past the hull."

"We're moving under a new type of propulsion. There are no moving parts to make noise. I can't tell you the mechanism because it is so unique and amazing that you would need to be a physicist to even imagine it. Also, it is classified at the highest level of secrecy we have."

"But we can't really be moving through the water at such speed, can we?" Cotes asked. Then his expression changed, and he suddenly appeared shocked. "Are we in a super-cavitation craft? I thought we only had that technology incorporated in torpedo designs."

"Aha," Ogoro said. "That I can tell you since it does not reveal the propulsion system. You are right. That is why we can travel at speeds usually associated with air travel. We are, in fact, traveling through a giant moving bubble of air. It reduces drag on the boat to minimal levels."

"Amazing," Cotes said. "I never dreamed I would see the day we could do this."

"And the hull? What is it made of?" Kayla asked with awe in her voice.

"A special type of organic plastic that has low drag characteristics. I can't tell you the name of it, but it is so secret that our military didn't even patent it so no one would know it exists," Ogoro said with pride. "It has the unique property of increasing strength when under pressure, which is perfect for a submarine. It gets stronger the deeper we go."

Logan marveled at the new information. "What is the crush depth for this submarine?"

"We have had it down to two thousand feet with no signs of distress. It is amazing," Ogoro said with obvious awe.

"That *is* amazing!" Kayla said.

"This new class of submarine is called a Hydra," the captain said. "You are on the *Hydra-X*. We're using this one and perhaps one other for diplomatic and courier services to the Western Pacific and a few other locations because of the danger posed by Chinese submarines and because we have lost so many communications and GPS satellites." He paused to look them each in the eye. "You understand the Chinese say they have no knowledge of our lost satellites, but we know for certain they have attacked many of the ones that cover the western Pacific Ocean. Our normally secure communications have all been compromised by the Chinese, so we do a lot of face-to-face and hand-delivery of documents now."

"How about the other boats?" Kayla asked. "Will they be available soon? Will they be used as couriers too or as warships?"

"They will come online soon and be used as torpedo boats. We intend to take the Chinese fleet down a few pegs."

"This is such a small sub. How can you carry enough torpedoes to do that?" Cotes asked skeptically. "I mean, even our newer torpedoes are twenty feet long."

"Sorry, Admiral, but you don't know about our latest class of Zebra torpedoes. They are only ten feet long and travel at up to one hundred knots under a new guidance system, propulsion, and warhead. It is another of our best-kept secrets. The Hydras will serve as lone-wolf, hunter-killer subs. Soon the Chinese will see their ships destroyed with no warning whatsoever."

"It's based on the MK-54 torpedo?"

"It goes beyond that technology, but the MK-54 is a good example of a lightweight weapon we have been developing," the captain replied.

"One last thing: if the hull is nonmetallic, it must be invisible to magnetic search techniques, right?" Logan asked carefully.

"I can't say more, but you are right that we are almost invisible to all radiation-sensing methods the enemy might use to find us," Ogoro said. "And just because I know you'll ask, Commander, we don't use GPS for guidance. We rely on a new, inertial guidance system, so we only correct our system when back at our home port."

"Well, I'm impressed, Captain. It's quite a boat," Cotes said with a smile.

"I'm damn proud to be her skipper, sir." Ogoro smiled himself and turned on his heel to exit. A crewman then entered the cabin with a tray of coffee cups that he politely passed around. He also handed them a half-page-size lunch menu.

"I'm Curtis. I'm the chef, steward, and host while you are on board. I don't really do a lot of cooking except for special occasions, but I can thaw and cook any of the specially prepared meals we have in our freezer. If you make a meal selection, I will prepare it at 1100 hours for an early lunch." He smiled. "We have a very small galley, so I hope you don't mind eating on the tray built into your seat. You can also sleep in your seats, which lie back like a first-class airline seat—one of the comfortable ones. We copied much of the design from Boeing."

The travelers sat somewhat mystified by all they had just heard. *It's remarkable,* Logan thought, *that the navy has been able to keep all this new technology under wraps for so long.* Usually, details of any new weapon system leaked out into the technical and intelligence communities long before the system could be commissioned. Somehow, they had managed to keep a lid on these developments. That must have meant they had new methods for managing information and procurement— something that had been needed for decades.

They feverishly chatted about the boat. At 11:00 a.m., Curtis appeared with trays of tasty food—certainly better than most airline food. He even offered them glasses of wine, something he said they did not usually provide, but a few bottles had been stocked because they had an admiral on board. Kayla and Logan toasted the admiral for their good luck in having him as a passenger.

After lunch, without much debate, they all agreed that they would try to nap to make up for the recent short nights they had endured. Before long, they were all snoozing in their reclining seats.

Logan awoke at about 3:00 p.m. and saw that Kayla was already sitting up and reading text on her cell phone. He smiled at her and received a grin in return.

"You're not getting a signal, are you?" he asked.

"Oh no," she answered. "I'm reading a document in preparation for our arrival in Taiwan. I have to be on my toes as soon as we dock. I will have to take our samples directly to the research labs at Taimmunology. They are an offshoot of the biggest vaccine maker in ROC. They will manufacture the vaccine for the whole island and for possible later distribution on the mainland, if they accept it. The CCP may not trust a vaccine from Taiwan and may use their own."

"ROC? The Republic of China on Taiwan?" Logan asked. "How long will it take for you to get them up and running?"

"It shouldn't take long, but I have another project I'm working on with them too. So it may be two weeks before I can leave. I guess you will be with me every day as my bodyguard, according to Cotes."

"Oh, I thought I was just protecting the vaccine samples," Logan said, somewhat surprised.

"Well, that's really it, but since I know how it was designed, I guess he's worried about my safety as well," she said. "A researcher was kidnapped from a Taiwan lab just last month by Chinese intelligence agents."

This was news to Logan, who had suspected that his boss was still hiding some things from him. It was the first he had heard of the possibility of a kidnapping. *Great,* he thought, *Chinese agents. Just what I need.* He thought about his limited Chinese speaking capabilities: he was at survival level thanks to a stint at the consulate in Shanghai a few years ago. He could possibly say something simple like, "Unhand that scientist, you lout." Not very convincing.

"You seem surprised. Is this another thing that the admiral forgot to mention?" Kayla seemed miffed that Cotes was hiding information from Logan. "Cotes has sprung a few things on me at the last moment too, like he won't be with us most of the time. We have to pin him down on that."

"Yes, we will," Logan said. "I guess I can't blame you for the secrets that Cotes keeps from us both."

At the mention of his name, Cotes woke up. "What did I miss?" he asked. He sounded like he was exhausted.

"Kayla was just saying that I'm her bodyguard and that you won't be with us in Taiwan. What gives?" Logan felt his blood pressure rising. "This had better be good after our last conversation, Cotes."

The admiral flinched and cleared his throat. "Well, it's true." He was trapped. "I received a text just before we left port that I will be required to travel on board this sub to Japan and Seoul to deliver their samples directly. It was news to me. I planned to hand over the samples to an intermediary who was supposed to take care of that."

"So you will be gone for what? Four or five days?" Logan asked.

"Or longer. That's why I thought I'd assign you to protect Kayla while she's on the island. I won't be around to do it. She will have a detail of Taiwanese specialists to guard her, but she needs someone very close for protection." He grinned in a cynical way. "You're it, Logan."

"You're kidding," Kayla said.

"Well, when your father was going to make the trip, I was to protect him and the samples. Now with this new duty, Logan will have to do it."

Logan and Kayla glanced at each other and shook their heads. It appeared that the situation was beyond even Cotes's control. They would have to live with it.

"But I thought all four of these packages of samples were going to Taiwan," Logan said. "Which ones go to the other countries?"

"I'll keep track of all that," Kayla said. "The bundles marked *J* and *S* will go with Cotes. The other two come with us to the lab. One is the vaccine, and one is a sample of the virus that it's based on so they can develop a therapeutic for it."

"Don't they have the new virus strain here yet? I thought it would be everywhere by now."

"No, we had to anticipate the next mutation," Kayla said nervously, "and we are the only ones to have it right now. It has to be carefully controlled, as you can imagine." She turned away to speak to Cotes. "And you will just keep going when we get off the boat? Who will meet us in Taiwan?"

"Unless things have changed, we will land at Tofu Cape Harbor at about 22:00 on Wednesday, a complete day jump because we cross the International Date Line. We will be met by Commander Chih-lung Lee of the ROC Navy. I will have to explain to him the change in plans. He will take you directly to the lab and on to your lodging on the campus nearby."

"He'll be our contact while we're there?" Logan asked. "He'll also be in charge of our security, then?"

"Presumably," Cotes said. "You will have to ask him about the arrangements."

Ogoro stepped into the cabin and smiled. "You will be dealing with exhaustion and a fifteen-hour time lag when you arrive. I suggest you eat dinner now, even though it's only four San Diego time. And take these pills to fight jet lag." He laughed. "You know, in the navy, we never had to worry about jet lag unless we flew somewhere, but *Hydra-X* has created new issues. Anyway, you will be surprised by how well the pill works."

"Where are we, Captain?" Kayla asked.

"We have just passed south of Hawaii. We are on course and on time."

They ordered dinners and wine from Curtis and enjoyed another surprisingly delicious meal. The men devoured beef burgundy with roasted potatoes, supplemented by a good bordeaux. Kayla had the chicken Kiev, which she ate with gusto after tolerating the simple camp fare they had eaten while on the convoy. They chatted about what conditions they might encounter in Taiwan. They also briefly talked about how smooth and quiet the ship was, considering they were traveling at about three hundred miles per hour. Shortly after that, they took their pills and fell into blissful sleep for the rest of their journey.

Chapter 15

Wednesday, March 22, 2023

Tofu Cape Harbor, Taiwan

The travelers emerged from the *Hydra-X* in darkness at a small pier on the east shore of Taiwan, Republic of China. They met Lee, who was head of security on the island. He had a brief conversation with the admiral, and then Cotes said a quick goodbye. He reentered the sub, and within minutes, there was no sign that a submarine had ever been there.

"Welcome to the ROC," Lee said. "I hope your trip was comfortable. When it is daylight, you will see how beautiful our little home is here. But now I want to immediately take you to deliver these samples to the lab." He smiled and pointed to a black limousine with mesh covers dimming its headlights. The sample cooler was loaded into the trunk, and Kayla let Logan hold the door open for her as they climbed inside the rear compartment with the commander. A black vehicle that looked a lot like a Humvee led their three-vehicle convoy as another brought up the rear. They drove out of the harbor and turned onto a two-lane, blacktop road that climbed over low hills.

Lee sat across from them, facing the rear of the vehicle while they occupied the bench seat. "I am certain that you are quite tired from your travels, but we must log these samples into the lab records for security purposes right away. There will be a few people at the lab to greet you, Dr. Grimley, despite the hour," he said eagerly. "I can assure you that you will be very safe during your visit. I have a team of specialists in my detail that will move with you wherever you go. There is also a security team at the lab that is very good at protecting the facility and its staff. There have been no incidents here, as there were at another lab recently. I will also be available at all times if you should need to travel from the campus."

"I wondered if it would be possible to go somewhere where we can see the Taiwan Strait to see some of the action that is taking place between your country and the PRC, mainland China?" Logan asked. "I have never seen the Strait and am interested in how the battle is going."

Lee appeared uncomfortable, but then grinned somewhat. "Perhaps we can find a day when we can make a short trip to oversee the Strait. I probably cannot take you anywhere near the fighting because it is restricted. But I can tell you all about the battle during your visit, if that meets your interest."

"Yes," Logan replied. "That would be perfect. Thank you."

They rode in silence for thirty minutes while Lee worked on his telephone, speaking in Mandarin, apparently ensuring that everyone was on the same page regarding their arrival at the lab. They drove steadily along the curvy road that wound its way over the hills and finally entered a valley that had been largely developed but still had some forest visible along its slopes. They passed a highway sign that announced *Taoyuan City* in English beneath a series of Chinese characters.

"We are entering Taoyuan City, where the lab is located. It will only be a short time now," Lee said cheerfully.

They made a number of turns and drove down a narrow alley terminating at a wall with a steel gate across it. The lead vehicle stopped, and its driver talked to someone in the guard station at the side of the gate. They were granted permission to drive through the gate, and it closed behind them.

"We are now entering the industrial campus. There are several laboratories here and housing facilities for staff and visiting personnel. We are going to building 153, which is the vaccine lab. That is where you can log in the samples."

They shortly came to a stop. A man held the rear door open for them to disembark. They crawled out and stretched their legs. Then Lee ushered them into a building and through its security check point, complete with a metal detector, hand scanners, ID checks, and briefcase inspection. The cooler with the samples was run through an X-ray machine and then partially opened. Once the inspector saw the biohazard stickers on the seals, he closed up the cooler and returned it to Kayla.

On the other side of the inspection station, they met Dr. Wu, who Kayla knew professionally, and two members of her staff. Kayla and Logan were issued ID badges for the building. They then followed Wu up a flight of stairs to a large lab full of experiment benches, analytical equipment, and specialized biohazard-ventilated compartments. It looked a little like the level-two area of Kayla's own research facility in Mankato.

Wu led them to the large, walk-in cooler room, where Kayla placed the cooler on a shelf. She then removed a package marked *T-A1*, which she handed to Wu, who accepted it with a perfunctory bow and thanked her.

"Thank you for bringing this vaccine sample and component to us here in Taiwan. I will now sign for it on your chain-of-custody form and sign it into our lab."

She ceremoniously signed a sheaf of papers and handed them to Kayla. She then entered the receipt of the samples into her own logbook and had all present sign as witnesses. Then Wu bowed to Kayla and smiled, saying, "I understand you have had quite a time getting here, my friend. You must be exhausted." She turned to Lee. "Commander, you must take my friends to their quarters so they can rest, and then we can get down to the business of making the vaccine in the morning."

They all bowed one more time, and Lee led Logan and Kayla back out to the waiting vehicles.

They drove the equivalent of about five city blocks, and Lee ordered the car to stop. "Here is the housing facility," he said. "I will walk you inside, and we will bring your luggage in for you."

They entered what appeared to be a long-stay hotel and checked in, again with building security similar to that they had just been through. Kayla and Logan were issued another set of keycards and ID badges for the building. Then a porter took them up to their room. Lee and his men came along, which surprised Logan.

At the door of their suite, Lee took the keycard from Logan and opened the door. One of his men walked through the apartment ahead of them to make sure it was safe, and then Lee had them enter. He handed the card back to Logan.

"We had originally expected Dr. Grimley senior to be traveling with Admiral Cotes, so we had a two-bedroom unit reserved," Lee said. "I'm afraid that is all we have available at this time. I hope these lodgings will be adequate."

Logan saw the surprise on Kayla's face. He said, "It works for me, but I would understand if you want your own quarters, Kayla. I can look for something else, maybe in a barracks or something similar." He turned to Lee for suggestions.

"Oh no, Logan," she said. "This will be fine since we have our own bedrooms. We won't be here very much anyway." She poked her head into one of the bedrooms and snickered. "And I see that this one has its own attached bathroom, so I claim it." She grinned and motioned for the man with her bag to place it inside.

"Hey, that's pretty sneaky. I guess I'm learning more about you." Logan chuckled as he pointed to the other bedroom. "This one has a better view anyway." He looked out the window at the gray shadow of an adjacent structure, hardly a view at all in the dark of night.

"If that is sufficient, then I will bid you good night," Lee announced. "You will be able to order room service for breakfast and anything else you may require. I will station one man outside your door for the night. Otherwise, I will be here to pick you up at eight o'clock. Is that good for you?"

"Yes, that's perfect," Kayla said. They all nodded, and the security team left the room.

"I don't know about you, but I could use a nightcap."

"A glass of chardonnay would be nice."

Logan picked up the phone and ordered a bottle of Chardonnay for Kayla and a bottle of Kavalan Whisky for himself. Many had said that Kavalan was the best of the Taiwan-made whiskies. They then set about unpacking their bags.

Just as Logan finished unpacking, a knock on the door signaled that the drinks had arrived. Shortly afterward, Kayla joined him in the living room. Logan was tired but happy to be settled in one location for a few days.

"I didn't expect to have a roommate on this trip, but it will be fun to have someone to talk to in the evenings," Kayla said. "It should also make it easier for us to keep track of each other, especially with you as my bodyguard." She smiled at him with a sparkle in her eyes as she sipped her Chardonnay.

"Yes, it will be easier to protect you this way, so in that, the arrangement has worked out well. Plus, I don't know anyone here—it might be nice to have dinner together, if you would like that?"

"Yes, that might be fun. But I think we may not be allowed to leave this campus for an evening out." She looked around at the confines of the apartment. "We may be staring at these walls quite a bit while we're here."

Logan laughed at the idea of being in such a secure facility. It wasn't the way he usually traveled. "Well, at least we're used to limited nightlife after two years of COVID lockdowns. I don't feel the need to seek out a discotheque."

"We could dance here in the living room—if we had music, that is." She chuckled at the idea. Then she evaluated the small, digital music and TV console that was lodged in one wall of the room. "This is rather sparsely decorated, isn't it?"

"Yes." Logan scanned the walls and came nearer to Kayla to whisper. "Say, you don't think they have this place bugged, do you? I've traveled places where I had to watch what I discussed in hotel rooms. I suppose we should assume that we're being listened to here, so watch what you say. They may even have a camera set up." His face tightened. "You know industrial espionage is a way of life in this part of the world. We shouldn't take anything for granted."

He held his finger up to his lips, signaling for her to be quiet. He walked around the room carefully, searching in the usual places for a hidden camera. He did the same in each of the bedrooms and the baths, paying special attention to the heat registers and light fixtures. After a few minutes, he approached

Kayla and led her to the smoke detector in the living room. He pointed at it, and she nodded her head.

They walked back and sat down. "I think that is the only one, but we can't be sure. There may be listening devices so small I can't detect them. But video devices usually have to be in the line of sight, so they are easier to find," he said softly. Then he checked out the TV screen and said, "Of course, many TVs were set up to have interactive speakers in them too, so that's always possible."

She came over to sit next to him. "Would our allies spy on us while we're here to help them? I only thought our enemies would be that bold."

"Well, these might be here to listen to commercial conversations too; maybe not specifically for us." He lowered his head close to hers and whispered, "No technical talk here. I would assume the lab is bugged too, so watch what you say."

"Do you suppose Commander Lee knows about this?"

"I don't know. He may not because he doesn't usually work at this facility." He stood up. "Let's see."

Logan walked to the front door and opened it. The guard who was standing outside was surprised and jerked to attention.

Logan addressed him formally.

"Ensign, can you ask for Commander Lee to call me immediately, please?"

The guard seemed worried, then nodded his head. He spoke Chinese into a microphone on his lapel. He appeared afraid to bother his commanding officer. He finished the conversation and then pointed inside the apartment to a telephone on the counter. Logan thanked him.

Within five minutes, the apartment phone rang, and Logan answered it. He said, "Thank you for calling, Commander. I was calling to find out if you had swept these rooms for listening devices. My colleague and I were concerned that our conversations might be recorded."

Lee responded quite formally, with a crisp sound to his voice. "I have been assured by the industrial campus that they have already searched the room for bugs, as you call them. If you like, I can arrange to have a team of my own men sweep the apartment in the morning."

Logan realized that he had caught Lee in a slight error. He should have already had the rooms swept independently. But maybe they hadn't had sufficient time to do so before he and Kayla had arrived.

"Thank you, Commander. A sweep in the morning will be excellent. Thank you for your kind assistance. Good night."

Logan gazed at Kayla and chuckled. "We can't take anything for granted here. We had best get some sleep before Lee turns up with a team of technicians." He chuckled, almost from exhaustion, and they shuffled off to their respective bedrooms.

Logan heard Kayla turn the lock on her bedroom door with a snap as he hung his clothes in the narrow closet by his bed. He commandeered the bathroom that led off from the kitchen area and laid out his toothbrush and shaver. Then he savored the last of the Kavalan and sat on the sofa to reflect on the day's activities.

After several minutes, he noticed that the sliver of light emanating from under Kayla's bedroom door had vanished, and he wondered how the next two weeks would play out. It was going to be either a boring slog, or something dangerous would happen that they had no way of anticipating now. He finally switched off the living room light and retreated to grab as many hours of shut-eye as he could before the sun signaled a new morning.

***

The next morning, Logan stayed at the apartment and observed Lee's team scan for bugs. The men were experts and detected a video device in the living room area, plus several listening devices there and in both bedrooms. Lee apologized profusely about the matter and said he would understand if Logan would like to move their quarters outside the campus. Clearly, he said, the campus personnel were untrustworthy.

Logan had anticipated the need to move and had made several calls that morning. American diplomats in Taipei had told him there were limited options because so many Americans had flown into the country to help coordinate US aid to Taiwan. Many of these personnel were undoubtedly spies collecting information about the Chinese forces that had been concentrated across the Strait on the mainland. In any case, now that the apartment had been swept clean, there was little need to move, and the convenience of being on-site outweighed other concerns for now.

Logan arranged with Lee that a man would remain stationed outside the suite at all times, even when Logan and Kayla weren't there, and that the guard would oversee the cleaning crew when they came to tidy up the unit. It would be hard to install new bugs while a guard watched. Lee went further and promised to sweep the premises every day before Logan and Kayla returned for the night.

After the sweep was finished, Lee accompanied Logan to the lab they had visited the night before. Kayla had spent the morning with Dr. Wu going over how the vaccine components worked and answering any questions she had about beginning production. When Logan arrived, they were having coffee in the break room.

"Oh, good," Kayla said. "We were just finishing up our first meeting, and you can help me take the second sample over to the virology lab. Commander Lee called and said he would be ready about now." She turned to Lee, and he nodded his head.

"If you recover your sample from the cooler, we can drive to the other lab immediately," Lee said.

"Excellent," she responded. "Let me call over there and be sure they are ready for us." She took out her cell phone and began to dial.

Lee held up his hand as if to stop her. "Since we have secured your apartment, let me provide you both with encrypted cell phones that will scramble your signal. The virology lab will detect the signals and decode your calls with the same level of protection. Please use them whenever you need to call that lab."

Kayla accepted her phone and spoke briefly with her counterpart at the lab. Then she walked to the secure, cold room and had Wu open it for her. She walked inside with Logan, confirmed that the seals on the cooler were unbroken, and carried the cooler out. She said a formal goodbye to Wu, and they walked out to the waiting convoy.

The cars wove their way through the campus to another checkpoint, where Lee conferred with the guards at a double gate. They passed through one gate and stopped so that the cars could be scanned for weapons and explosives. When the search was complete, they drove through the second gate and over to the portico of the virology lab.

Dr. Ming Wang, the head of the virology lab, met them by the door. He wore an N95 mask on his face but still appeared friendly. He was a gracious host and led Kayla, Logan, and Lee, all in masks, up to his office while Logan carried the sealed cooler. His office was opulent compared with Dr. Wu's austere place of work. He had a mahogany desk and comfortable chair, with an ancient-looking tapestry of a Chinese Lake District scene, perhaps the Li River, on the wall. He offered them hot jasmine tea in classic ceramic cups with small wafer cookies on the side. He bade them to sit down on embroidered chairs set in a circle around a small tea table. An assistant poured tea in traditional Chinese fashion and then withdrew to stand along the wall by the door. Logan figured Wang's office had been either swept for bugs or he had special ones installed for meetings like this.

"It is a pleasure to meet you at last, Dr. Grimley. I was expecting your father but am happy that you have come instead," Wang said. "We have much to talk about." He noticed the cooler in Logan's hands. "This is the sample?"

"Yes, it is," Kayla replied.

Wang nodded to his assistant, who then walked to the office door and stepped outside. Within seconds, she returned with two masked men following her.

"Let me introduce the virologists who will be working with the sample," Wang said. "This is Dr. Kuan, who will develop the treatment or therapeutic for the virus."

The taller of the two men with a long, thin but friendly face stepped forward and bowed to the others all around. He smiled at Kayla and said, "It is good to meet you, Dr. Grimley. We will have much to discuss in the coming days."

"And this is Dr. Chin, our virology characteristics expert," Wang continued. "He will also work with the virus and will be in touch as needed."

"It's a pleasure to meet you, Dr. Grimley," Chin said. He was a short, heavyset man with a determined look on his face. "I also might have questions that you may be able to help me with, if that's OK." His English was smooth and less formal, like he had lived in the United States at one point in his career.

"It's nice to meet both of you. I look forward to working with you," Kayla said. She introduced Logan as her associate and Lee as her head of security while in the country. They all chatted briefly, and Logan was aware that the men immediately wanted to take possession of the sample and get to work. After a few pleasantries, Wang suggested they walk down to the lab so that Kayla could sign off on the sample delivery. They did so, and after she handed over the cooler, the men quickly departed.

Wang gave them a short tour of the lab—at least, the unsecured portions of it—and they returned to his office. They arranged for Kayla to return the following morning to meet with both researchers.

Lee, Kayla, and Logan returned to the vaccine lab in time for lunch in the cafeteria. The room was big enough for ten plastic tables and accompanying chairs, with the service counter set up along one side of the room and a few vending machines along the opposite wall. The walls were painted that dull, cream color so often favored by government facilities, and an acoustic ceiling muffled much of the clatter coming from the kitchen. Lee left them to themselves and said he would return when they planned to return to their apartment.

They walked through the cafeteria line, and each picked one of the bowl lunches and hot tea to drink. They selected a table away from the more spirited conversations in the room and sat down.

Kayla said, "Logan, I don't think you need to be with me all day on the occasions when I work with lab personnel. It's just a waste of your time to sit around and wait for me, especially since one of Lee's men is always accompanying me too."

"I think you're right. I will check out security at both labs, and then I can feel comfortable that you will be well cared for," Logan said. "The problem is, I don't really have much else to do."

They both tasted their meals and smiled. Logan added salt to his rice bowl. He often found that Chinese food was very mildly spiced and needed salt and other condiments to bring it up to his American palate.

"I heard back from the general in Chicago about how things are going there," Logan said as he savored his rice. "Our guys managed to hold back Antifa from invading the Cabrini-Green area. We lost some men doing it, but bloodied the anarchists badly. Otherwise, things haven't changed that much. The Caliphate and Antifa are still tearing up the city."

"I heard that they have already moved a portion of the government to Denver per our old Cold War contingency plan in case Washington was attacked again," Kayla said thoughtfully. "There will be no reconstruction of DC until rescue teams have searched everywhere for survivors and bodies of the dead. The place is under martial law with a general in charge for now. Extensive field hospitals were built to deal with all the injured.

There are a lot of radiation burns and people with radiation poisoning. Between New York and DC, all the health resources of the Eastern Seaboard are overloaded. And that's on top of the COVID problems."

"That's the same in NYC. According to reports, an estimated two million have died, and another million are injured. Rioting continues on top of that. I guess a lot of the Antifa people there were killed, but others have started looting the suburbs now. The police forces are completely overwhelmed. There are fires everywhere."

"It's not much to go home to, is it?" she said mournfully. "Well, at least we aren't in a world war yet."

"Not officially," Logan whispered. "But we might be soon. The aircraft carriers are expected here in two days. Their arrival may lead us into a war with China. Then all hell will break loose."

They ate the rest of their meals silently, engrossed in thought.

Chapter 16

Saturday, March 25, 2023
Outside Taoyuan City, Taiwan

Three days passed by quickly as Kayla worked with virologists in the two laboratories and Logan served as her constant guard. After that amount of time, Kayla and Logan had become closer and ate most meals together. They didn't have a lot of choices about the dining arrangements and made the most of the limited selections on the room service menu. They found out from Lee that his men could bring in food from outside sources if they gave him two hours' notice. This made their dining a bit more adventurous.

The minutes passed especially slowly for Logan, who had little to do except oversee their security. He did get outside the campus once to see where it was situated on the island. He had told Lee that he needed to be sure they had an escape route if the campus came under attack in the increasingly violent bombardment the island suffered from the Chinese People's Liberation Army, the PLA.

Logan had convinced Lee that he should take him out to observe the action that would occur when the two US aircraft carriers entered the north end of the Taiwan Strait. That was scheduled for today, and would no doubt lead to plenty of aircraft activity. After some argument, Lee had agreed to drive to a lookout point where they could see along the coast and out onto the Strait. They would have an unobstructed view of the giant carriers as they entered the Strait close to the Taiwan shore. Logan guessed that Lee gave in because he also wanted to witness the event.

The Communist Chinese had threatened to attack any ships that entered the Strait because they claimed that would be an act of aggression. This was outrageous because they were the ones hurling missiles at Taiwan daily. The threat was clearly intended to get the newly appointed US President, President Callahan, to back down.

Logan learned from Cotes that the commander of the US Pacific Fleet had assured the president that the ships could always be removed if they were threatened. Of course, the US Navy had already promised a show of force four weeks before when the mainland forces had begun their bombardment of Taiwan's shoreline and military installations. The president had been told she couldn't back down now.

It was 11:00 a.m. before Logan and Lee reached the observation point that Lee had in mind. They were on one of the mountain peaks just south of Taoyuan City that was not very high, but afforded an unobstructed view of the sea west of the island. It turned out that the point was being used as an observation post for the Taiwanese Army, and Lee was able to gain access for the day. The view was impressive, overlooking the northwest coast south of Taipei and as far south as Hsinchu City, which had been the target of some of the bombardments for the last few weeks.

The soldiers on top of the peak were excited because Communist China's People's Liberation Army Navy, called PLAN, the naval component of the PLA, was active today. They had organized a show of force of their own with some twenty ships traveling north up the Strait, supposedly just on their side of the median line that officially separated the side of the channel that China claimed from the side that Taiwan claimed. Of course, Mainland China had really claimed all of the Strait as part of their country, but, in practice, had kept mostly to their own side. The fleet appeared to be too close to the island to be following the rules of the channel.

The fleet consisted of three frigates, six destroyers, ten missile boats, and a supply ship. While all of them were relatively small, they bristled with anti-ship missiles. Each ship in itself wasn't much of a threat to an aircraft carrier strike group, but if they concentrated for an attack on a few targets, they could be very effective. The Chinese strategy of attack on US capital ships was to overwhelm them with relatively inexpensive anti-ship missiles. The idea was to strike with so many missiles that American defenses couldn't respond to all the incoming threats.

Logan watched the north end of the channel, where three Taiwanese destroyers flanked the first escort vessels of the American aircraft carrier strike group as it appeared on the water. The American ships stayed far away from the median line, because the Strait was at its narrowest width there. Several fighter aircraft flew in to occupy the airspace over the channel where the ships would patrol. These included some Taiwanese fighters, as well as US fighters from the carrier.

"Look, Commander," Logan said, pointing to the ships sailing into view on their right. "That's the *Roosevelt*, I think."

As they watched, the first carrier, the USS *Theodore Roosevelt*, sailed south close to the island in Taiwan waters. Then the other ships of the strike group, two American missile cruisers, six missile destroyers, and other escort ships followed at half-mile spacing. The carrier bristled with aircraft on deck that was ready to deploy. Planes were taking off as a few craft landed to refuel.

The group of ships slowly sailed south along the coast. Then the leading ships of the second carrier, the USS *Ronald Reagan*, appeared, following the same course as the *Roosevelt*. The two carriers were about three miles apart, and their escort craft were only separated by about a mile. It wasn't clear if they intended to sail down the length of the channel or simply to patrol the Taiwanese side. Lee wasn't sure, but he thought they were going down the Strait first and then would return on patrol.

"Look over there, Commander," Lee said. "There are more PLAN ships coming from the northwest."

Logan swung his binoculars to look northward. Sure enough, a fleet of some twenty-five surface ships were advancing south along the median line. From what little Logan knew of the Chinese navy, these ships seemed like more of the missile-laden craft that were in the fleet, with a few frigates and destroyers mixed among them. They appeared to be heading to a point just west of where the *Reagan* was cruising.

Then Logan noticed a sudden change of course of the first PLAN fleet. They had veered eastward and were heading toward the *Roosevelt* at speed. The *Roosevelt* escort ships started to reposition into a screening force on the offshore side of the aircraft carrier, placing themselves between the PLAN ships and the *Roosevelt*. More aircraft began to launch from the *Roosevelt*. It wasn't clear yet if the Chinese were making an attack run or simply provoking the allies. It would be right out of their book of tactics to provoke an incident and then blame it on the Americans for interfering in their so-called territorial waters.

"The other Chinese fleet is turning this way as well. It's a coordinated action," Logan said as he tracked the ships through his binoculars.

Some of the *Reagan*'s sixty-eight F/A-18 Super Hornet fighters began to launch, and its escort fleet started to re-form. Logan imagined the scramble that was taking place on all the ships. The captains of the carriers would be calling all men to battle stations, as well as sending out warnings to the PLAN vessels in Mandarin and English to turn away from the American ships or face defensive measures. Someone would be communicating with Taiwanese naval officials about the action and coordinating with the Taiwanese destroyers. Meanwhile, the missile cruisers within each strike group would take charge of the coordinated defense of the group.

"Look," Lee said as he pointed. "Our destroyers are turning into the attack."

It was clear to everyone on the hilltop that the Chinese were either going to attack or provoke someone to fire on them. The CCP loved international incidents and could create a situation that would either embarrass President Callahan or make her blink. But they may have miscalculated here because there was no time for either side to back off once the shooting began.

"Our navy has strict rules of engagement," Lee said. "We cannot fire until fired upon—unless there is an imminent threat of attack and loss of life."

They strained their eyes to see the three Taiwanese destroyers as they closed the distance to the approaching ships. A pair of Taiwanese fighter jets flew toward the northern PLAN ships, no doubt issuing warnings that the ships had crossed the median.

Then a missile rose from the PLAN frigate that led the antagonistic maneuver, and within seconds, the first of the ROC jets burst into flames. The second jet veered off but was chased by a second missile from the same PLAN ship. It dropped what appeared to be chaff and dove to escape the missile, then flew back toward the island at a low elevation.

If this was to be a full-blown attack, the PLAN ships would likely want to come within ten miles to launch their missiles. The class of anti-ship missile carried by most Chinese ships had an effective range of about twenty miles, but their accuracy would be increased by a shorter launch distance. The trick for any captain was to come close so his shots would count and that any defenses the American ships had wouldn't be able to react fast enough to shoot down all the incoming missiles.

When the PLAN ships got too close for comfort, one of the American destroyers fired its five-inch gun and placed a shell across the bow of the frigate as a warning. The first round landed two hundred yards from the PLAN ship. A second landed right next to the frigate's hull. The frigate responded with its equivalent to the five-inch gun, and the shell landed four hundred yards from the US ship. The PLAN frigate fired an anti-ship missile from one of its launch tubes.

Then all hell broke loose.

Suddenly, the sky was filled with incoming aircraft from the mainland, all fighters from land-based airfields. Nearly fifty PLA fighters came in low over the water and then jetted up to combat height as they approached the carrier strike groups. These were the kind of air attacks the Taiwanese had been defending against for weeks.

Logan shouted, "Shit!" He was sure that Lee shouted something similar in Chinese. They glanced at each other as if wondering what they should do. The two men used to taking action were powerless to react to what they knew was impending disaster for many of their ships.

The carrier defensive patrol jets began to engage the newcomers as soon as they were within ten miles of the carriers.

More Hornets took off from the carrier decks and rose to the attack. They were joined by ROC fighters who flew their version of the F-16 Fighting Falcon and other planes that Logan didn't recognize. Both sides fired air-to-air missiles at each other as soon as the PLA planes crossed the median line. Nearly twenty planes began to smoke or blew up outright from missile strikes. Then, at closer range, they began a massive arial brawl, with undamaged planes tangling with the enemy. More missiles were launched, and individual planes fired their cannons at enemy fighters in dogfights.

"Those are fighters we designed and built here. They are F-CK-1C fighters," Lee said proudly, pointing to the ROC aircraft. "Don't even think about making fun of their name," he said grimly as Logan was about to speak.

In minutes, the sky was filled with PLAN missiles that were launched from sloping tubes on the decks of the missile boats. Those ships were able to fire a missile every few seconds from multiple tubes. The destroyers and frigates also launched missiles, but at a slower interval. They rocketed toward the American ships at hundreds of miles an hour, the newer ones flying at thousands of miles per hour. White smoke tracks from their exhaust laced the air as they gained elevation and then dropped to fly just above the sea's surface. It was clear that some of them had already locked onto a target.

The American guided-missile cruisers spun up their Aegis Ballistic Missile Defense systems and began to launch the newest antimissile projectiles. These self-propelled missiles with blast fragmentation warheads, called SSDS, reached the speed of Mach 5 in seconds. The SSDS missiles on the aircraft carriers had smaller but faster missiles that could accelerate to Mach 8 with only kinetic warheads, meaning they simply collided with any incoming missile and tore it to pieces, much as a bullet would do. They traveled the distance to impact in seconds, even though the ships they launched from were still ten miles apart. It happened so fast that all Logan could say was, "Holy shit! I don't believe it."

American and ROC fighters fled the area directly between the enemy and friendly ships to avoid the friendly missiles. They scrambled away to fight the remaining PLA jets down the channel.

The American destroyers had launched anti-ship missiles within seconds of the beginning of the attack. Those missiles struck the leading ships in both PLAN fleets, forming huge fireballs as they penetrated the superstructure. Three missiles struck the frigate that had fired the first shot, and one of the powerful blasts blew the bridge off. In this first salvo, six PLAN ships were hit within minutes of the first shot being fired.

"Look over there!" Lee shouted. "More missiles were launched."

Within a few minutes, the sky was filled with nearly four hundred Chinese anti-ship missiles. They raced toward the American vessels, most of them obviously targeting the *Roosevelt* and the *Reagan*. The antimissile projectiles that the US destroyers and cruisers continuously fired knocked down about one-third of the incoming threat. Then as the PLAN missiles closed on the screening ships, Gatling guns of the Phalanx CIWS defense system on the US ships began to roar to life. This close-in weapon system used radar to target incoming threats and fired 20mm cannon rounds at a rate of seventy-five per second. The extremely accurate guns simply tore missiles to shreds with a stream of bullets. But no system was designed to deal with what the allies were encountering. The sheer number of incoming threats led to different systems simultaneously targeting the same missile while a few were able to slip through the defensive fusillade.

One of the US destroyers was hit by a blast that tore a huge portion of its forward structure and tower off the ship. It was largely out of commission after that. The cruiser nearest the *Roosevelt* was hit twice in the forward structure and caught on fire. Another destroyer took a hit right at the waterline near the bow. The damage was limited, but it was taking on water.

The worst damage was that the *Roosevelt* sustained eight missile strikes, two of them to its island, the superstructure that housed the bridge, the communications tower, and all above-deck structures. The bridge wasn't hit, but the tower was hanging inverted off the structure. One hit was on the flight deck, which damaged several planes waiting to take off. Another missile struck the starboard side of the ship, causing moderate damage to smaller structures, such as one Phalanx gun, but with no real damage to the hull. The ship was still operational, shifting flight operations to the secondary catapults.

The *Reagan* was hit twice with little damage. Two of its destroyers were hit, with one on fire.

"My God!" Logan shouted as he shifted his binoculars from one ship to another, trying to keep up with the battle. "What the . . ."

As the last PLAN missiles approached, the American cruisers and destroyers began to retaliate with swarms of their own anti-ship missiles that decimated the PLAN ships. The Taiwanese destroyers fought too, firing their own missiles and cannons. One of them fired two torpedoes at the lead frigate of the southern PLAN fleet, causing a huge explosion amidships that tore the frigate in two. It sank quickly as the two halves took on water.

The two carriers now had sixty planes in the air attacking the rest of the PLAN ships that were trying to flee. The planes fired several missiles that attacked each ship's air defense system and then dropped thousand-pound bombs directly onto their decks until all the remaining PLAN ships were on fire or sinking. Thirty minutes after the attack had begun, dozens of smoke plumes were rising from stricken ships.

What had started out as a potentially relaxing day of watching venerable ships sail through the Taiwan Strait had turned into a devastating, modern sea battle. Many ships and planes had been lost, and many men and women had clearly died. The show of force that the mainland Chinese had hoped to gain had turned into a rout, and the PLAN had lost face in battle. That fact might have been the single lesson that the PLAN would remember: not that they had lost nearly fifteen thousand sailors and aviators, but that they had lost face.

Logan stared at Lee, and they both nodded. "This is horrible. They will want to retaliate and regain face," Lee said.

"As if we didn't already have enough to worry about," Logan said, shaking his head.

"All-out war looms nearer."

Lee's cell phone chirped, and he tapped the screen. His face noticeably tightened as he read a text message. He looked up at Logan and said, "Trouble. We have to go." Then he pushed a button on his lapel and spoke rapidly in Mandarin. Men began to rush toward the convoy vehicles.

"What's happened?" Logan asked as he followed Lee at a fast march toward their car.

"There is a bomb at the virology laboratory. They are evacuating the building now. We must hurry."

Chapter 17

Logan and Lee arrived at Dr. Wang's virology lab forty minutes after dashing down the mountain and speeding through light traffic. There was a crowd of people wearing white lab coats standing outside the building in the street, which had been cordoned off by emergency vehicles. Members of the campus police force were providing crowd control and keeping people together for safety. Two of the lab's internal security men were standing with a small cluster of people across the street from the building entrance. Logan noticed that Kayla was in that cluster, which included Dr. Wang and Dr. Kuan. They were speaking in animated fashion to one of the guards and pointing toward the building.

Lee and Logan immediately jogged over to the group where Kayla was standing. She noticed Logan right away and stepped over to speak to him.

"They found a bomb in the lobby and had to evacuate all of us. We only had a few seconds to get out of the lab." She nodded her head toward Wang. "Dr. Wang is concerned that the lab may not be secure because we all left so quickly. We may not have locked everything down properly. He wants a few people to reenter the building right away to be sure everything is safe and all security protocols have been followed."

"I take it the police don't want to let anyone in," Logan said.

Lee said, "Let me intervene. Security of those samples is the highest priority. If we have to send a few people in, then that is what we must do. They can still deactivate the bomb whether we're in there or not."

Lee marched off and joined the conversation with the lab security people and Wang. Shortly afterward, Lee, Wang, Kuan, and one of the security guards reentered the building with the other guard left to explain to the police what was happening.

"Are you OK?" Logan asked Kayla. "Was anyone hurt? Did they catch whoever left the bomb?"

"I'm fine. I was in Wang's office when this all happened, and we got out right away." She quickly glanced at him, her face somewhat flushed. "It was darn scary."

As Logan was about to say something comforting, a large truck that had a huge steel box mounted on the back deck pulled right up onto the sidewalk in front of the building. Two men wearing heavy protective clothing stepped out of the cab of the vehicle and walked to the rear to open the doors on the box. They pulled out a large toolbox the size of an Igloo cooler and marched into the building with one of the policemen in the lead.

"Looks like the bomb squad has arrived," Logan said. "I wonder who did this."

"I don't know, but Dr. Wang said they have never had a bomb threat before. One other building had one, but no actual bomb was found. They're really nervous about it."

"I wonder if it's because of the vaccine you brought here. Maybe someone knows about it."

In a few minutes, Wang and his entourage exited the building, looking relieved. They walked over to where Logan and Kayla stood.

"All is in order," Wang said to them. "I was concerned that we may not have followed protocols when we had to leave."

Logan smiled at Wang and wondered if Wang had had other things he needed to do in his office, like put away some classified papers that he might have been reading at the time. He imagined that a lot of the top-secret work that should have been secured had been left on lab benches and in offices. These all were legitimate concerns for a manager of a laboratory.

Logan's phone vibrated as he told Kayla and Wang about the sea battle he and Lee had seen unfold. He briefly read a text message and then continued with his story. He told them how surreal it was to stand on the hilltop and watch such a panoramic scene in real time. He still had difficulty believing what he had seen. They were surprised because they had been in the midst of the building evacuation, so the news hadn't reached them yet.

Kayla asked what the text message was about out of curiosity, and he said he would tell her later, downplaying the matter. He stood there impatiently waiting for the bomb situation to be resolved.

The two men from the bomb squad came outside carrying their toolbox between them to the truck and placed it inside the steel box before closing the doors. They then began to take off their padded suits and looked relieved.

Lee walked out of the building and stood in front with a megaphone. He had apparently taken charge of the situation.

"All is safe now. The bomb specialists have assured us that the device wasn't dangerous. It was only a replica of a bomb and contained no explosives. It was only meant to scare us." He stopped and surveyed the crowd, looking carefully along the perimeter. "It may have been a hoax of some sort. We can all go back to work now, as the building is secure."

Wang called for everyone to return to their work, then led his colleagues inside. Lee walked over to join Logan and Kayla. He continued to scan the crowd, as did his security team.

"Are you looking for the potential hoaxster?" Logan asked quietly. "Sometimes they lurk around to see how effective their attempt has been."

Kayla looked at him, surprised. "Do you think someone might be out there?"

"I don't know. People do that if they are seeking attention," Lee said. "But I think this might be a test of some kind to observe our reactions. Why else leave a dummy bomb?"

"Good point," Logan agreed.

Lee walked away to talk to his men, leaving Kayla and Logan to themselves on the sidewalk. When he was gone, Logan said to Kayla, "The text was from Cotes. He's in San Diego."

"San Diego? He was supposed to come back here," Kayla said, concerned.

"Apparently, he has been redirected there to pick up more vaccine samples that your father has prepared. Cotes and the *Hydra-X* have been requisitioned to deliver samples to our allies in the Western Pacific. The brass thinks the vaccine must be distributed quickly because, even before today's attack, they thought China was getting more aggressive."

"But then we'll be stranded here."

"Only for a while. He will make a run to Australia and New Zealand and other southern oceanic partners. He said Australia is setting up to produce millions of doses for all the smaller countries that will need the vaccine." This fact impressed Logan.

"Yes, that's logical. It's not the easiest vaccine to make, so centralizing production makes sense."

"How are things going here?"

"Dr. Wu is really amazing. She and her team have already begun production of the vaccine for the island's first responders and seriously threatened groups," Kayla said. "She has started working with two companies that will manufacture the vaccine on a large scale—literally ten million doses per month at first. They only have twenty-five million of their own citizens. They will create a surplus within two months and will distribute the vaccine to other countries, like Vietnam and Thailand."

"How about mainland China? Are they making their own vaccine?"

"Yes, they have one that they used last year, but it is only about fifty percent effective for the old version of the virus. It won't work for type 2—at least, not very well."

"And the new vaccine? How effective is it?" Logan asked.

"Our vaccine is ninty-seven percent effective for the type 2 variation. It is over ninety-five percent for the newest version we expect to see. It will work differently for different populations."

"Oh, ninety-five percent?" Logan asked. "That sounds really good."

"And we expect to have some herd immunity working for us too. Most vaccines are only in the sixty-to-eighty percent range. If you have a lot of people vaccinated, then the chances of contracting the disease are much lower than the efficacy rate itself suggests." She gestured as she tried to make her point.

"That's why it's so important to get as many people as possible immunized. Then the overall effect is nearly ninety-nine percent or better."

"So if parents refuse to have their kids get shots, they cut into the herd-immunity equation," he said. "What happens if only half the population gets the vaccine?"

"Well, for seventy percent efficacy, the people who get the shots have approximately a seventy percent chance of avoiding the disease completely, plus some herd effects." Kayla waved her arms in the air to indicate a graph of the population as a whole versus a portion of it. "But the remaining thirty percent of vaccinated people will probably have a milder case of the disease if they contract it. They are likely to survive with few side effects."

"And statistically, what happens?"

"If you don't get herd immunity, people without the vaccine are likely to get the disease and suffer full-blown cases of it. For the flu, that means they may have severe cases, and kids will die unnecessarily. Of course, we can't guarantee that no one will get sick, but the illness should be less aggressive, and many will not even catch it. The same is true for the coronavirus, but more of the infected people will ultimately die compared with flu cases."

"I never liked getting shots when I was a kid," Logan said.

"Me neither, but now I'm a zealot for vaccinations," she said with a smile. "I just hope we can produce enough of this vaccine before fall. We need to make it for so many people in poor countries that can't make their own. Billions of doses."

"How are we doing in the States?" he asked. "And why do you say by fall?"

"We have several facilities manufacturing our vaccine, mostly in secret so far, to avoid public fear and a mad rush for doses. We have production in several plants in different parts of the country. We are already dosing first responders and those over sixty years old in most states. We lost a facility in New York due to the bomb, so others have had to pick up production."

"And fall?"

"That's usually flu season, and people catch respiratory diseases more often then. We'll still have to wear masks for another year or so, but if everyone gets the shot, we may beat this thing, and life will get back to close to normal."

"OK. Enough of the science talk. Are you going back to work or going home now? I mean, to the apartment?"

"I need to finish a discussion with Dr. Kuan, but then I could go back. If you want to wait, we can ride back together."

Logan made a few calls on his secure phone while he waited for Kayla. They rode back to the apartment by 5:00 p.m. Logan enjoyed her company, and she seemed to enjoy being with him as well. They were beginning to appreciate each other's humor about their situation and the limited dining and entertainment choices. The TV in their apartment carried only local news and shows in Chinese. They tried to make the most of being in a country with strict COVID lockdown rules and civil defense requirements.

The civil authorities were concerned about the frequent missile attacks being launched from the mainland. One missile had landed in the campus a week before, killing six people. Since then, they had instilled a siren alert system, and citizens were advised to run to safe zones in their buildings if there was time.

Three missile attacks had triggered alerts since Logan and Kayla had arrived, but with no hits to the campus.

Bomb siren began to blare shortly after 8:00 p.m. when they had just finished their favorite repeat meal of chicken and rice. They scrambled to put on their shoes and grab their phones, laptops, and other valuables. They reached the door of the apartment just as the guard outside knocked loudly. They ran after him as he rushed to the nearest safe zone: the staircase built to earthquake code.

Other residents also raced to the stairs until there were eleven people from their floor sheltering there. Then there was a loud explosion nearby, and the building shook. Dust flew up from the concrete surfaces for a little while.

Logan reached out and put an arm around Kayla, who was shaking. She nestled beside him, but despite his protection, her shaking intensified.

"It will be OK," he said. "The missile struck a couple of blocks away, by the sound of it. We should be fine."

After a minute, the siren stopped, and everyone smiled sheepishly at one another, acknowledging their fear and relief. Logan and Kayla walked back to the apartment and thanked the guard for his assistance.

"I need a Scotch after that," Logan said and pulled a glass from the cupboard. "Care to join me?"

"Sure, why not? Look, I'm still shaking." She held out her hand to show how it wouldn't keep still.

Logan poured a couple of fingers of Kavalan into each glass and handed her one.

"To exciting times," he said as he raised his glass. They saluted and sipped for the toast.

Kayla moved to the sofa and flopped down in the middle, kicking off her shoes as she did so. When Logan was about to settle into the chair nearby, she patted the seat next to her. He raised his eyebrows and sat down on her right.

"I don't want to be pushy," she said uncertainly, "but I wouldn't mind it if you put an arm around me again right now. I think I need someone to hug me a little until I get over the fact that someone tried to bomb us twice in one day."

"Yes, I see." He put his arm around her, and she snuggled into him. "It is scary, isn't it?"

They sat that way for the rest of the evening, occasionally rising to pour more drinks or to turn on music. They told each other about their childhoods and how they happened to be in the careers they had chosen. It was pleasant conversation.

"So you don't have anyone special waiting for you back in the Windy City?" she asked playfully. "Or do you not like being tied down?" She glanced at his face to see how he would respond to such a personal question.

"Well, you kind of put me on the spot here, Dr. Grimley," he snickered, surprised by the sudden interest in his personal life. "I would have to say no. I don't meet many interesting women in my line of work. At least, no one outside of the job. And I haven't been back in Chicago long enough to develop any other friendships." He felt self-conscious as he spoke. "We don't have the same wild lifestyle you appear to have in Mankato."

She laughed loudly as his response. "Wild lifestyle? Not in Mankato." Her face changed and she seemed to reflect internally for a few moments. "My life is far from wild these days. In fact, I don't have much of a life at all lately." She grinned at him as she finished her glass of wine. "I don't have anyone special either." She smiled at him and blushed.

Logan realized he was falling for this captivating woman and felt she might feel the same way toward him. They talked a few minutes about music they liked and he noticed that the hour was getting late. By 10:00 p.m., Logan noticed that Kayla was dozing off, and he gently roused her so she could get to bed. They stood up and hugged, their lips touching briefly in a gentle kiss, before retreating to their separate bedrooms.

Logan lay in bed afterwards, unable to sleep for some time, thinking about that kiss.

Chapter 18

Monday, March 27, 2023

Taoyuan City, Taiwan

The sunrise shone golden light through Logan's window, waking him to another day of routine protective duty. He knocked on Kayla's door to wake her as he ambled toward the bathroom for his shower.

Shortly afterward, Kayla emerged fully dressed in a cheerful mood and joined him for a quick breakfast of a soothing rice pudding. They hurried to be ready for the knock on their door that they should head to the convoy to the virology lab. Kayla was to work with Chin today, who was developing a different application for the virus.

Kayla was secretive about the work Chin was doing, not telling Logan anything more than the basics of his project. When he inquired further, she said it was need to know only. At lunch, he tried to coax more information out of her as they sat at their own isolated table in the private dining area of the building. She resisted. She had a firm professional side that wasn't easy to crack.

"Can't you tell me at least why his work is important? What does it involve?" he asked in his most charming manner.

"All I can tell you is that he's investigating how transmissible the disease is, how it could be spread under different scenarios. That sort of thing."

"I thought we already knew that."

"We do for type 2, but not so much for this variant—type 3. And social and cultural conditions are different here in Asia.

There's still a lot to learn, and it might help Dr. Kuan with the therapeutic he's developing."

Logan persisted, "Has anyone actually contracted type 3 yet, or is it all theoretical?"

"There have been a few volunteers who have had it under controlled conditions," she said quietly so no other people could hear. "I think Dr. Chin will do more of those types of experiments later when there is a therapeutic available for testing. But that's his work, and I don't know everything he has planned."

"But you work with him all the time. You must discuss what he plans to do, don't you?"

Visibly upset with this line of questioning, Kayla sat up straight, and her expression tightened. "Look, Logan, there are some things I'm not able to share with you, OK? You are getting into areas that you shouldn't and which I cannot discuss." Her eyes tightened more as she angrily glared at him. "Let's talk about something else, shall we?"

"OK, OK," he said. "I can tell you that I heard a rumor that President Callahan may declare martial law for the entire country at home. Then she can direct the governors of some states to stop the violence in their cities or send in the national guard to do it. It will be a real mess politically, but so be it. There has to be an end to some of these long-term occupations of cities and the senseless killing."

"Really?" she said as she finished eating. "Well, that's good news, I guess. Too bad the governors didn't have the moxie to do it themselves."

"In any case, if that happens, it means we will finally get help straightening out Chicago. That would be great. The general said he needs me back there soon if that breaks loose."

"Oh?" She looked up. "So soon?" I thought you would be here as long as me."

"Well, Cotes is running around the Pacific with our only means of transportation."

They both laughed. Logan escorted her to the third floor to Chin's lab. She went inside, and he took his post outside with the guard. He pulled up a chair and began to read text messages from Jorgensen.

At 2:00 p.m. sharp, an explosion erupted close to the lab, shaking the building violently. Glass shattered from windows on the ground floor, creating a loud crescendo of sharp shards striking concrete. Alarms were set off throughout the building and in cars parked along the street outside.

Smoke began to fill the hallway as Logan jumped up from his seat. He and the guard moved to the lab's entryway while the guard shouted instructions in Chinese to someone on a radio.

The lab door flew open, and the first of several panicked scientists ran out into the hallway. They were all wearing blue, surgical masks; surgical gowns; and face shields. When they saw smoke arising from the stairwell, screams of fear and terror echoed in the halls.

The building shook again, and the panicked lab workers began to race for a spiral staircase that wrapped around the circular elevator shaft. The guard ran over to calm them, but many had already begun to run down the steps in their flip-flops and shoes, some wearing blue, surgical booties over them. Shrieking came from below, where other escapees must have been huddling in the staircase.

About forty people came out of the lab, and finally, Dr. Chin appeared, looking shocked but not panicked. Logan grabbed his arm when he walked by and asked where Kayla was.

Chin gaped at him and said, "I saw her earlier, but not just now. She must have come out already." He pressed on toward the staircase with his assistant by his side.

Smoke was building in the stairwell by then, and the stream of people leaving the lab had trailed off. But still no Kayla. The guard was busy assisting an older gentleman who had fallen and twisted his knee. It sounded like complete chaos down below.

Logan was sure he hadn't seen Kayla leave; she was taller than most of the Chinese scientists, and her blonde hair would stand out in the crowd. He stopped the last person he saw coming out to ask if there was another fire escape that she could have used.

The man said, "No, only one way. Secret lab, so only one door." Then he ran to the stairs.

Logan had no choice. He grabbed the lab door just as it was about to close. He turned back and saw no guard on duty any longer. He made up his mind. He pulled the door open and ran inside, into the strange smells of disinfectants and something else: the smell of C4 explosive mixed with concrete dust.

He saw a pack of plastic, surgical gloves on the wall and pulled out a large pair to wear. He put on his own mask and began to search the lab through the haze of dust. He couldn't see anyone in the first room and walked on to an interior hallway that ran directly back from the main entrance. He worked his way along it, calling out Kayla's name as he went.

He came to the room where he had seen her working the day before and surveyed it thoroughly. He found her purse and jacket still at her desk. She was nowhere in sight. But there was a fine dusting of gray concrete on the desktop. He smelled a hint of ether.

The smell of the explosive was stronger here than in the front of the lab, and there was more dust in the hallway than on her desk. He noticed that there were a few footprints in the dust on the floor. They were visible up and down the hall and in her room. Most were oriented to the end of the hallway, with a few pointing toward the main exit. He followed them to a steel door at the end of the hall.

He opened the door and was struck by a cloud of dust that blew outward. The door had led to a storeroom. Chunks of concrete and fine powder littered the floor. He stopped to check that it was all inert material and not a chemical that had been blown out of its container in the explosion.

"Wait," he said out loud, "the explosion was outside—not in here."

Then he saw it—a rough, square hole about four feet across in the back wall of the storeroom. It had been neatly blown through the concrete, leaving the stench of C4 lingering in the air. This was the work of an explosives expert. Footprints led to the hole.

He ran to the hole and peered through it into a service staircase that led downward. He heard muffled Chinese voices below and the shuffling of feet. There was a thud and then swearing in Mandarin. Someone was running away.

Logan pulled out his handgun in anticipation. He climbed through the hole and onto the stairs, then quietly glided down the steps in the cloud of gray dust.

He heard a fire door being thrown open with a clang as the door hit something. He reached the last flight of steps and saw a sharp movement of something white—a person wearing a Tyvek hazmat suit carrying a heavy container. He was swearing a blue streak as he manhandled the container.

Then as Logan landed on the last stair and could look out through the fire door, he saw Kayla. She was unconscious and slung over the shoulder of a taller man who was carrying her toward a van. The man reached the vehicle and opened the rear doors, apparently ready to throw Kayla into it.

"Xioǎxīn!" an accomplice shouted, holding the door open when he saw Logan. "Look out!"

He let go of the door and reached for a handgun he had strapped to his hip. He raised his gun, but Logan fired first, hitting him in the leg with two rounds before the door swung closed on the second man holding the container. Logan was right on the second guy, so he reached forward and clubbed the man over the head with the butt of his automatic. The man dropped the container on the second blow and fell to the ground, unconscious.

The wounded man pulled the door open again and blindly fired several shots inside. The shots scattered all over the place before he stuck his head inside and saw that Logan had lodged himself against the wall inside the stairwell. Logan shoved his gun in his attacker's ribs and pulled the trigger twice. The man dropped onto the doorsill, blocking the door open and screaming in pain. Logan kicked his loose gun away, stepped over the man, and threw himself out the door, rolling on the concrete outside.

He saw that the man carrying Kayla had dropped her into the van with the rear door still open. He had also produced in one hand a short, black machine gun, which he fired at Logan. Luckily, the shots pulled up high with so little hand control, and the bullets struck the wall over Logan's head. He had just enough time to fire a few rounds back at the man and dropped him by the van.

A fourth man ran out from the side of the van to get into the driver's seat. Logan heard the engine come to life with a roar and the sound of the escapee revving the engine. The driver put it in gear, and the van jumped, then stalled.

Logan ran to the rear of the van and grabbed Kayla's ankle with his left hand while he held his gun hand up to fire. The van roared to life again and lurched forward with the sound of screeching tires. Logan held on to Kayla, and she slid out the back as the van peeled away. He was able to cradle her head in his hands just before she fell to the pavement. She was lifeless. Maybe dead.

"Oh shit, no," he murmured out loud.

Seeing the threat was gone, Logan set his handgun on the ground and cradled Kayla in his arms. He stared at her slack face and felt overwhelmed with emotion. He straightened a lock of her hair on her forehead with one dusty, gray finger and felt his eyes water as he searched for life in her features.

"Kayla," he said as he repositioned her body in his arms. "Don't you go and die on me."

He checked for a pulse on her neck and thought he felt a weak flutter. He put his face close to her mouth to listen for breath— just a faint inflow. Then a blue eye blinked open.

"Kayla," he whispered as tears came to his eyes. "It's all right. You're safe now."

Chapter 19

Monday, April 3, 2023

On Board *Hydra-X*, Pacific Ocean

Logan, Kayla, and Admiral Cotes were seated in the comfortable seats of the *Hydra-X* once again, speeding their way toward San Diego. They had left Taiwan at 4:00 a.m. and had dozed for three hours. Now they sipped coffee and ate fresh eggs that Cotes had requested Logan bring. Cotes had had enough of the meals that the boat had to offer. He had been on board the secret craft for nearly two weeks on his mission to allocate the vaccine to most of the US allies in the Western Pacific.

"I have to say it has been an honor to deliver these samples, but I can tell you I'm not so fond of submarine life. I would rather be on the bridge or on deck for at least some portion of the trip." He glanced at Kayla and smiled. "But you have had quite an adventure while I was at sea, haven't you?"

"I wouldn't call it an adventure, Admiral. I'm lucky to be alive." She smiled at the two men and nibbled on a breakfast cracker similar to Swedish Wasa bread. "I still smell ether in my nose once in a while, and every time I do, I feel terrified all over again." She paused for a moment and teared up. "But the work was very rewarding and the people wonderful to work with."

"We were all surprised when the PRC spies broke into the lab like that," Logan said. "We were lucky to capture the thieves in the act. I hate to think of what they would have done."

Kayla was silent for a moment, and then reached over to place her hand on Logan's. "I was terrified when they grabbed me during the attack. It was timed so that we would all evacuate the building as we had earlier. The second explosion was lost in the pandemonium after the first bomb went off." She gazed at Logan again. "I suddenly had an ether-drenched rag shoved over my face, and I passed out almost immediately. I didn't have time to fight them off. I saw the men in white hazmat suits and didn't realize they weren't part of the lab personnel."

Logan saw her looking distressed at the memory and squeezed her hand. He had thought he had lost her for a few moments, and the thought had scared him deeply. He hadn't realized how much he cared about her until he had pulled her from the van.

Logan's mind flashed back to the scene a few days before. Lee and his men had arrived just as she had begun to wake up, and they had arrested the Chinese spies. They were able to stop the van a short distance from the lab and grab the driver, who hadn't resisted. One man was dead, and the other two were wounded and out cold thanks to Logan's actions. It turned out they had stolen a virus sample and had stashed it in the container they were carrying. They had intended to kidnap Kayla as someone they could interrogate later. Lee's men had tracked down three more accomplices who had worked at the campus and supplied the blueprints of the building. That was how the spies had known they could blast their way into the storeroom.

An ambulance had arrived and checked Kayla out for injuries, taking her to the on-site hospital for further evaluation. Logan had stuck to her like glue to be sure she was safe. He had her discharged and took her back to the apartment to recover. They had spent the night in her bed, clutching each other and talking through the terror she had felt, then finally fallen asleep and slept in each other's arms. Since then, they had become lovers and spent every night together in his bed.

The next days had been hectic as Kayla had tried to wrap up her work in time to catch the *Hydra-X* when Cotes came to collect them. Then they said goodbye to Lee and his guards and the scientists at the labs. This morning, they had left all that stress behind as they headed for San Diego.

"I'm going to be on this diplomatic assignment for the next few months, they tell me," Cotes lamented. "I'd rather be back running special ops."

As they finished their meals, Captain Ogoro entered the room with a smile on his face. He stood next to the admiral and said in a loud voice, "One of our sister boats, the *Hydra-5*, just sunk the Chinese carrier *Shandong* this morning near the Spratly Islands. She took out two of the escort ships as well, one a frigate."

"There seems to be a lot happening in the South China Sea over the last two weeks," Kayla said. "A lot of Chinese ships are disappearing."

"That's because we finally launched four of our Hydra-class subs to go hunting," Ogoro said gleefully. "The commander of the Pacific Fleet declared a limited war on the PLA Navy after they attacked our carriers. We're on schedule to sink every one of their fighting ships within the month, if we can find them." His smile broadened. "We're finally kicking some ass."

"How can we do that without being officially at war—I mean, *really* at war with them? So far, neither side has actually declared war on the other," Kayla said.

"It seems to be the new way that wars are fought," Cotes said. "Nobody wants to admit they are conducting acts of war. It's part of the asymmetrical warfare thing. At first, it was cyberattacking, where there was some plausible deniability. Then small incursions and minor attacks that didn't seem like enough of a provocation to initiate a declaration of war. Then we fight whole wars in the Middle East without calling them that." He searched the faces of the others. "Now it's secretly sinking ships but not admitting it."

"But the Chinese know we're behind the attacks, don't they?" she asked.

"Oh, I'm sure they do. And it must piss them off to no end knowing we are doing it but being unable to catch us in the act," Ogoro replied, chuckling. "It just looks like they keep losing ships for no reason. They can't really blame anyone, except indirectly claiming it's us somehow."

"They are losing face each time it happens," Cotes commented.

"And they are still pounding away at Taiwan with their missiles and now air attacks. This won't end well," Logan added. "We need to get another carrier over here to support the island's defense."

"By the way, what happened to the aircraft carrier that was attacked? She was badly damaged," Kayla said.

"The *Roosevelt*'s crew was able to complete repairs to make her seaworthy. She still had navigation and power, so she is on her way back to San Diego for a more complete refitting," Ogoro said. "She should be back in action in a few months."

"Geez!" Kayla exclaimed. "Do you think we'll still be fighting for months?"

"Let's hope not," Cotes said. "Let's hope we can end this misery soon. Especially the COVID pandemic."

"How long will it take to distribute enough vaccine to make a difference, Kayla?" Logan asked. "If all our allies are making it, then we should see everyone vaccinated, right?"

"It will take time, but we should see a dramatic decrease in the number of cases in three to six months and a reduction in the severity of the cases that do occur."

Ogoro turned to go. "Well, I just wanted to let you know the good news about how our sister ships are doing. Enjoy your coffee." He left the room.

"Does he know about the virus work?" Kayla whispered to Cotes.

"No. He hasn't been read in, so we can't talk about it here," he replied.

"What about the virus?" Logan asked. "He must know that we delivered it to Taiwan too, right?"

"Not the work that Dr. Wang's lab is doing," Kayla said cautiously. "The work directly with the virus, V108."

"But they are just developing a therapeutic, right?" Logan asked her. He wasn't sure what was so unique about that.

"Yes, but we can't talk about it here," Cotes said quietly but with a harsh tone in his voice, staring at them both.

They sipped their coffee in silence for a few minutes. Then Kayla said to Logan, "I will be in San Diego for a few days to see how my dad is doing, but then I need to get back to my own lab. I don't know yet whether my father can return with me." She added hopefully, "Maybe we could return to Mankato together. I don't know how we will manage it without you, Logan."

Logan smiled as she squeezed his hand. "I understand that the skies are a lot safer now, so we may be able to fly back if we have the right conditions. Isn't that right, Admiral?"

"Yes, things have improved considerably in the last two weeks. Air travel is safer now that air traffic control has been reestablished. There have been fewer Stinger missile attacks on commercial jets lately, thanks to local law enforcement." He sounded pleased with these developments.

"Can Williams fly into San Diego now to pick us up? It would save us the cross-country travel problems," Logan asked.

"I'm not sure he can do that, but the navy has regular flights to Houston now. If you can get there, I can have him pick you up and deliver you to Mankato and then Chicago." Cotes seemed happy with that possibility. "I heard from someone that there's a flight to Houston in four days, so maybe that will work out for you." He smiled at Kayla.

"That would be great!" she said.

"By the way, Logan," Cotes said, "I promised I'd get you some help for your fight in Chicago." He paused. "I heard that the national guard has finally been activated in Illinois. And I have lined up a SEAL team for you to help with the leader-decapitation task."

"Decapitation?" Kayla said in surprise.

"It means knocking out the leaders of the terrorist groups, not actually chopping off their heads," Logan explained, chuckling. "Although some of these bastards deserve the guillotine."

"I'll text you the contact info when we get into port," Cotes said matter-of-factly.

"Great," Logan replied cheerfully. "That will give us a shot at winning this urban warfare game." He smiled at Cotes and added, "Well, I hope that I have contributed enough to this mission to deserve that reward, sir."

"Logan, you have been just the man for this mission. Without you, we would have lost a sample of the virus to the enemy, not to mention you saved one of our top virology scientists from being captured and tortured. You did well, Commander. And don't you forget it."

They settled into their seats, Cotes scanning messages on his cell phone until he gave in to an awkward sleep and Logan and Kayla holding hands until they napped. Meanwhile, the *Hydra-X* plunged ahead beneath a restless sea.

***

Four days later, Logan and Kayla lay in bed at her home in Mankato after a day of constant travel. But they still had retained the energy to roll around in her comfy, designer bed, even after eight hours of flying.

"I'm sorry you have to leave in the morning, Logan. I'll miss you," she said.

"I wish we had a few more days together, but General Jorgensen needs me at the CNF. We're going to make an effort to push Antifa forces south so that they will have to push on the Caliphate. Maybe we can get them fighting against each other some more."

"Why can't you just attack them and destroy them?" she asked.

"They have fifteen thousand members now. Not all of them are soldiers, but there are at least ten thousand terrorists to deal with. It will take a concerted campaign to dislodge them completely."

"It sounds terrible."

"And it's street fighting. We don't have many men who have experience with that. It's a different kind of warfare than most ex-military guys have encountered before," Logan said.

She raised up on one elbow to kiss him. "Be careful, my love. I don't want to lose you."

They kissed warmly and then snuggled into each other again. He felt torn by his call to duty and his desire to stay there with the woman he loved.

"If things work out, I can try to get you on a transport in about two weeks. We will be coordinating our work now with the militias in Minnesota and Wisconsin," he said. "And if all goes well, we may be able to eliminate Antifa in all three states."

"How about the national guard? Can't they help?"

"The guard has been activated in Wisconsin and Illinois so far. We hope the new governor in your state will see the light and get on board with clearing out these terrorists. Until now, your governor has been reluctant to do anything useful."

"Our previous governor was too afraid to act," she said. "This state is politically very leftist. And we have a large Muslim population now that is anti-American. Any attempt to get federal help is dangerous."

"You'll come see me?"

"Oh yes. But I have to get the lab in order before I can leave for even a week or so."

"Well, we'll have to plan for the worst and hope for the best."

Chapter 20

In the three weeks since Logan had returned to Chicago, he had fought to catch up with the constantly changing events both locally and across the nation. Now, five weeks after the first bombs had struck the East Coast, the fires in the targeted cities were nearly under control. Massive camps had been constructed to house the injured who required medical care from the pure force of the bombs and the fires and radiation that had accompanied them. Tens of thousands had been relocated to other cities and towns while the chaos surrounding the beleaguered communities was dealt with. Radioactive fallout was being cleaned up by the simplest means available, and mass graves filled swaths of the region surrounding the damaged cities.

Meanwhile, the West Coast dealt with raging wildfires in the Sierra Nevada Mountains and other coastal ranges. Power lines were under repair, but the outlook was for an extended period of little or no power for large portions of the affected areas. Luckily, loss of life from the EMP attacks had been limited. The whole nation had been mobilized to support recovery operations, even though many larger cities were still overrun by fanatical gang violence.

In Chicago, the CNF had made a push into Antifa territory and met fierce resistance. The fighting had been heavy and sustained for the last six days, with the CNF gaining ground in the western portions of Antifa territory—South to West Grand Avenue on the west side of the Chicago River. They had met implacable force east of the river, holding them north of the Chicago Avenue line.

It turned out that the crackdowns on Antifa and BLMX in both Minneapolis, Minnesota, and Madison, Wisconsin, had caused many of those terrorists to migrate to Milwaukee, Wisconsin, and Chicago, where they could avoid prosecution and bolster the defenses of their comrades in arms. As the Wisconsin National Guard cracked down on other cities, including Milwaukee, Antifa simply moved south to the Windy City. Thousands of fighters flooded the city via any number of routes because there were no real roadblocks on any of the highways except the one that the Illinois State Police maintained along Interstate 90 near Rockford at the Wisconsin state line. The only other impediment to the movement of Antifa troops was the local militia control points at some county boundaries in Wisconsin and Northern Illinois. The militias simply didn't have the manpower to shut off that kind of traffic.

This created a problem for the CNF because the ranks of Antifa had increased significantly. There were now about twenty thousand fighters in northern Chicago, and the new fighters were more adventurous than the ones who had settled into a routine of raping and pillaging the neighborhoods. The new blood escalated raids into surrounding neighborhoods and then withdrew to their strongholds south of Chicago Avenue and east of the river. They kidnapped women for sport and killed a lot of defenseless citizens, redoubling their efforts to slaughter anyone who got in their way. Violence was their main form of entertainment, or so it seemed.

Antifa zealots had recently changed some of their tactics. Instead of holding people and soldiers they captured for trade or ransom, they simply executed them. This violated the code of conduct they had maintained with the CNF up until now. Given the aggressive nature of the gangs, the CNF was forced to change its modus operandi. General Jorgensen had decided that under certain conditions, they wouldn't take any prisoners either.

"I don't like it," Logan said tersely. "That isn't something we should do. It's barbaric." He glanced at his reconnaissance buddies Cal Barker and Jasper Reynolds to see where they stood on the issue.

"But it's what we must do until we can get some support from the national guard," Jorgensen disagreed. "We can't afford to have men tied up guarding these vicious swine while we're being overrun by the very barbarians we want to arrest."

"Besides," Cal said, "Even if we arrest them, there's no active court system to turn them over to. We've got no cops, no judges, no working jails except the ones we've activated. And our jails are filled to capacity."

"Logan," the general said with concern, "we can't just take their guns and turn them loose. They'll come back the same day and kill someone else." He stared at Logan, apparently sizing him up. "As a practical matter, we have to be ruthless. We will make the anarchists fight to the death, just as they have treated our men. They shoot us if we surrender. We must do the same, at least until there is some sort of system in place to deal with prisoners."

"I still don't like it," Logan said. "How about a military court of some kind? Under martial law, we can establish a means to deal with them. Maybe we could get someone from the military justice system to handle them once we have them in custody."

"First of all," Jorgensen said, "I'm not sure we even have the right to arrest these people, even though they are prisoners of war, so to speak. It isn't a declared war, and we may not have any legal standing since most of them are US citizens." He stood up and paced around the conference room, where seven other members of the CNF sat for the meeting.

"How about a military tribunal, sir?" Jasper asked. "We used that in Afghanistan and then at Guantanamo. It was legal."

Jorgensen stopped and considered this idea. "That's a possibility since we're under wartime conditions. It would allow us to create a more formal system under military law." He looked at Jasper in surprise. "How do you know about tribunals?"

"I was studying law before all this hell broke out, sir. At Northwestern." Jasper appeared to be shy about his background. "I thought I might be an attorney one day."

"I want you to stay after the meeting is finished so we can discuss this idea more thoroughly." Jorgensen then moved on to the subject that had brought them together for the meeting. "As you know, we have been having our asses kicked lately. Much of that is because we are now fighting twice as many terrorists as we were before. The new BLMX and Antifa people from outside our state have changed the game. And that doesn't include the Caliphate with an army up to fifty thousand insurgents, some of them foreign." He took his seat at the head of the table again.

One of the other men spoke up. "Some say Antifa is more like thirty thousand strong, sir, with more streaming in here every day. But that might include the women, who aren't all combatants."

"Damn right, they aren't combatants," Cal said loudly. "Some of them are the women they kidnapped and use for sex. They let them go after a while, but many have died due to poor treatment and brutal conditions." His anger about the way the gang treated their captives was obvious.

"Yes, yes," the general said, "this is all deplorable, but I wanted to talk about something new today." He scanned the faces in the room to get everyone's attention. "It's a secret right now to avoid a public panic, but the president was assassinated in Colorado yesterday," he announced solemnly. "She was meeting several people at a venue called Red Rocks when a sniper got her. The secret service captured the shooters as they tried to make a run for it. The sniper was part of a special team of Antifa assassins. Anyway, she died instantly from a single shot."

Everyone in the room sat stunned by the news. *Things just keep getting worse*, Logan thought. *We're being overrun by Antifa, and now they go and kill the president. What will happen next?*

"How did they know where she would be, sir?" Cal asked with a puzzled look on his face.

"The presidential party had just arrived at the natural amphitheater," Jorgensen said cautiously. "Someone knew they were going to be there. There must have been a leak."

"Jesus! That's just shit," Jasper said. "These damn terrorists have to be taken down."

"Well, we're working on it," Logan said grimly as he thought about how desperate their situation was.

"Now, this isn't to leave this room either. Within the hour, there will be an announcement that General Navarro will be appointed acting president until an election can be carried out to replace the executive officers and members of Congress that were killed last month. He will declare the plans for an election as his first act in that role."

"Why Navarro? He's chairman of the Joint Chiefs of Staff, but he isn't elected."

"Well, he was appointed and confirmed by the Senate, so he's legit," Jorgensen said. "Nobody anticipated the situation we are in now."

"When will the next election be, then?" another man asked.

"Unknown. Probably in the fall, since it involves so many offices. The parties will need time to line up a roster of candidates." Jorgensen looked like a caged animal with the weight of the world on his shoulders. "In the meantime, we must carry on with our mission to rid this city of the plague within our borders."

"One bit of good news, sir," Logan said. "I learned from a verified source that the new COVID type 2 vaccine is working well and is being widely distributed. We may be in line to get our shots in a month or so."

"Well, that's good news, Logan," Jorgensen said. "And your source is who I think it is? That should be accurate information."

Jorgensen's phone chirped. He read an incoming text on it, then declared, "General Navarro is now the acting president. He confirms that the entire country is under martial law, and he will make further announcements later today."

Everyone in the room sat up straight. They had been waiting for the government to act. It would change a lot of things.

"Illinois is under martial law, and that places the national guard under military control. The president can order governors to follow his orders. I have been told that the CNF may be incorporated into the Illinois National Guard as a division."

"That's great news, sir," Logan said loudly. "In that case, we would have new resources and new authority."

"It's only in discussion, but either way, we will see the guard start to push back on some of these gang activities," Jorgensen said optimistically. "The first place they will tackle is the capital in Springfield, I am told."

"How quickly can they get up to speed, sir?" Cal asked.

"They can mobilize two or three companies right away, but it will take months to get all units organized and combat-ready. Many of the men and women of each unit have been back in civilian life for a while. They have to be recalled and activated."

"We have a month or two to hold out," one man said.

"Or to make some progress," Logan added. "When the guard takes over, we may have a lot of constraints on what we can do." He looked around at the other men at the table. "Sometimes, the brass doesn't listen to the people who have been fighting the war."

"What are you saying?" Cal asked.

"We can't be sure that we'll stay together as a unit when the guard is involved. We may be broken up and delegated to existing companies." He turned to Cal and Jasper. "I think we need to carry out an operation to show that we can and should stay together as one fighting force."

"How would we do that, Logan?" the general asked.

"Suppose we could do something big—something Antifa would never expect. We could do it before the guard gets here. Then we would have proof of our effectiveness." He glanced around to see if the others were interested. "I mean, this is our fight more than some officer in Springfield. And our general is our leader. He would be in a stronger negotiating position if we had a big victory to prove our mettle."

Jorgensen smiled at the idea. "We would be more than just a collection of militia rednecks, you mean." He laughed. "It would be a surprise for Antifa. They think they have us back on our heels."

The men began to discuss the idea among themselves as Logan pulled Jorgensen aside. "I'm thinking we might be able to drive them out of the east side of the Loop, if we can surprise them. They expect us to continue to press on the west now, but we could change it up easily enough. And we could use the lake as access at night."

"That's interesting," Jorgensen said. "We would have to keep it very tight so no word gets out." He turned and perused the men at the table. "I think these men can keep it quiet. Why don't you present the idea to them and see how much support there is for it? Then you can lead the working group to plan it out. You can have anyone you like for the mission. Just run their names past me first so I can confirm the choice. Some men have a few shortcomings you may not know about." He smiled at Logan and shook his hand. "It's good to have you back, Logan."

***

Logan spent the next few days meeting with the group of men he had selected to plan the operation to invade the Loop and reclaim part of it from Antifa. He picked Cal, Jasper, and a man named Harley, who, like Logan, had experience fighting door-to-door in an urban setting in Iraq. Logan devised the overall plan with input from the others and the general. Harley worked on the logistics needed to support the operation. He also worked out how to train militiamen with no city combat experience except in residential neighborhoods. Cal and Jasper helped recon the area with night stealth-drone flights with Logan designated as gunner for their Bayliner craft.

They named the operation Stonewall in honor of General Stonewall Jackson. The farthest south they planned to go was East Jackson Street, a major east-west corridor that marked the boundary between Antifa territory and that of the Caliphate. That section of the city, between Lake Shore Drive on the east, Chicago Avenue on the north, Michigan Avenue on the west, and the Chicago River on the south, was generally referred to as Streeterville. It was an area of high-rise buildings and high-density living—or it had been, before Antifa had cleared most of the buildings in their murderous way. It included the Magnificent Mile, the most glamorous part of downtown Chicago a few years ago, now largely vacant and devastated by two years of rioting, arson, and vandalism.

They would attack from the lakeshore and from the north down Michigan Avenue in an attempt to divide the Antifa forces in two. With the element of surprise, they would drive the wedge south and cause the Antifa troops on the east side of Michigan to worry about being cut off from their men on the west of Michigan. Hopefully, they would withdraw, and the CNF wouldn't have to fight them all to a standstill. Since Antifa's headquarters was a few blocks west of Michigan Avenue at city hall, it made sense that their troops would withdraw in that direction. The plan worked well in theory, but there were a lot of details to clarify, and that required legwork to spot enemy positions and decide how to allocate CNF troops.

By the end of the month, they had devised a basic plan that they presented to the larger' operations command group—a group of ten leaders from the different militias that formed CNF, Jorgensen being one of them. The concept and plan of action were accepted, with two major additions that improved the implementation of the plan and allowed buy-in from the leaders. They would create two diversions to distract the Antifa leaders early on the same day, striking the west side of Antifa's perimeter where the CNF had already been pressing the terrorists. In addition, they would launch a preliminary attack from the east at the lakeshore in the dark. Between those two actions, they hoped to divide Antifa forces for an hour or so until Operation Stonewall began with a bang.

The command group meeting broke up at 9:00 p.m., and the leaders dispersed into small groups for either a late dinner or a nightcap. Logan had time to write out his take on the meeting before he had to meet Cal and Jasper for a recon mission. He sat at his table in one of HQ's back rooms and made his notations. When he finished, he locked up his notes in his file cabinet, then pulled out the gear he would need for the night's activities.

As he organized his gear, he had a chance to think about how things had been with Kayla during the last few weeks. Both of them had been swamped with work after returning from overseas. She had extra duties at her lab, even though her father had returned to Mankato. It turned out that her father had not yet recovered from his minor heart attack and was on light duty until he could fully recover. That had added to Kayla's workload, making it difficult for her to travel to Chicago as they had planned earlier.

Meanwhile, Logan had helped shore up defenses in Chicago against the increasing strength of Antifa. Then he had been engaged to spy on Antifa's disposition throughout the downtown area, and the fight to gain ground on the West Side had diverted his attention from his recon activities. Now the planning of Operation Stonewall had him completely occupied.

Even though they talked by phone every other day, he felt the loss of the intimacy they had enjoyed only a month ago. He decided he had time to call her before going out for the night.

"Hello, Kayla?" He started the call cautiously in case her father was asleep.

"Yes, Logan," she said pleasantly. "How nice to hear your voice. You have a few minutes to talk? That's great."

"I just wanted to see how you are," he said. "I've been buried in work. I can't talk about the particulars over the phone, but it's big. How about you?"

"I've been busy with the vaccine. I have to travel to Houston tomorrow for a week. I wanted to let you know I'd be on the road. I can fly there on a commercial flight, I guess. They tell me it's safe to fly now. What do you think?"

"Geez, I don't know. I can make some calls if you want. Check it out." He was worried about her security. "When do you leave?"

"Tomorrow night, about six. Our lab security people said it would be fine, but if you could verify it, it would make me feel better."

"Sure, I'll do it first thing and call you. Why are you going?"

"We have a company there who will also manufacture the vaccine, and they need samples and expertise. I have to go because Dad can't travel until he recovers from his heart problem."

"Is a security detail going along with you? I mean, you should have an escort to be safe."

"Yes, I have one man traveling with me. He has been at the lab for years, so I trust him." She paused and then sounded like she was unsure. "I'm scared, Logan. Things are so tense everywhere. More doctors kidnapped. It's not like when I had you with me. I felt safe."

"Well, that doesn't sound like enough manpower to keep you safe." He thought to himself and then said, "Let me talk to your head of security there at the lab tomorrow. Maybe they can up your security team." He paused. "They can't expect you to travel if you're afraid."

"OK, thanks." She was silent for a few seconds. "I'd rather be coming to see you. I miss you."

"I wish you were here too." He hesitated and then said, "I'm going to be busy for the next two weeks, but then I'm going to find a way to come up and see you, Kayla. I miss you too."

She fumbled to get out words, "I'd better go. I love you, Logan."

"I love you too. Bye."

He felt terrible. He knew she was suffering from PTSD, and now she had to go into another lab without her team. He made a note to call her lab in the morning and to check on Houston air traffic. He fell into a bad mood, stomping around while he dressed. He had to protect her. How could he do that from Chicago when she was in Minnesota?

Chapter 21

Logan's team finally got into position after midnight. They had cruised quietly along the lakeshore from Montrose Harbor using a small but quiet outboard to propel the boat along the shoreline, just far enough away so that they weren't visible unless someone was wearing night-vision goggles. They ran dark, as usual, using a compact radar set on the bow of the Bayliner. It let them avoid other boats and anything else that would go bump in the night. It also revealed the shoreline relatively well so they could keep their position as they motored along. They switched off the outboard and turned on the electric motor to proceed in absolute silence.

They had reached the point just offshore from the Chicago Street and Lake Shore Drive intersection, the farthest south outpost for the CNF. There was a barricade of buses parked across the drive, and sandbag bunkers were located on both sides of the road. They made radio contact with the CNF guards manning the bunkers.

"Acknowledge Dark One is passing at 12:36." Dark One was their call name while on patrol.

"Acknowledged. Safe travels, Dark One."

They continued south slowly past the building complex that was Northwestern University until they were just off Ohio Street Beach. There the huge, landfilled headlands projected out into the lake to form the water treatment plant pier and Navy Pier. Both were artificial-fill areas constructed by the placement of massive numbers of timber piers and rock fill to project a half mile out into Lake Michigan.

They sailed far out into the lake to avoid detection by Antifa lookouts stationed on the piers. They passed them both without incident, videoing the defenses as they went along. They rounded the far side and crept back to shore along the south flank of the piers, staying in the shadow of the east-west breakwater that ran all the way into the north side of the river locks. This breakwater was unmanned as far as they could tell and provided excellent cover in the nighttime for their progress. At the west end of the breakwater, they were only one hundred feet from the north pier of the Chicago River channel. East of that point were the famous locks that allowed inland access for shipping to move from the lake level into the river.

They crossed the last area of open water to the north face of the north pier and tied up the Bayliner. Carefully and silently, they climbed off the boat and clambered up the rocky ballast that had been thrown up against the pier to stabilize it. From here, they had an unobstructed view of the mouth of the river where it penetrated the shore. The Outer Drive Bridge loomed out of the darkness where North Lake Shore Drive crossed the river. It was the largest and easternmost bridge in the series that ran across the westward-flowing river and connected the north bank to the south bank.

Their objective tonight was to surveil the first three bridges along the river from the lake going inland. They needed to find out how Antifa defended the bridges and if any of them had been rigged with explosives for demolition. They would need these bridges to remain intact in order for them to advance with truckloads of men and equipment into the North Loop area. They also needed to learn how many men would have to sneak up the river from the lake to capture and hold the bridges until reinforcements could arrive.

Jasper stayed with the boat in case a quick getaway was required while Logan and Cal climbed onto the north pier with their gear. Cal held his laptop and the night-vision stealth drone while Logan carried night-vision binoculars, his silenced Glock, and an AR-15 rifle with a silencer and night scope mounted on it. They found a place where they weren't obviously exposed, and Cal launched his drone.

Cal muttered to himself as he flew the drone directly toward the Outer Drive Bridge while skimming the water, careful to not attract attention. He managed to guide it right under the bridge without being observed. Once there, he scanned the understructure for both major spans, looking for any obvious explosive placements. There didn't seem to be any, so he slowly brought the drone up to road level on the west side, looking for sentries. He observed one man on each end of the bridge, both favoring the lake side.

"No explosives visible," Cal whispered. "Only two guards standing up. Easy targets for a sniper."

"Good, they can be picked off when the time comes," Logan whispered back. "No sandbags or defensive barriers?"

"Not that I can see without drawing attention."

"Good. Move on to the next bridge."

Cal wasted no time dropping the drone down to water level and skimming west to the William P. Fahey Bridge, which crossed the river at North Columbus Drive. This was a modern drawbridge with clean lines that would make it difficult to easily destroy with explosives, but it could be raised to render it impassable. Cal performed the same observations there and then pulled up to inspect the street level. It took about five minutes before he finished.

"Same here. No explosives," Cal said. "And I don't even see anyone on the bridge, but any guards may be hunkered down."

"OK," Logan whispered. "Move on to the next one on Michigan Avenue."

Cal flew the drone downriver another half mile to where Michigan Avenue crossed the Chicago River via the DuSable Bridge, a historic drawbridge with double decks. It was more difficult to recon because the lower deck was hard to see in the dark. He dared not fly right through the open space between decks because the drone might be spotted. He was able to fly below the lower deck and over the upper deck to some extent but didn't see anything to indicate it was rigged to blow. There were guards at street level on both ends of the bridge, sitting in small, wooden guardhouses.

Cal said, "We're done. It's all on video to show folks later." He began to fly the drone back up the river and toward the lake. The drone had just passed under North Shore Drive when a pickup truck started to drive their way along the top of the north pier. It appeared like it could be a regular patrol and was in no hurry.

"Get the drone back and collect your gear. I'll move up and distract them if needed."

Logan moved in a crouch past Cal toward the oncoming truck. Cal flew the drone as quickly as he could without being obvious. He managed to get it back to the north pier before the truck's headlights swept their area. He shut it down, packed up his laptop, and scrambled over the side of the pier onto the boulders next to the Bayliner.

Logan laid down on the ground and steadied his rifle as carefully as possible, using one hand as a rest for the weapon.

Then he lined up the crosshairs on the left front tire and squeezed the trigger. The one shot sounded like a cough and went directly into the tire, causing the truck to jerk to the left abruptly just before it illuminated Logan with its headlights. The truck quickly came to a stop as the driver lost control of the vehicle.

Logan crawled to the edge of the pier and slipped over the side to join his men in the boat. Jasper started the electric motor and guided the craft along the pier, staying as much as possible in shadow. They followed the pier and didn't see any other lights from the patrol as they motored away into the dark waters of the lake. At the end of the breakwater, they turned north and swung wide around the end of Navy Pier and out into the night.

***

The CNF group carefully planned the invasion of Streeterville, making decisions about how they would advance down North Shore Drive to Ohio Street Beach and simultaneously down Michigan Avenue to reach the Chicago River. This area was a major commercial district in Chicago that Antifa had occupied for over a year, looting and savaging it during that time. Most of the residents had left the area due to the endless violence and murders, so the CNF forces didn't expect to encounter many civilians except those held as hostages or Antifa sympathizers.

The problem was that the area they would have to capture was huge, enclosing about seventy city blocks that contained mostly the high-rise properties. The district included Northwestern University and its hospitals, various clinics, and specialty schools. The surrounding blocks contained the remains of office buildings, commercial establishments, residential buildings, dormitories, and museums. Of course, the Antifa goons, being as destructive as possible, had destroyed much of what had previously stood there, leaving vacant buildings and ransacked homes and shops, as well as structures that had been partially burned.

There were also logistical issues to work through. The CNF forces could expect to encounter about ten thousand Antifa soldiers, many with little experience but lots of attitude. If they carried automatic weapons, then they could do a lot of damage, even if they had no combat expertise. The group, therefore, wanted to have at least as many men in the fight as the enemy. Ideally, they preferred a two-to-one advantage, but given their resources, one-to-one was as good as they could field. They expected to have superior training and weapons, but would be fighting a ruthless enemy who had been entrenched for over a year and knew the area. It would be hard fighting in this urban environment.

They had decided that since they must drive Antifa west away from the lake that they needed clear tactics and the supplies to support them. Experience told them they needed fragmentation grenades in abundance because they would have to enter rooms, hallways, and stairwells of many configurations. There would be lots of nooks and corners where the retreating enemy could hide and return fire. Grenades were one of the favored tools to oust an assailant from a cubbyhole. Flamethrowers like the ones used to dislodge Japanese soldiers that were dug in on the Pacific Islands in the Second World War were another. They were grisly, but effective. If all else failed, gas could be used, but they would have a hard time getting ahold of the right stuff on short notice. It was also dangerous to work with, even for the good guys.

"Logan," Harley said, "how many grenades will we need down there? I'm concerned about the number of buildings we'll have to clear as we move along the streets. I'm assuming we'll have to clear all the first-floor shops, bars, and restaurants, and any business lobbies and offices. I figure there will be a hundred hiding places for bad guys per city block. I'd like to have a hundred M67 frag grenades for every block, assuming we have to clear them all and find an Anti in half of them." He grinned. "What do you think?"

"That's a lot of grenades," Logan said. "Maybe seven or eight thousand. And that's just for Streeterville. We'd need nearly as many for the East Loop too, although there are fewer residences there."

"You know, I wonder what to do for the residential structures," Harley said. "Our intel says that the big, residential tower called Lake Point Tower still has some people inside who are paying ransom to Antifa to leave them alone. That's a seventy-story building with hundreds of apartments and condos, meaning hundreds of potential residents when full. We'll have to bypass structures like that, won't we?" He glanced at Logan with interest. "I mean, we can't storm into the building and drag everyone out."

"Yeah," Logan agreed. "We may have to just station several guys there to hold any Antis upstairs so they can't come in behind us."

"The key to this operation is to bypass as much as possible and cordon it off to deal with later. So that includes the water treatment plant and Navy Pier, the tower, any hotels that are not used by Antifa as residences, and a few other buildings that would take too long to clear."

"Then we send cleanup teams of fifty men each in behind them to flush out any Antis, building by building," Logan said.

He felt the operation was getting too complicated because of the number of massive buildings they would have to clear. "The more I look at it, the more I think we have to draw the Antis out into the street to fight. If they resist and try to fight building by building any more than beyond the first floors, we could bog down rapidly."

"Jorgensen had the right idea to break our incursion down into nine block groups as we go along to be sure we don't bite off more than we can chew," Harley said with appreciation. "It's sure not like busting doors in Fallujah, is it?"

"No, sir, it isn't." Logan chuckled. "We were younger and dumber then. Didn't know how much danger we were in."

"Damn right!" Harley said loudly. "But we lived to tell the tale."

They both laughed and returned to their planning duties. They had a lot to do in the next ten days: finalizing plans, presenting them to the command group, and then explaining the details to division and company leaders; passing on the supply lists and personnel breakdown to leaders and officers; and then preparing their own troops for the tasks they had to perform.

Logan was still waiting to hear if a Navy SEAL team would be coming to join them in time for this operation. They had been delayed because they were involved in the Middle East, possibly in Syria. Cotes had told him that they were helping collect evidence tying Iran to the East Coast bombings. They would be deployed to Chicago after that.

Logan's adrenaline was already rising in anticipation of the danger ahead. They would be hard at it for two or three weeks to make it work and capture Streeterville—or die trying.

Chapter 22

As the CNF group prepared for the invasion, they received disturbing reports from some CNF soldiers that something peculiar was happening in the Antifa army. They had observed that the ranks in the front lines along West Chicago Avenue were staffed with fewer Antis than normal.

The street was cluttered with the usual barricades of concrete traffic barriers, crude wooden fences, and abandoned, often burned-out cars. Junk and remnants from burned furniture and other trash littered the streets. Here and there, canvas and nylon tents had been thrown up behind the sidewalks to provide shelter for Antis who were watching the street for any incursion into their territory. Armed men and women hunkered down behind concrete block walls that protected their makeshift barracks. Many heads showed just above the concrete barriers as some guards smoked dope and carried on heated conversations about unintelligible topics. But there were fewer guards manning the barriers than usual.

A soldier had also noticed that a portion of the Northwestern University campus in Streeterville was being activated, especially the hospital area. They couldn't explain what was happening, but it was apparently something significant.

Logan was concerned because this was right in the area where they intended to kick off their operation. Could it mean that Antifa was increasing their defenses there? Why would they do that? ?

He brought this up with the general, and Jorgensen said it could be important enough to affect their plans.

"Do you suppose they have gotten wind of our plans?" he asked Logan. "Very few of our troops know about the operation, but could someone have unwittingly leaked something?"

"I don't know, sir," Logan replied. "The men said they had seen trucks driving along Fairbanks Court to and from the university hospital. It's not clear what they were doing."

"So all we have to go on is that there's increased truck traffic?"

"Apparently, but one man said he had also seen ambulances going back and forth to the hospital," Logan added. "Maybe they're reactivating the hospital. We know that they evacuated the area about six months ago."

"I don't like it. Suppose they've beefed up manpower in the area and are billeting men in the university buildings?" Jorgensen suggested with concern. "That would give us trouble moving through the area—an area we had hoped to bypass quickly."

"It's a potential problem," Logan agreed. He tried to think of any purpose that the Antis would have to reenter the campus. "Maybe we can run one of our drones down there to see what they're up to. Let me talk to Cal and see if he thinks we can do that. It might have to be in daylight, so it would be tricky."

"Well, see what you can do. I don't like unknowns at this point," Jorgensen said. "By the way, there's a possibility that we can get satellite coverage of the whole east side where we will be operating. I'm supposed to hear back from my contact at the Pentagon today or tomorrow. It would be helpful for planning purposes."

"That would be great, sir," Logan said eagerly. "I'm not used to the possibility of having such resources available."

"Me neither."

***

"OK, we're airborne," Cal said as he held the drone control panel on his lap.

They were sitting on the roof of Pierson Condominiums on the corner of Pierson Street and North DeWitt Place. They had a view down to part of Fairbanks Court as far as the parking ramp on Erie Street. The street itself was partially blocked off by a collapsed building on the corner of Huron Street and Fairbanks Court. Apparently, the Antis had decided to demolish one of the medical buildings for unknown reasons. Or they had stored explosives in the building and it had suffered an accidental detonation. The rest of the street was littered with the usual abandoned cars. In one place, a mountain of black garbage bags had been stacked ten feet high all along the pavement. Antis didn't care to perform basic services like trash collection and disposal.

From that vantage point, they could see vans coming and going up Fairbanks and turning into Erie Street. The vehicles were ordinary-looking delivery vans, and occasionally, they saw an ambulance drive in as well. But they couldn't see what the vehicles were doing once they were on the side street.

"I have to come in high so nobody hears the drone, and then I can fly over to snoop on their activities," Cal said nonchalantly. "I'm at five hundred feet now, and the drone is barely visible from the ground." He worked two control sticks on his control panel and then flipped a switch to turn on the camera. "OK. We're right over that big, vacant lot across from the parking garage. It's all covered in shrubs and stuff."

"Oh, I remember seeing that once. Always wondered what was in there—an arboretum or something?" Logan said.

"The old VA hospital site."

Cal held his altitude and swiveled the camera for a better view. He was preoccupied with the drone while Logan was riveted to the screen of the laptop computer that showed the camera view.

"Wait right there," Logan whispered. "It looks like they have a backhoe and are digging. It's a trench of some kind. It's too wide for utility work. What the hell are they doing?"

"I'll drop down a little for a better view." Cal thumbed the sticks on his control board, and the image became larger and clearer. "They are unloading something like bundles from the vans and carrying them to the trench," Cal observed. "They're throwing the bundles into the trench."

As they watched, one of the bundles split open, and a human body slid out into the trench bottom. They both gasped.

"They're burying bodies! Shit! Look, there's a stack of bundles over there on the left. Must be corpses too," Logan said.

"Jesus, that's a lot of bodies."

"Why are they burying them there? Why not somewhere else? I mean, they've killed so many people, you would think they must bury them all the time."

"Wait a minute. See how everyone has the same-color clothes on? Why is that?" Cal maneuvered the drone lower to one hundred feet. "Those are blue Tyvek suits, aren't they? And look, they're all wearing masks and something else on their faces."

"Face shields?" Logan asked. "They're in full PPE. These must be COVID victims they're burying." He surveyed the area next to the trench. "It looks like there's more than one trench."

As they watched, they saw one of the people on the ground look up, and they could see that he was wearing a face mask and safety glasses. Then he pointed right at the drone.

"Shit!" Cal said. "We've been spotted."

Soon, all the people on the ground were looking up at the sky. One man appeared to be shouting something, and a man with a rifle came out from under a tree to look up. He pointed his rifle directly at the drone.

Cal swiveled his control sticks, and the drone shot north as it climbed into the air. The camera now just showed a wild collage of views as the drone headed toward Chicago Avenue. It whirred over the tops of buildings with what looked like very little clearance. In a minute, Logan heard the machine approaching, long before he could visually pick it out of the cloudy sky. Almost as if the device had teleported, Cal brought the drone in low to settle next to them on the roof.

"What the hell did we just see, Logan?" Cal asked. "Why are they dressed in hazmat-level clothing?"

"Maybe they have a lot of COVID deaths and had to get rid of the bodies? But why there?"

"Well, the area has been vacant the since the VA tore down the old hospital years ago. Maybe they needed a new place to bury corpses. It's a big site, all right."

"I think this is important. I want to call the general and let him know what we found." Logan was already calling the general on his secure phone. He arranged to meet with him in thirty minutes at HQ.

It took ten minutes to get down off the building and to Logan's car. Another twenty minutes put them at CNF headquarters. They walked directly to Jorgensen's office. He told them to enter and close the door behind them.

"What important information do you have, Logan?" Jorgensen asked as he perused a document from behind his desk. "Oh yes, please sit down."

"Sir, we flew a drone down Fairbanks Court and got a look at what all those vans are doing," Logan said. "We took video." He motioned for Cal to set up the laptop so Jorgensen could see the footage. Cal arranged the laptop on the general's desk, and he and Logan shifted around to the side of the desk.

"Here, sir, you can see a backhoe digging a long trench in a vacant lot next to the campus hospital. Men are unloading long bundles from a van and placing them in the trench. There were many more bundles stacked to one side, as well as over here." Logan pointed to one side.

They watched for a minute and viewed the body roll from the bundle.

"My God! They're bodies," Jorgensen said. "They're burying bodies out there."

"Yes, sir," Cal confirmed. "And they are wearing a high level of PPE like they are handling hazardous materials."

"Hazmat gear? Why?"

"Sir, I think they are burying COVID victims in a mass grave."

"Oh, I see. Why so many, do you suppose?" Jorgensen mused. "Why here? They must have other burial sites."

"We were discussing that on the way over here and think maybe they have had a bad outbreak of COVID," Logan said. "Think about it, sir. They have just had a large influx of extra

Antis from other cities. Maybe they had a super-spreader event. Lots more COVID cases and deaths."

The general sat back in his leather chair and stared at Logan. "What does this do to our invasion plan? Does this mean that we're sending our men into a plague-ridden area? If they have a lot of the disease, we could be exposing all our troops to COVID."

"That's what I'm afraid of too, sir. If many of the Antis are infected and we have to go into confined spaces to drive them out, our men would be exposed. The casualties from COVID could be as high as from combat."

"And if we have to police the bodies and recover them for burial, we would be exposed again," Jorgensen said, looking troubled. He drummed his fingers on the surface of his desk as he frowned in the general direction of the two men facing him. Then he grunted and slammed his fist on the desk. "Damn it," he said loudly. They all knew this news added an extra dimension to the operation at hand.

"We need to know for sure before we go any further on this course," Jorgensen said. "Logan, I need you and your team to find out for sure what's going on, ASAP."

"Yes, sir," Logan said quickly. "We may have to capture one or two Antis to interrogate about this. Do you want to know of our progress as it happens, sir, or should we proceed on our own?"

"Proceed and let me know the results, Commander." Jorgensen returned to his document.

***

It was 11:00 p.m. at the intersection of East Chicago Avenue and

Fairbanks Court, one hour before the usual change of Anti lookouts at that location. There were two Anti outposts so that guards could surveil both the street corner and the wide parking lot of one of the university buildings on its west side. The parking lot was as trashed as most of the open areas that the Antis occupied, with mounds of trash bags and what looked like debris from interior walls ripped out of the adjacent buildings. Who knew what they had been working on in those structures?

Both outposts were on the south, or Antifa side, of Chicago Avenue. The CNF had two corresponding posts across Chicago Avenue to watch the Anti outposts. Each side had about twelve men in each pair of sandbagged bunkers.

The CNF had a smash-and-grab planned for 11:05 p.m., led by Logan, with twelve additional men scattered along the avenue. At that precise moment, six men opened fire on the Antis manning the outpost on the west side of the intersection, tossing grenades and lurching forward to run to the south side of Chicago Ave. The CNF outpost opened fire on the same Anti outpost, drawing the attention and support of the Antifa men stationed on the east side of the intersection.

The Antis all responded to the CNF men who were scrambling to cross the street. At the same time, Logan and five other men, all wearing masks, sprinted silently across the avenue, a hundred feet east of the Antifa eastern outpost, unnoticed by the enemy. They approached the unsuspecting Antis from their side of the street and captured two men for questioning before their targets responded with some gunfire. They hit the captives over the head to subdue them and wire-tied their wrists together behind their backs. A few moments later, Logan and his men dragged the two captured Antis across the street to the CNF line.

The diversion force retreated with only one man injured by rifle fire.

Logan had the captives brought to the Chicago Avenue control station for questioning in separate rooms. One was a young man with a black beard and thick, unkempt hair. The other was fortyish and thin, with sparse, dirty-blond hair. Logan and his men donned masks, plastic surgical gloves, and plastic aprons for the task. Once they were propped up and tied to wooden chairs, Cal threw water in the prisoners' faces to wake them up for interrogation.

Logan entered the room where the young man was seated. He snarled at Logan when he regained consciousness.

Logan began with, "What's your name?"

There was no response, only a glazed look on the man's face. He was sweating profusely and had a bad cough.

Logan tried to be friendly. "You can tell me your name. You're allowed to state name, rank, ID number. You'd know that if you ever watched any war movies."

"Jim Bridger. I hate you assholes."

One of Logan's men punched Jim in the mouth twice to get his attention. Jim spit at him in response and received two more blows for his trouble.

"You look sick to me, Jim. COVID type 2? How many days before you die?" Logan asked.

"I ain't going to die, asshole. I just got sick like the others." Jim glared at the man who had hit him. Then he coughed violently, and he appeared to realize that the other man was wearing gloves.

"Look, Jim. I just want to know why you guys are burying so many bodies down in that vacant lot on Fairbanks. Did the new guys from Minneapolis give all of you the fever?" Logan kept his face neutral. "We just want to know if you all have COVID or not. That's all."

"So what if we do? What's it to you? You'll get it too. Just watch. We're all goin' to die from it in the end."

"Not us. We're too careful for that." Logan acted like he didn't really care about the disease. "How many came to join you here in the city? We heard it was up to a thousand men and women. That true?"

"No way. We got another twelve thousand, they say. But some of them was sick." Jim stopped and seemed nervous. "Lots of them sick."

"So why are you burying bodies up here? Don't you have a regular place to bury your dead?"

"Yeah, but it's full now." Jim looked like he realized he shouldn't have said that.

"Where was that? Over by the Merchandise Mart?"

Jim straightened up quickly. He stuttered, coughed, and then said, "No. Not there. We got lots of places to dump bodies. What do you care?"

"Aha. Thanks for confirming that." Logan chuckled. "We have spies in the sky. We're watching you guys all the time."

"Fuck you!"

"OK. Let's talk to your buddy and see if he can confirm everything you just told us."

"Fuck you! I didn't say nothin'. You assholes."

Logan walked to the room where the other captive was waiting. The older prisoner was looking around the room as if searching for a way out. He glared at Logan when he entered. His hair was matted down, and he also coughed occasionally. Wasting no time, Logan told him directly to answer a few questions.

"How many of you are sick with COVID?" he asked. "We saw you burying lots of bodies. Did you guys have a falling-out with the new people from Minnesota? Kill each other?"

"You can go to hell. We ain't fighting nobody except you shits."

"Why all the bodies, then? Accidents? You guys learning how to use your rifles?"

"Like hell. We can shoot you shits just fine," the man said.

"You're saying it's COVID, then. Don't you guys know about masks and distance? You're pretty dumb, aren't you?"

"We know how to do all that stuff. And we know how to shoot your asses off too."

"Your buddy said you're dying right and left from bad food and syphilis. Is that right?" Logan asked.

"I ain't saying anything to you. Now let me go, or my friends are going to come for you. They'll kill you real slow," the man said.

"Well, by the looks of you, you'll be dead of COVID in two days. Just like those other COVID cases." Logan then had an idea. "Or wait. They didn't tell you about the deaths, did they? You're too low on the totem pole to know about it. That's what this is, isn't it?"

"What're you talking about? I know all about it. We were OK until those new shits showed up . . ." He stopped talking, trapped. "I ain't saying no more."

"That's all we need to know." Logan stood up. "Thanks for your cooperation."

Logan directed his men to take the captives back to the guards at Chicago Avenue until they could be taken to the quarantine holding center near headquarters. His men marched the two Antis outside. He waited at the command post with Cal until his men returned.

Shortly after the men left, there was a commotion and the sound of shouting outside the building. A burst of gunfire, followed by two others, signaled that something was wrong. Logan and Cal grabbed their weapons and ran outside in the dark to see what was happening. One of Logan's men ran back to the station.

"What happened?" he asked the man.

"We were just opening the holding cell when the thin one lunged at me and knocked me on my ass. Then the second one broke loose and ran for it. My buddy shot him as he ran. Killed him dead. Then the second guy got away and ran to the avenue. Our guards shot at him as he crossed Chicago, but he kept going and ran toward his side. Then his own people gunned him down. I guess they didn't recognize him." The man shook his head. "What a way to go."

"Yeah," Logan said. "That's a bummer."

Chapter 23

At 1:00 p.m., the Minnesota National Guard C-130 Hercules airplane landed gracefully on the military-designated runway at Chicago O'Hare International Airport. It taxied back to hangar 12B, where Logan, General Jorgensen, and Major Sanjay Sarabhai, the CNF's chief medical officer, stood.

The plane approached the hangar and made a turn to allow access to its cargo bay. The hinged loading ramp was lowered and secured as the pilots cut the engines. Seven people marched down the ramp, six in drab, olive camo uniforms and one woman in slacks and a red blouse. They all wore face masks and plastic gloves, as did the three men waiting near the hangar door. The woman turned to scan the welcoming party and then smiled. She waved a hand and walked quickly to them.

"Logan!" she cried. "I finally made it." She walked up to him, lowered her mask, and threw her arms around his neck, planting a substantial kiss on his lips.

He kissed her back, but then realized that his commanding officer was standing right next to them and pulled away.

"Sir, this is Dr. Kayla Grimley," he said. "Kayla, this is General Jorgensen and Major Sarabhai. The major is our chief medical officer."

They all shook hands and greeted one another cordially.

"Pleased to meet you, Dr. Grimley," Jorgensen said with a slight smirk on his face. He turned to Logan. "No wonder you wanted to get her down here. She's beautiful, and smart as well."

He turned back to Kayla. "I welcome you to Chicago. I'm glad to meet you and want to thank you for your help getting us the vaccine. We sorely need it with this damn disease spreading again."

"Well, General, Major, I'm happy to say I managed to get you even more vaccine doses than I originally promised." She paused, which added effect. "I have a hundred and twenty thousand doses on board, and I'm ready to turn them over to you, Major. The shipment should be enough for all the CNF soldiers and the national guard in Northeastern Illinois, as discussed.

"That is marvelous news," Sarabhai said. "We will off-load it and begin distribution today. You have arrived just in time to deal with the recent outbreak we seem to have here. I have been reading about your cutting-edge work and wish to congratulate you on your development of the vaccine. You have performed a very valuable service for our people."

"Thank you, Major," she said with a smile. "I hope we will have time to talk about your work here in the city—maybe after you get started with the vaccinations."

"Oh yes. That would be excellent. How many days will you be with us?"

"I'm here for a week until there's another flight back to Minneapolis."

"Very well," Jorgensen said. "Please excuse us while we unload the vaccine. We need it urgently at our medical facility. Perhaps you could sign off on the transfer now, and we can inspect it, per standard procedure."

They walked over to the transport plane, and she showed them all the pallets of coolers with the vaccine. Satisfied that all was in order, both she and Sarabhai produced chain-of-custody documents for signature. Once that was finished, men began to transfer the pallets from the aircraft onto the beds of four trucks. Logan helped, and Kayla paced, waiting for nearly an hour.

Logan had driven his own car out to the airport, and when they were free to leave, he whisked Kayla away to the parking structure, where they could be alone. Once out of sight of the general, he swept Kayla up in his arms, and they wrapped around each other as close as they could get in clothes.

"I'm so happy you're here, Kayla," Logan said. "There's so much to talk about."

"Oh, me too. I've missed you so badly since Taiwan. The telephone is just no way to stay in touch with someone you love."

They climbed into his Toyota, put her bag in the back seat, and made out like teenagers. After reluctantly tearing themselves apart, Logan drove out to Interstate 90 and continued to the North Avenue Exit. He drove east along East North Avenue to North Clark Street near the lakeshore. Then he turned north onto Clark for a few blocks, driving past Lincoln Park, the large park that backed onto the North Avenue Beach.

It was a beautiful day, the trees had leafed out nicely, and the flowerbeds were overflowing with early-spring blossoms. This was one part of the city that the uprising hadn't reached, so it looked like it would have on any other May day before the COVID pandemic and the terror inflicted by the fascist Antifa and BLMX.

Logan veered left on Lincoln Avenue and made a sharp turn into the parking ramp of the Hotel Lincoln. He parked in a space near the staircase, and they took her bag upstairs to the lobby.

"Oh Logan, you got me a room?" Kayla sounded surprised to be in a hotel. "I thought I would stay with you at your place."

"I didn't want you to see my motel room. It's pretty run-down, and I'm not a great housekeeper." He smiled as he walked her to the elevator. They stepped in and rode upstairs to the top floor. "I got us a room with a view for your visit. It's safe here, and there's a lot we can walk to nearby."

They walked into a mini-suite that overlooked the park to the east and had a partial view of downtown to the south. The view was fabulous on such a fine, spring day. The combined sitting/dining room contained a couch, a work desk, and a breakfast bar and with a half-size refrigerator and a microwave oven. The separate bedroom had a king-size bed that allowed a guest to see the lake first thing in the morning. Logan had placed his small geranium on the windowsill in the bedroom. Kayla walked over to admire it.

"It's a cute plant. I like the red ones like this," she said quietly. "And I see a very comfortable-looking mattress." She took Logan's hand and led him toward the bed. "Maybe we should see how comfortable it is. I think I will like it."

"Me too."

Two hours later, they were shown to a table in the rooftop restaurant with a view of the lakeshore. They ordered cocktails and settled in to enjoy the environs. The day had turned out to be warm and bright, transforming the lakeshore into a luscious strip of green vegetation standing in sharp contrast with the deep blue of the lake water.

"Wow, Logan," Kayla said. "You know how to pick a romantic hotel. Do you bring all your girlfriends here?"

Logan swallowed hard and then grinned. "I get a frequent-visitor discount."

They both laughed.

"Actually, my family used to come here when we were all together in the old days. It was a lot of fun because the zoo is nearby, and the beach was great. I always associated this place with good times."

"Did you have any siblings?"

"No. I grew up alone. I had a few good friends, but no brother or sister." He felt sad for a moment. "I always wished I had a brother to play with. It's hard to play army alone." He smiled wanly. "But now I have you."

They smiled at each other, and he wondered how fate had brought the two of them together. It was fortunate for them both. And right now, they needed a break from all the stress and drudgery of their lives during this bloody, domestic war that he hoped would be over soon.

"We're fighting a civil war, you know. We have these anarchists who want to destroy our way of life and the Caliphate that wants to change our country into something entirely different based on one religion—and power and greed, of course. But neither of them believes in America or what it stands for."

He stared, first at her, then let his eyes drift out over the lake. He wondered how she viewed the present conflict. Did she see it in such stark terms? Or was she, sheltered in her lab, too far removed from reality and the violence to be so cynical?

"Have you heard about how things are going in Taiwan?" he asked. "The Chinese have started their invasion, but they aren't making much progress."

"I heard that from Dr. Wu," she responded. "She said that the Communists had started to land at one of the cities on the southwest coast. It's an air invasion, with lots of airplanes bringing in men and equipment. No ships."

"That's because we control the waters of the Strait," Logan said as he leaned forward to speak softly. "Our friends with the dark subs have been sinking most of the PLAN ships, even the first of the troop transports the Chinese tried to get across for the invasion. So the PLA had to try an airlift operation. It's much slower to move equipment and troops that way."

"But don't we control the sky over there? How about the ROC Air Force and our carrier, the *Reagan*?"

"The ROC Air Force has been decimated after months of battle. The Taiwanese have lost so many pilots they have a hard time keeping up a defense. And the *Reagan* is running low on munitions right now. It had to pull back toward Taipei just to help defend the capital. We have a convoy of supply ships and another carrier on the way, but it will take a few days."

"That sounds awful. I liked the people I worked with there," Kayla murmured. "I feel so sorry for them. They're good people, and all they want to do is live their lives freely." She began to tear up and pulled a Kleenex out of her handbag. "I still have nightmares about being kidnapped, Logan. I think of those awful people who took me, and I wake up afraid."

Logan had wondered if she had been able to shake off the fear that the mainland spies had subjected her to. He hadn't wanted to bring it up. He was afraid that the feeling would be with her for a long time, if not forever.

He changed the subject. "How is the vaccine work going over there? Have they got enough made yet to vaccinate the whole country?"

She brightened up as she replied, "Oh yes. Health-care workers have already vaccinated everyone on the island that didn't have a religious conflict. The government made it mandatory to get the vaccine. They have herd immunity now."

"How long does it take to be immune, or at least have some protection, once you take the vaccine?"

"About two weeks in most people. For instance, when all of your CNF people have received the shot, they will be protected in two weeks, three weeks tops." She smiled at him. "And Major Sarabhai said he would have it distributed to the national guard within four weeks. So all your fighting men will be protected, along with all the police departments and other first responders in Northern Illinois. We will start regular shipments to Illinois soon from our unit in Minnesota and the one in Wisconsin as soon as they have vaccinated all their people."

"Is everyone in Minnesota covered already?" he asked. "I thought that would take a while."

"We have vaccinated most people in Minnesota except in the far northern counties, which are getting it this week, and a few pockets in the Twin Cities that are still too violent to enter."

"I thought Minneapolis was cleared of Antifa already?"

"Nearly so. But there are a few holdout neighborhoods. The guard will occupy them in a week or two."

"We're working on it here too, but it's slow going. We hope to take out Antifa within a month or so and then tackle the Caliphate in the fall when the guard can deploy troops to help us."

"A lot is going to happen in the fall, if the Taiwanese can hold out that long," she mused, seeming miserable.

"What do you mean? What happens in the fall?" he asked.

Kayla looked at him with glassy eyes. Her lip trembled. "That is when the final wave will begin."

"The final wave?" He glanced around the restaurant to be sure no one had overheard her remark. "Be careful what you say here, OK? What is this about another wave? I thought that was just a possibility. If people hear that, they may get scared. We don't want to start a panic." He grinned and gazed at her face, which flushed.

She turned away, saying, "I never meant for it to come to this." Then she gazed sadly at Logan. "All I ever wanted to do was to do good science. And now . . . what have I done?"

"What are you talking about, Kayla?"

Kayla stood up abruptly, bumping the table and spilling a few drops of her wine. "There's something I have to tell you, Logan. I can't do it here." She looked around at the few people sitting at other tables. "Let's go back to our room. I need to tell you something important."

They left the restaurant and walked to catch the elevator. They rode it down one floor and hurried to their room. Once inside, Kayla stepped over to the window that overlooked the lake. She turned, and when Logan stepped beside her, she pulled him in for a hug and then a long kiss.

"I have something I must tell you about the virus work we did in Taiwan. I wanted to tell you sooner, but I couldn't. The admiral insisted it had to be kept a secret." She stared at Logan with wet eyes, and her lip trembled again. "I hope you don't hate me when I tell you."

Logan gaped at her in confusion. "What secret?"

"It's about the virus we took to Taiwan, V108. It has the mutation that can start the final wave of COVID. That's what Dr. Chin's work was about. He was supposed to weaponize the virus to use against the mainland Communists, if all else failed."

"What? He weaponized it? Why? How would that help anything?"

"The plan was to develop V108 into a weapon that the Taiwanese could use if they were invaded. They would be overwhelmed, and many would be slaughtered by the invading PLA forces. It was to be their backup weapon instead of using their nuclear weapons."

"They would consider using nukes to fight off the Communists? That's pretty extreme."

"But you don't understand. To the nationalists in Taiwan, invasion by the PRC poses an existential threat. If the Communists came in and took over, millions would be executed, and their whole way of life would be wiped out in a matter of months. Look at how brutally Hong Kong was treated when the Communists took over there in 2020. They destroyed the people and their way of life. That is what Communists do, Logan. They would change the system to their own way—a totalitarian way."

Logan was shocked at hearing these words. He couldn't believe what she was telling him.

"So they developed a virus weapon—V108—to use against the mainland?" he asked. "But how would that work? Wouldn't it be just as deadly to the Taiwanese as to the Communists?"

"Normally, yes. But I engineered the vaccine for COVID type 2 to include protection from V108 too. For instance, you and I have had the vaccine and are immune to type 2 and

V108—which is really type 3. I invented V108 because it was the logical next variant if the virus mutated. My father said it was extremely unlikely to mutate in that way, but you could say the same thing about type 2."

"Wait a minute," Logan said as he tried to wrap his head around all this new information. "You're saying you made a dangerous virus in order to develop a vaccine against it, right?" He shook his head and stared into her face. "But that's crazy. It could be used as a bioweapon. Did you know that?"

"Yes, but I'm not the only person to do such a thing. researchers do things like that all the time to see what effect the change has on the virus and how it works. It's called gain-of-function research. That's one way we find out what works for a vaccine. I just found a new variant that is very infectious and lethal but initially has few symptoms. It's asymptomatic in most people."

"If it's asymptomatic, then how can it be dangerous?" He didn't see how that could be true.

"It gives you a mild cold at first, but as it becomes more dispersed throughout the body, it begins to change how your immune response system works. It takes months, but eventually, your body loses all ability to fight off the virus infection. That makes it sneaky and dangerous." She seemed resigned to the fact that she had created something that made perfect sense scientifically, but that could be misused by unscrupulous people.

"But why give it to the Taiwanese at all if it's so dangerous?"

"They knew they were going to be invaded and how awful life could become. They secretly knew they couldn't rely on the United States to defend them completely—partly because we have abandoned allies before and because our policy toward mainland China drives most of our decisions. They knew how many of our politicians have already been compromised by Chinese money and blackmail."

"Well, most of our national politicians are dead. But it's our business leaders who favor the CCP now," he commented.

"The Taiwanese also knew that, even if we tried to defend them, we would be hard-pressed to do so, considering the distance involved and the might of the PLA." She stopped as if she was thinking about how to proceed. "Even if we used nuclear weapons."

"You're right there. We would be afraid to unleash our nukes," Logan noted.

"Yes, exactly. Well, the ROC didn't want to rely on nukes because the PLA has many more of those than the ROC does. The Communists would just bomb the hell out of Taiwan and annex it in fifty years when the radiation levels fell off. Their concept of time is warped, and they wouldn't mind if all the Taiwanese perished in a firestorm. Once the Communists begin, they will stop at nothing to win. We know that." She stared out the window and seemed overwhelmed by her thoughts.

"So they felt like they had no choice. I get that. But how would a weaponized virus help them?"

"If they infected everyone on the mainland with the virus, they would all die. Only the Taiwanese have the vaccine, you see. They wouldn't be affected, except in a few rare cases. There is no downside to using the virus."

"They'll release the virus, then. They'll use it as a way to retaliate for the invasion," Logan said reluctantly. "But it won't save them from losing their homeland."

"At first, the ROC rejected the idea, but then they realized that they could use it as a bargaining chip to force the CCP to give up the fight. If they didn't surrender or at least give up their claim on Taiwan, then the virus would be unleashed. The Communists would pay heavily. It would be like mutually assured destruction, like during the Cold War."

"I see. Very clever. But if the virus is so slow-acting, it wouldn't pose much of a threat ahead of time. The CCP would have time to come up with their own vaccine or treatment, right? It wouldn't be a very effective threat. They would need something that spreads and acts faster."

"Exactly. That's why they have already released the virus on the mainland. That is what Dr. Chin was doing. He came up with a way to distribute the virus all over China in only a few weeks. The whole country has already been thoroughly infected."

"What!" Logan shouted. "They did it already? Oh my God! That's genocide."

"No, wait," she said, putting her hands up in front of her. "Remember, I said it's slow-acting. Everyone is infected and has the asymptomatic disease. No one will die for a few more months. There is time to negotiate and, if the CCP agrees to stop their aggression and give up all claims to Taiwan, then they can have the therapeutic."

"What therapeutic? There's a cure?" Logan wondered if he was getting this right. Could this really be true, or was it some movie script-like fantasy?

Kayla started to cry. She laid her head on his chest and let months of dread drain out of her system. She shook with violent sobs of despair.

"How did they spread it so fast?" Logan asked incidentally.

"Dr. Chin infected a hundred volunteers with the virus and secretly sent them all over China, coughing and spraying aerosol in public places. It was a very effective and discreet method of dispersal. Once a large number of people were infected, it just spread everywhere. That's why we spent all that effort to get our vaccine out to all our allies in neighboring countries. We had to protect them. Our vaccine is over ninety-five percent effective for both virus types. If people are vaccinated, they are generally safe."

"That's why we made vaccination in this country mandatory: to protect our citizens."

"And we have shared the formula for the vaccine with all our allies around the world under the guise that it protected against COVID type 2. Only China will be affected. But the other leaders don't know about the infection of China. Not yet."

"When will the Taiwanese bring this up for negotiations to begin?"

"Soon, according to Dr. Chin. And Dr. Kuan has reported that he is making great progress on the therapeutic for the disease. It's in final testing. They don't want to threaten the CCP until they have a treatment in hand and deaths begin in China."

"So when is that?"

"In August, most likely. Kuan predicts results for the therapeutic will come out soon, and the first deaths will start about that time. Until people start dying, Chairman Zi will not take the threat seriously. Given his view of himself as a demigod, he may need to see large numbers of deaths before he will admit that he has to negotiate. Thousands will die until then."

They both stood there, silently staring out the window and holding each other. Somehow, the world had just gotten much smaller and more dangerous. It felt like it would never be the same again.

Chapter 24

Friday, June 2, 2023

Chicago, Illinois

The FC 470 Zodiac slipped through the water quietly as they approached the Outer Drive Bridge. The inflatable boat weighed more than they had expected once they had loaded it with all the ammo and gear that they needed to hold the DuStable Bridge. They piloted the craft with its standard 30 horsepower Evinrude engine down the lakeshore in the dark until they drew close to the breakwater. They then switched to the electric motor to propel them silently along the edge of the breakwater to North Pier. When the coast was clear, they huffed the boat up and over the pier and into the Chicago River.

Logan waited anxiously as the other boats in the advance force followed them to North Pier and completed the same procedure. There were six men per boat, eight boats in all, four boats per team, one team per bridge. He stealthily led his expert team of twenty-four men downriver to the DuStable Bridge. The other team under the command of Captain Francis Harrison quietly drove their four boats to the William P. Fahey Bridge. Both teams positioned their boats under their respective bridges and unloaded their men and equipment along the abutments. Then they waited for the signal to occupy the bridges and hold them until relieved.

That was the theory, at least.

At dawn, a heavily armed force would storm the Outer Drive Bridge and break through the Antifa barricade on Lake Shore Drive at Chicago Avenue. That team would roar down the lakeshore to Jane Addams Memorial Park at the neck of the peninsula where the water treatment plant and Navy Pier were located. The force would occupy the park and the rest of the peninsula to cut off those areas from the rest of the city. Twenty men would simultaneously move in to occupy the first floor of Lake Point Tower Condominium. Four trucks would continue to the bridge and capture it. If all went well, the CNF would control the neck of the peninsula, the bridge, and the Ohio Street Beach. That would give them access to bring in more troops via water, if needed. The whole operation was timed to take less than fifteen minutes from barricade to final positions.

A second convoy would roll down the lakeshore immediately after the first force broke through to capture and hold North Shore Drive from Chicago Avenue to Ohio Street, securing their supply line. They would effectively control a seven-block length of North Shore Drive. From positions along the drive, CNF troops would begin to work westward into the Northwestern University campus. This would all have to be accomplished in less than thirty minutes.

It was a great plan.

Logan hoped all would go well with their part of the operation. He waited until 4:45 a.m. Then he did a quick comms check and waited for the text message authorizing him to proceed. The waiting was nerve-racking because they had their boats tied up under the bridges and hoped no one would see them as the first rays of daylight began to brighten the sky. At any moment, one of the early risers in the Antifa army could look down and wonder what four boats were doing floating along the bridge abutments. All it would take was for one of them to ask the Antifa guard at street level what was happening. Then they would lose the element of surprise and be in a firefight.

The text arrived silently. It read: *GO*

Logan led two men up the concrete stairs at the base of the northwest bridge abutment and surprised the guard who sat at street level, smoking a cigarette. Logan shot him twice with his silenced Glock and looked for anyone else who might be guarding that side of the bridge. Seeing no one, his men dragged the dead guard away to his sandbag bunker and stacked his body next to it. Then he stood guard while his men shot the enemy soldiers posted at the other corners of the bridge at street level. Two more of his men cleared the second level of the bridge to make sure there were no guards unaccounted for.

In five minutes, they had seized control of the bridge. They set up .30 caliber machine guns on either end and rearranged the sandbag stacks to provide them with better protection from attack. He sent four men to find and overtake the north control room for the drawbridge.

Logan pulled out his binoculars and surveilled the Fahey Bridge to confirm that Harrison's team was also on schedule. He breathed a sigh of relief. Then he heard gunfire coming from Lake Shore Drive as the CNF convoy broke through and occupied the peninsula, the tower condominium, and the third bridge. He checked his watch: 5:18 a.m. Not bad. So far, no one had noticed that the bridge had been taken over. He hoped it would stay that way as long as possible.

At 5:20 a.m., he heard a loud barrage of gunfire issuing from the lakefront. He figured that was the thrust of the second attack. The hostility raged for nearly a half hour before it broke off into more sporadic fighting.

He received another text: *WP AND NP TAKEN. LAKESHORE SECURE. MOVING WEST AS PLANNED. BE PREPARED.*

The message preceded the sound of trucks driving rapidly up Michigan Avenue toward the bridge. He could see seven or eight trucks with men hanging out of their beds holding rifles. They drew near the bridge without slowing their speed, apparently suspecting nothing.

When the first truck was about a hundred feet away, Jasper stepped out and fired a grenade launcher at it. The M79 grenade went low and bounced in front of the truck and then rolled under the frame before exploding. The force of the explosion lifted one side of the truck off the ground and sent the driver, who had his eyes wide open at that point, careening into the curb at the side of the street. One of Logan's men began to strafe the truck with his machine gun as men tried to climb out. Meanwhile, Jasper had a clear shot at the second truck and sent a grenade its way.

One of the ironies of the situation was that the Antifa soldiers had cleared the area adjacent to the bridge on both sides of the river, so there were no parked cars standing along the street. The Antis had no cars to hide behind as the .30 caliber rounds from the machine gun sought them out. Everyone in the first two trucks was killed quickly. Jasper lobbed more grenades at the other trucks, setting three of them on fire and killing a few of their occupants. He then retreated to the safety of the sandbags before the Antis organized a counterattack.

They had made about eighty to one hundred men angry and eager to kill them. About four- or five-to-one odds. *Not too bad for before six o'clock in the morning,* Logan thought. They were making a difference by holding back Antifa reinforcements south of the river. That would give the CNF time to push the terrorists out of Streeterville and the Magnificent Mile.

Logan and his men settled into the combat, firing only when they had clear shots and were reasonably sure of hitting an Anti. He watched as more Antifa trucks filled with reserves from their headquarters drove up Michigan Avenue to support their comrades. He watched as even more trucks showed up at the Fahey Bridge and tried the same type of attack. Harrison and his men held out well as wave after wave of Antis charged their position. They repelled them every time, but like Logan's position, they were getting worn down by the fighting, and they were likely using up their ammunition faster than anyone had planned.

Soon, Logan's team started taking incoming shots from the north side of the street as Antis began to attack from that side too. RPGs were an addition to the fight he didn't need. He hoped that the relief force was working its way toward his position. If not, he would have to consider his options. Could they retreat via the river? Or would they have to fight to the last man? He had not contemplated that this morning.

He settled into a fog of overwhelming mental stress for a moment. His mind shifted focus to how things had ended with Kayla three weeks before. They had discussed the implications of the virus work she had done and decided that much of what would happen was out of their control. They had looked at Kayla's work on the virus from all sides and could find nothing they could do to change the course of events now. They had tried to let it go and enjoy the time they had together.

An RPG struck one of the sandbag revetments, injuring two men on the south side near the bridge house. Cal reported that he had two injured, one severely and the other with minor shrapnel wounds. Then three more RPGs struck them, one killing a man on the north side this time. Their situation was getting even more dicey as more and more Antis flooded the area on both the north and south sides of the bridge.

Logan contemplated their options. He had a fallback plan in case they couldn't hold the bridge from overwhelming force. That was to open the bridge partway so that it couldn't be used for any form of traffic. To make that happen, he needed to find out if the bridge was functioning properly.

"Jerry, I need you to check out the controls for the bridge!" Logan shouted across the deck. "Join me in the northwest bridge house."

Logan then ran toward the building that housed the controls for the northern half of the drawbridge. Shortly after he scrambled into the building, he was joined by Jerry, an older man who had worked for the City of Chicago in the maintenance department for twenty-three years. In that time, Jerry had worked on the bridge and had personal knowledge of its inner workings. He could raise the bridge.

Inside, the two men jogged up the stone stairs to the control room and searched for the control panel. Jerry said, "When I was here a few years ago, they kept the key on a lanyard. We need it to start her up."

They searched the small room and finally saw the key hanging on a nail above the control panel. Jerry grabbed it and inserted it into the panel. With a twist of the key, the panel came to life. He pushed on a lever, and the bridge reacted slowly by rising up an inch at the leading edge of the southbound lanes.

"There are two sections on the north side and two on the south side. We can open the north-side sections from here. You have to be in the southeast bridge house to control the south sections. How high do you want to raise it?"

"About ten feet should be enough. Just enough so no one can drive across," Logan said hurriedly. "Our guys will have to evacuate down to the boats." He radioed his troops that the bridge would lift up next to them.

"OK. Here goes," Jerry said as he pushed the levers forward slightly. The two northern sections of the bridge slowly rose up until the far edge was about ten feet above the level of the rest of the bridge. No one could come across under those conditions.

"All set," Jerry said. Then he took the key from the control panel and threw the lanyard around his neck. "Best not leave the key here, or they might figure out how to lower the damn thing." He chuckled as he descended the stairs and exited the stone building.

"Team One, prepare to abandon positions," Logan called out over the radio. "Cal, that means you on the south side. Take your guns and ammo and load onto the boats in five. We'll give you cover fire and then be right behind you on the north end."

Logan waited as Cal disengaged and got his men with their gear moving down the stairs to the Zodiacs on his side of the bridge. He gave him about three minutes to load his wounded men. He radioed to Harrison that they were abandoning their site and would motor over to join him on the Fahey Bridge. Then he led his men down the stairs as bullets zipped past them and ricocheted off the bridge deck. They loaded their boats on the north side with their wounded, guns, and ammo as bullets whizzed past them on all sides. It appeared that hundreds of Antifa fighters wanted them dead.

Logan shouted over the radio, "Go!"

All four boat motors started up, and the Zodiacs sped out from beneath the abutments as fast as they could go. The boats were lighter than they had been at the start of the day, but they still seemed underpowered to run the half mile to the Fahey Bridge. As soon as the watercraft lurched out from under the safety of the concrete structure, the Anti fighters began to pepper them with rifle fire. Bullets streaked around each boat, splashing up mini-fountains of water and piercing the sides. Rounds hit a few of the men, killing two of them outright and wounding five others during the two-minute voyage upriver.

There was nothing Logan or any of them could do to prevent it once they were in the open. He felt rotten to have led his men on this deadly retreat.

Logan directed his men to bring the Zodiacs in on the north-side abutment of the Fahey Bridge. He ran up the staircase to find Harrison on the deck, meeting him behind the sandbag barrier on the north side.

"Where do you want my men positioned, Major?" he shouted above the constant rifle fire.

"Spread your men out to support all positions. How's your ammo situation?"

"We're about out. How about you?"

"Down to the last belt of .30 caliber for the machine guns. Can you get us resupplied real quick?" Harrison asked grimly. "Or be prepared to fight with your Bowie knife."

Logan chuckled at the reference to Davy Crockett and the last stand at the Alamo. "I'll see what I can do, Major."

Logan backed into a secure position and radioed to the commander of the North Lake Shore Drive contingent of CNF. "Team One to Third Base. Are you there?"

There was a lot of static, and then a voice broke through the electronic haze. "Third Base here. Team One, come in?"

"Right, Charlie. This is Team One. We're desperate for ammo of all kinds. Where is our resupply unit?" Logan asked.

"We're a little bogged down out here, Team One. We got our ass high in the grass and are hard at it." Charlie was stressed yet jovial at the same time. "What do you need, Lone Ranger?"

"We need .30 cal belts, maybe forty of them, and twenty cases of .223 ammo. Grenades too. M67s and M79 ammo. We need it delivered to the Fahey Bridge ASAP. Can you spare a few trucks with troops to defend?" Logan asked.

"Holy shit, Logan!" Charlie cried. "You got a war going on or something? You'll have to sign a requisition order or some such bullshit for all that." There was silence. "I'll see what I can do. Out."

Logan stayed by the radio but got a few shots off at Antis on the north side of the bridge while he waited. He scanned the surroundings and saw that his team had less structural protection here because of the more modern bridge design. They had more exposure to high-rise buildings than at the DuStable location, which meant they wouldn't be able to hold out for more than twenty minutes at this rate of attack.

The radio chirped, and he answered, "Team One, this is Third Base. Come in."

"Third Base, this is Team One. Hear you loud and clear."

"I have three trucks coming your way in twenty minutes. They are driving up the north bank on that little walking trail. Give them cover. The lead vehicle has hellfire, so be prepared."

"Roger that. We will cover. Thanks, Charlie. I owe you one."

Logan dodged lead in order to get to Harrison to let him know that help was on the way. The fighting intensified for several minutes and then slacked off a little. Logan kept tracking the time on his watch. The northwest outpost radioed in that they were out of belt, so someone on that end of the bridge ran a box of .30 cal ammo over to them. Soon, the sound of the northwest machine gun sliced through the air again.

Bullets were flying everywhere, not hitting his men at all times, but close enough to chip concrete close to everyone. Some rounds zipped by really close to Logan's head, and RPGs came their way often enough to keep them in place. The sound of gunfire was overwhelming. He hadn't been in the midst of such a violent firefight since his worst days in Afghanistan.

It was then 9:00 a.m., with bright sun glaring. Logan radioed in a sitrep to Jorgensen. "Where the hell is my backup, General? They should be here by now," he asked.

"Look, Logan," Jorgensen said over the static. "We've got our headaches too. We've moved through the university sector just fine, and we control everything north of Ontario Street, including that vacant block where the Antis have been burying bodies. But we've bogged down north of Ohio Avenue, and they are pouring troops in over the river east of you via the State Street Bridge."

"We're just barely holding on here, sir!" Logan shouted over the noise of battle. "We must have four hundred of these crazies trying to dislodge us."

"Well, hang on. I'll get someone to you as soon as I can. Maybe an hour." Jorgensen sounded like he was trying to be optimistic. "Hell, just hang on and kill those bastards as fast as you can. I may need to send you over to State to shut off that bridge."

"What the . . ."

The radio went dead.

Chapter 25

The fighting became more desperate. They ran out of ammo on the southeast side of the bridge, where the bridge house was. Logan took three men, and they dodged bullets for what seemed like ten minutes as they worked their way over to resupply the machine gun. It was their last belt of .30 caliber ammo.

Logan radioed his men on the south side. "We have more ammo on the way. If you have more belt, can you hold on for an hour?"

"Jesus Christ, Commander," one private said. "Now you want miracles?"

"Yeah. We need one of those." Logan stared at the dust-covered faces of the men, some with minor cuts from the flying concrete chips. "Our backup is running late because they're having trouble in Streeterville, and the Michigan Avenue battalion is tied up. We have to hold for an hour." He turned to go.

"We'll do our best, sir. Just get us some ammo."

Logan and his men scrambled to the next cover, a stone bench on the side of the roadway. Just as they reached it, they were showered with automatic weapons fire, sending bullets ringing against the bench and chipping off dozens of tiny, granite projectiles that struck all of them. Logan caught three chunks on the left side of his face, deep enough to draw blood. One cut in his forehead dripped blood into his eyes that then ran down his face. It hurt like hell.

When there was a brief lull in shooting, he and his men ran back to the north-side sandbag revetment. They found another man wounded there, being tended to by their team's medic. The medic slapped a gauze square over the worst of Logan's injuries and used bandages for the smaller cuts. He gave Logan a questioning look and then spoke up.

"Sir, we have six dead now and eight seriously wounded," he said. "I can't do much for them here. We need to get them back to the base for better care."

"Noted. Maybe we can get them out on the supply trucks that are supposed to be here already." Logan scanned the medic's face and made a decision. "Look, I need you to get the wounded and dead down below the north abutment ASAP. We'll send them back to Lake Shore. They can handle them there."

Logan's radio chirped, and he raised it to his ear.

"We're a block away and under fire, so be ready to greet us. Over," a man stated. "Where do you want us?"

"The trail drops down under the bridge abutment, so pull in there, and we can unload," Logan shouted into the radio. "Do you have hellfire on your truck?"

"Yes, sir. We surely do. You want us to light up the place as we come in?"

"Yes, I do."

"You got it. You'll hear us in about thirty seconds."

Cal grinned at Logan's request. "Those Antifa bastards are going to be surprised. With the different angle, our guys should hit a bunch of them."

Just then, they heard the roar of the twin M60 .30 caliber machine guns of hellfire blazing away on the north side of the river and swinging west to cover the intersection on the approach to the bridge. The five hundred and fifty rounds per minute from each gun created chaos on the street. Antis were either shot where they hid behind vehicles or concrete barriers or were caught running away from the blazing death. The lead truck fired until it dropped down under the bridge onto the walking trail that served as an underpass below Columbus Drive. All three trucks sheltered in the relative safety under the bridge.

The driver's door of the truck flew open, and a large, Black man jumped down from the two-ton with a grin on his wide face. He was laughing as he asked, "Which one of you is Logan?"

Logan stepped forward and took the meaty hand that was offered. "You made one hell of an entrance, soldier. Nice shootin'."

"I'm Wendleson, Commander. Pleased to meet you. We got a shitload of stuff for you, courtesy of Mr. Charlie himself." He walked to the back of the truck and threw up the tattered canvas tarp that covered the load. Several of the steel ammo boxes had been dented by bullets on the drive in. "Lots of goodies all right here."

Harrison took charge of unloading the truck and distributing the ammo. "Hey, you brought us Claymore mines too. We can use those right enough." He was tickled at the discovery.

"We have some wounded who have to get out on your return. Can you do that and a few bodies too?" Logan had to duck as a stream of bullets ricocheted around them. He picked up his rifle and shot back at the source of the trouble.

"Yeah, sorry to hear it, but you boys look like you've been through the wringer here already," Wendleson said. "Where's your backup, man?"

"They're an hour out, they say. How's it going on your end of things?"

"We've got the lakeshore pretty secure, and our battalion has pushed in past North McClurg Court now, so they are halfway here from the lake side. You'll know it when they push the Antis out into Columbus Drive over here. You can cut them up when they try to cross the drive."

"How about the clearing operation?" Logan wondered how the teams were doing that had to go into buildings and make sure no enemies were still hiding inside.

"The university area was good, but it got tough over by McClurg. Nasty fighting. Lots of sick buggers in there. They had nothing to lose."

Wendleson broke away to see how the wounded were being loaded into his trucks. Only the truck he was driving was enclosed, so they placed the wounded in there. The bodies of the dead were unceremoniously strapped onto the two flatbeds.

"We're loaded and out of here, Commander. Hope you get your relief soon." The big man climbed into the cab, and he leaned out the window. "We'll scare the hell out of those buggers again on the way out." He laughed heartily as the vehicles turned around and roared up the slope from under the bridge. The dual machine guns of hellfire came back to life as the trucks pulled away under heavy fire. They kept driving and made good time along the riverbank. Soon, they were out of sight, and only sporadic gunfire trailed them.

Harrison had his men running up the stairs with ammo, distributing it to the sandbagged outposts. They had received twenty boxes of grenades in the shipment, so they deployed them as well.

"What should we do with the Claymores, Logan?" Harrison asked. "Put them facing the north intersection? We could use them if we're overrun."

"That shouldn't happen, but we need to make the most of them. I guess the Antis will rush in at some point, and we can use them when they're bunched up." He glanced around their surroundings. "Ask some of the men to come up with placements. They'll have creative ideas."

"Good point. I have a couple of guys that can think of crazy stuff. We'll put them out just in case." Harrison half grinned and walked away to join the men on top of the bridge deck.

Logan thought about their predicament. He wasn't sure if they would get reinforcements in time, but he thought they had better plan for another withdrawal if things got out of hand. He didn't relish another escape by slow boat, but they had to be prepared.

He crawled up the stairs and was surprised to see that they were under even more intense fire than before the supply trucks had shown up. Antifa troops were closing in from all sides now, as if they had received orders to overtake the bridge. Maybe they needed it to allow more vehicles to cross and join the battle north of them. Then he realized that most of the new Antis were streaming out from the city blocks to their north, probably being driven back by CNF forces pushing into Streeterville.

He saw Harrison and his men attaching Claymore mines to the concrete barriers that separated the street-level traffic from the riverside trail to prevent drivers from running wild along the riverbank. They worked fast, with three men laying down suppression fire while two others attached the mines via straps. Once they had them attached, they scrambled back behind cover, running electrical wires behind them as they did so.

"Good work, Harrison. I think we might need those after all." Logan pointed to the Antifa soldiers who were beginning to creep out from side streets and onto Columbus Drive from the neighborhoods. "Our guys are pressing them from the east, so they're emerging here. They may try to cross the bridge to get back to their stronghold on the south side."

"Yeah, that's what I figure too, Logan. Might as well have extra firepower if they push it too hard."

As they crouched there, they could hear gunfire approaching from up Columbus Drive, seeming to drift out of the side streets. Then they saw a large group of Antis back out of the nearest side street, North Water Street, fighting as they retreated. The men were firing into the street and taking fire at the same time. They shot back, using the corners of buildings as cover, but several were hit as they tried to escape the oncoming CNF troops.

"Hey, Harrison!" Logan shouted above the noise of the fray. "Our guys are driving them back!"

As he watched, about a hundred men ran out of Water Street and onto Columbus Drive. They were in full retreat now as more and more Antis cleared out from neighboring streets. Soon, the whole drive was filled with armed Antis, some of whom began to flee toward the bridge. They apparently thought it provided an easy way out of the fight and a route to the south side.

"Let's lure them in, shall we?" Logan said.

Harrison grinned and shouted for his men to hold their fire until the enemy was close enough to use the Claymores. "Duck down and wait for it, men!" he shouted into the radio.

Logan got on the radio and tried to contact the CNF commander who was driving the Antis forward. "Team One leader to leader of CNF Force on Water Street. Do you read me?

Team One leader to CNF on Water Street. Come in." He hoped they were on the same frequency.

"Team One, Force Six, over. Where are you, and what do you want? I'm busy here."

"Team One is holding the bridge on Columbus just south of you. We're about to engage Antis headed our way. Be advised." He didn't want the CNF force to come into his line of fire or think they were the enemy.

"Team One on the bridge? You holding OK?"

"Yes, please keep in contact as you sweep onto Columbus so we don't shoot you."

"Roger that."

Logan surveilled the situation. They were hunkered down behind the sandbags so the oncoming Antis couldn't see them. They simply waited and confirmed that they had enough ammo within reach. They gazed at one another with impassive faces, strained and somewhat hopeful, but also aware that this could all go very wrong.

Logan checked out the positioning of the Claymores. Harrison and his men had laid them out well, facing outward at a forty-five-degree angle so that the ones in front formed a kill zone about twenty feet ahead of the sandbag revetment. Others were located to fire straight forward and the rest to blast outward and to the sides. Triggered in the right order, they would clear the whole forward area.

The Antis jogged toward them, slowing when they didn't see anyone on the bridge. It may have seemed odd not to see sentries protecting such an important facility. On the other hand, they had just seen a hell of a lot of strange shit. *Maybe it's not so much of a mystery. Maybe they're just scared out of their wits and aren't thinking,* Logan thought. *Maybe they'll run onto the seemingly empty bridge without wondering if they're being chased by soldiers.*

A few Antis slowed to a walk, scanning all sides to see if it was safe. When they were within fifty yards, they could see numerous bodies lying alongside the road and a dozen or so lying completely still in the middle. Then one of the Antis who had been shooting at Logan's men called out, "Look out! There are assholes on the bridge."

Harrison blew the first two Claymores, the ones that shot straight ahead. There was a loud explosion, and steel balls shot out from the mines at ballistic speed. The first twenty Antis were hit immediately and dropped where they were. Once they had fallen, Harrison fired the next set, and steel balls shot across Columbus Drive at high speed, cutting into the next rank of Antis, but with fewer direct hits. Another twenty or so men dropped, and the balls still had enough energy to wound forty more men farther away. Harrison fired the last set of mines, and more balls shot forward and to the sides, ricocheting off the walls of the surrounding buildings and bouncing back onto the pavement. More Antis fell, but a smaller number were killed outright. Profuse screams broke out from the injured on the ground as some of their comrades helped drag them to the little cover there was on the street.

"Open fire!" Harrison shouted.

The CNF men rose from hiding with the M60s and began to shoot down the street at the confused Antis. The Antis fired back, but Logan's men were protected by the sandbags. They fired their machine guns until the belts ran out. Then they reloaded and continued until there were no more obvious targets. Columbus Drive was littered with bodies by then. Any remaining

Antis ran west along Water Street to escape the avenue of death and the advancing CNF troops.

"Team One, Force Six here. Hold your fire, Commander," the voice on the radio said. "We are emerging onto Columbus Drive."

"Roger that. You are clear to enter," Logan said with relief.

He stood up to use his binoculars to scan the road to the north. He could see that Antis were emerging from the other side streets up Columbus Drive, where it became North Fairbanks Court. That was the street he had looked down three weeks before from the other end when he was checking out the Antifa body-burying detail. The Antis were on the run, crossing Fairbanks quickly and continuing west on the side streets.

A Humvee drove out from Water Street and headed toward the bridge. Two support vehicles flanked the Humvee, and they all pulled up together in front of where Logan stood. Additional CNF troops ran along the side of the street and engaged the few Antis remaining there. A detail marched directly over to the side of the Humvee and stopped as an older, distinguished-looking gentleman stepped out of the passenger side door. It was Jorgensen.

"I told you that you would be relieved in one hour, and by God, we're here," the general said. "Logan, you are hereby relieved. Captain Sanchez will take over the bridge defense." Jorgensen indicated to an officer standing nearby with his men. "Take your men back to Third Base and resupply. Stand by for orders. We aren't out of this yet."

"Sir, thank you. I am grateful." Logan saluted him. "Looks like you have the Antis on the run. Great work."

"We'll see how this plays out, Logan. They will probably regroup over on Michigan Avenue. But we have them in a tight spot. They may not want to fight too much more. These troops are pretty green from what we have seen. They can fight, but they don't have good leadership."

"All right, sir. We will withdraw." Logan saluted again, and Jorgensen climbed back into his Humvee. The truck and support vehicles turned and drove toward Water Street, where they headed west.

Captain Sanchez and his troops moved in to take possession, and soon, Cal and his men were released from their end of the bridge. Fighting carried on, but at a slower pace on the south side.

"Gentlemen, load your boats and return to Third Base," Logan instructed them. "We will leave the M60s here and all the ammo. We'll take our last dead and wounded with us. Meet on the north bank by North Pier." He paused and then added, "Good work, everyone. We accomplished a major victory today. We held the southern perimeter and won. Good job."

They loaded their boats and motored east on the Chicago River with only light gunfire directed at them from the south bank. Logan and his men looked at one another in relief. No "Oorahs" were heard like in the movies: they were just tired warriors, glad to have survived another battle. Deep breaths were audible in the boat after the long morning.

Chapter 26

The day dawned warm, sunny, and wonderful for Logan and Kayla. They were back at the Lincoln Hotel for a few days of R & R. They had both been busy throughout the whole month of July with their jobs and the challenges that came with them. Now they could be together again after five weeks apart.

Logan awoke first and quietly lay in bed, looking out the window at the sun as it rose over the lake while Kayla slept peacefully at his side. To him, sunrise had always represented a sign of renewal and hope for the future. His potted geranium seemingly transmitted the same vibes as it practically glowed in the morning sun. He thought about all that had changed since he had met Kayla. In some ways, the world was a better place. He reflected on how much progress they had made in Chicago to expel the extremists who had plagued the city since the mission the CNF had conducted in June. He had lost good men and nearly all his troops had been wounded to some extent in the desperate action. But they had prevailed.

In the space of only a few days, CNF forces had occupied all of Streeterville. While clearing the buildings, they had been shocked to discover the extent of the enemy's cruelty. There were far more dead people hidden away in the Antifa-controlled high-rises than they had expected. The terrorists had executed many of the residents. Rotting bodies had been stashed there in sealed-off offices for disposal. Until then, the CNF had assumed that most of the residents had run away to safety elsewhere. Apparently, many had never had a chance.

Clearing teams had also found the remains of several Antifa cohorts who had died from COVID type 2 and other diseases and injuries. The terrorists had also piled up these dead in sealed rooms, at least in some areas. The burial of corpses that Logan had seen at the Erie Street vacant lot had apparently been an attempt to permanently dispose of the bodies.

It had taken four weeks to clear all the buildings. Several occupants had holed up in their apartments and paid the gang for protection. Most of them were ill and undernourished. Others were insane from captivity and mistreatment. Some had been recent captives whom the Antis had used as sex slaves, and the rest had been held hostage for ransom. It was a major undertaking to rescue these people and find them help and new housing. That work was still continuing two months later.

The CNF had been preoccupied for several weeks with burying the dead. In this, they had been advised by Kayla, as a virus expert, to bury the bodies outside the city in mass graves on vacant land, preferably on a hill with good drainage. She said they had to bury COVID victims deep, at least six feet below ground, to prevent the virus from escaping from burial sites that were too shallow. The virus could live on for months or even years underground, and someone might still get infected if gases from bodily decomposition were released from the soil. She had cited the Black Plague pits of England as an example of disposal. The CNF took her advice and found a farm considerably west of the town of Gilberts on which to dig several mass graves.

All this unexpected work and responsibility delayed the CNF from carrying out further incursions against Antifa. They simply didn't have the manpower to prosecute battle and deal with the tragedy of the occupation. In addition, many of the CNF soldiers were middle-aged men who did not have the stamina to keep up a long-term campaign. They could sustain a limited engagement but couldn't be expected to keep on the go for extended periods of time. *That's why armies are manned by energetic young men and women,* Logan thought. Although all the soldiers played their parts, with many older ones taking on the vital processing and care for the innocents whom they had rescued, the younger troops bore the brunt of continued fighting with the Antis and picking up new ground in smaller actions.

The toll on the CNF had been severe: 257 men lost and 569 wounded. It would take a while to recover from such losses. But they had inflicted much greater casualties on the Antifa army, with twenty-nine hundred dead as far as they could tell and at least twice that in wounded.

Jorgensen had decided that they would hold their position for now and observe Antifa's actions. They had learned from the few prisoners they had captured that the enemy ranks had been decimated by disease, especially COVID type 2. Drone observations showed that the Antis were dropping like flies and had work details busy stacking up bodies daily or burying them in shallow graves on any grassy area near their headquarters. Something about the level of sickness that Antifa experienced worried Jorgensen. He wondered if they had encountered a new disease that was even worse than COVID type 2.

Logan worried that CNF forces would bog down now that they didn't have a clear objective. Jorgensen told him to enjoy the respite. He hoped that by waiting, the COVID pandemic would do more damage to Antifa than any attack they could muster. Logan had to agree that letting attrition reduce the enemy ranks was a good idea.

"You're awake already?" Kayla stirred under the bedsheet and wriggled over to place her head on his shoulder. "You should have woken me," she said and then kissed his neck.

"You were sleeping so peacefully."

Her eyes closed again for a moment, then fluttered open. "What time is it?"

"A little after eight. Go back to sleep. You're on vacation."

"I could, you know, but it's late. I should get up and drink some coffee." She gazed at him devilishly. "Unless there's something else you would like to do first?" She giggled and kissed his neck again.

**

"I heard from Dr. Wang that the first virus cases have most likely been detected in China already, but no one is allowed to talk about them," she said between bites of croissant slathered with strawberry jam. "It seems early to me for V108 to show symptoms, but it's possible."

They had moved to a table at the hotel restaurant to have breakfast. Sunlight was streaming in beneath the outdoor umbrellas. They were eating omelets and sipping Columbian coffee.

"How is the treatment coming along? That other doctor was developing it, right? Kuan?" Logan asked. "I hope he has it ready soon."

"He said they had some setbacks but are on track now. At least, that's what Wang said."

"Well, you said you expected the first cases to show up in August, so you were right," he commented. "Did Wang say when negotiations would begin?"

"No. But the invasion has bogged down for some reason."

"I heard about that from Cotes. He said the PLA has had trouble moving men and materiel across the Taiwan Strait." He grinned at Kayla. "You know they landed at Tainan City on the southwest coast to gain use of the airports there." He used his hand to indicate that the city was located on the lower part of the island. "We sent the ROC an abundance of Stinger missiles and other replacement gear. They have small fishing boats out on the water, and when one of the PLA planes makes its approach to the airport for a landing, they fire a Stinger at it. The PLA's losses have been extensive."

"Oh, so they aren't really getting anywhere on the invasion? Maybe they will want to talk soon." She smiled at the thought. Then she seemed uncomfortable about something as she asked, "What's the plan here? Are you going to finish off the Antifa army soon? And then what about the Caliphate?"

"We're regrouping, and at the same time, we're still putting pressure on Antifa. Jorgensen thinks we should just wait it out and see how many of them die from COVID. They have it pretty bad." Logan looked south over the city. "We haven't developed a real plan against the Caliphate yet except to keep an eye on them. Word has it that they're smuggling in military equipment on freighters that dock in Gary, Indiana. We have no control over that port since it's within the Caliphate. But we may start intercepting vessels heading there from the St. Lawrence Seaway or the other Great Lakes. We need to get the coast guard involved, if they can disengage from the southern coast. They're overwhelmed down there, even with navy support."

"Sounds difficult. But you're getting part of the city back. That's good news."

Logan's phone beeped, and he read a text that had arrived from Jorgensen: *Israel attacked. See TV now.*

Logan nearly dropped the phone. He stared at the text again and then looked up at Kayla.

"What's wrong, Logan? You look upset."

"We have to go back to our room and watch what just happened." He checked around the restaurant to see if any other guests had noticed his reaction. "Let's take our coffee with us."

They left the restaurant and took the elevator down to their room. Once inside, Logan turned on the TV and checked the local channel he watched most often. A large, red banner flashed on the screen that read *Breaking News.*

A female announcer said, "Reports just sent to us indicate that the state of Israel has been attacked by Iran. Apparently . . . and we have not been able to verify this yet . . . three missiles were fired at Israel from a site in Iran early this morning, our time. Only one of the missiles is known to have struck the country, and where the other missiles landed is unknown. The missile struck northwest of Jerusalem near the West Bank town of Beit Horon." The announcer stopped speaking, looking shocked. She sat there staring at the camera with her mouth open.

A generic map of the Middle East appeared on the TV screen with a dot showing where Jerusalem was located. It was a useless map because nothing else was labeled and did not indicate where the bomb had fallen relative to the city. Then a short video clip came on the air showing what appeared to be desert with a large, black cloud spiraling upward above it several miles away. Logan immediately knew it was from a nuclear blast.

The announcer began to speak again. "My God! It was an atom bomb." She visibly tried to control her emotions. "I'm being told it struck near a small town, and there is no information about the extent of damage. Witnesses said that at least seven missiles have been launched from an undisclosed location in the south of Israel. Our contact in Jerusalem claims they are Israel's nuclear response to the attack." She stopped talking again and was apparently listening to someone speaking into her earpiece. "Israel has gone on high alert. That is all we have at this time." She looked confused, and then the programing returned to a soap opera.

"Holy shit!" Logan said. "The Iranians finally broke all the rules."

"Oh my God!" Kayla whispered. "This is awful."

Logan's phone rang, and he answered quickly. It was the general. "Logan, I need you down here ASAP," he said. "We're having an emergency meeting at HQ."

"Yes, sir," Logan said, and the call ended.

He turned to Kayla. "I have to go to a meeting. Can you wait here until I get back? I'll call if it will be long."

"OK. Sure," she said reluctantly. "Please hurry."

***

"I was going to call you together this morning anyway, but the Iran news has added impetus to our situation," Jorgensen began. "I trust you are all aware of the situation in Israel. I have news that the bomb missed Jerusalem almost entirely, but struck in the hills of the West Bank. It almost hit Ramallah, and there are numerous casualties. The new Iranian ayatollah has claimed victory against the Little Satan, even though only one missile made it near the target. One missile crashed about a mile after launch, and the second exploded in the Iraqi desert southwest of

Baghdad. No reports on deaths yet, but it must have been devastating."

"On the news, we heard that Israel had launched a response. Is there any update on that?" one of the men asked.

"Yes. The Israeli military launched seven missiles with nuclear warheads. One hit Qom, where the Iranians operate a nuclear bomb factory deep underground. They hit other nuke-related targets too, but I don't know which ones," Jorgensen muttered. "Another important development regarding Iran: The Pentagon and CIA have completed their assessment of the attack on our East Coast last spring. The missiles were certainly launched by Iran and Syria in a combined operation. Acting President Navarro has released the report and issued a statement that we hold Iran and Syria responsible. He, in essence, declared war on Iran, but our response is considered a defensive action, so it falls under the War Powers Act."

"What will he do, sir?" Logan asked.

"I've heard, but have not confirmed," Jorgensen said sternly, "that he will launch ICBMs at specific targets in Iran in retaliation for the attack upon our soil and in response to the attack on Israel, whom we have sworn to defend from external forces. The targets are being selected as we speak."

Logan's secure phone beeped, and he excused himself to talk to Admiral Cotes. He stepped out of the conference room and spoke quietly.

"Sir, I just learned we're going to launch missiles at Iran. Is that true?" Logan asked cautiously.

"Yes, a combination of continental- and submarine-launched weapons, all on military targets. In a few minutes, there won't be any Revolutionary Guard or Quds Force left in the country," Cotes replied.

"But they have good air defenses, even for some missiles, I think."

"Yes, but we have the Hermit. It will go in first and destroy all electronic communications, networks, and radars. Hell, our cyber guys already wrecked a lot of their internet and commerce this morning."

"Hermit? Never heard of it."

"You're not supposed to know about it."

"Oh," Logan grunted. "Did you call about Iran, then?"

"Yes, I wanted you to know that the SEALs you have been waiting for will now be tied up even longer doing some nasty shit to Syrian assets. You may not see them until the fall. They did good work collecting the data we needed to tie the Iranians and Syrians to the East Coast attack. We should be proud."

"Yes, sir. I'll have to call you back later to talk more." Logan checked his watch. "Are you still traveling?"

"No. I finished that assignment and am headed back to Falls Church. Back to counterterrorism for me."

"That's good news, sir."

"Yes, it is. I'll be in touch, Logan. Out." The line went dead and Logan felt as if his whole world had been pulled out from under him. Was this the beginning of World War Three?

Logan rejoined the meeting and sat down, his hands shaking. When Jorgensen saw him enter, he changed topics. "Logan, you will be happy to know that because of our successful operation to clear the Streeterville area, we have been declared a functioning division of the Illinois National Guard. We have full status. Thanks for helping put us on the map."

The men gave Logan a hearty round of applause. He felt a little sheepish because they had all contributed to the successful outcome. Still, a little praise went a long way toward lifting spirits.

"And I've decided we should begin to push on Antifa again," Jorgensen announced. "Let's drive them south of the river into the western portion of downtown this time, and then take a few weeks to clear up their mess. We know that we need to plan for that after seeing up close the death and destruction they leave behind."

"At least we know what to expect now, sir. And we have a method to deal with the bodies," one man added.

"If this works well, we can do the final push on Antifa in late September and eliminate them as a force entirely by October." Jorgensen surveyed the eager faces around the room. "Hell, when we started this in May, there were thirty thousand of them. Now, there must be less than ten thousand. It should go better this time."

The men clapped their hands and started chattering optimistically about the plans among themselves.

Logan brought up the elephant in the room. "When do we take on the Caliphate, sir? They are just getting stronger as time goes by."

"One enemy at a time. Besides, we are going to need help from our brother guardsmen to deal with that menace. It will take time."

The meeting broke up after that, with a few men stopping by to talk to Logan about the upcoming operation. He begged off from further discussions so he could return to Kayla. He got in his car and drove back to the hotel.

When he opened the door to their room, he found Kayla sitting on the sofa in running shorts and a T-shirt, watching TV. He sat beside her, put an arm around her shoulders, and drew her close. She turned her head and kissed him warmly on the lips. Her mind seemed elsewhere, and a shiver ran through her from the physical contact.

"All this news-watching—it's depressing, isn't it?" he asked.

"Yes, it's surreal to see bombs exploding a world away. It's like watching a war movie, but in this case, it's really happening."

"It's weird, I agree. And we aren't even calling it a war."

"I'm scared, Logan." She threw her arms around his neck. "What will happen now? Has the whole world gone crazy?"

Chapter 27

Logan stood at O'Hare, waiting for Kayla to arrive. The national guard now occupied Minneapolis-St. Paul International Airport, and service to Chicago had been restored two weeks ago. She was visiting him once again, and they planned to spend a few days at their favorite hotel. The intensity of their lives made separation difficult to bear, even if they could talk on the phone. So much was happening that the miles between them seemed too vast to contemplate. Try as they might, her visits to Chicago were few and far between, and his one visit to Mankato had been cut short by duty.

Two months had passed rapidly. She had made only two trips between the cities in that period, mostly to visit Logan, but also to help with vaccination oversight in Illinois. Everyone in the Midwestern states who would submit to inoculation had been vaccinated. Most people wanted the vaccine, of course, yet there were those who refused it, either on religious or other unscientific grounds.

Eighty-one percent of Illinoisans had been vaccinated, but not the people of the Caliphate. They believed that the vaccine was poison from the Great Satan. As a result, many within the Caliphate contracted COVID and died. They considered themselves a separate country with different beliefs and laws—Sharia law, to be specific. But the CNF, including Logan and his team, noticed that more and more foreigners were filtering into the Caliphate from abroad. And some of those people were seen bearing arms and inflicting violence on the citizens of the cities that the Caliphate occupied outside of Chicago; Gary, Indiana; and their suburbs. Fortunately, the leaders had stopped beheading people in Grant Park, although there were rumors of many executions still taking place in less glamorous settings.

Kayla stepped out of the arrivals hall, towing her carry-on bag. Logan flagged her over, and they embraced warmly. He grabbed her bag, and they exited the building to where he had his car ensconced in short-term parking. He whisked her away for a pleasant, sunny drive to Lincoln Park, where the trees were showing off their fall colors.

As soon as they reached the hotel room—they stayed in the same one whenever possible—they dove into bed to make up for the missing weeks. An hour later, they were sweaty but happy. They sat up in bed and gazed out the window as they had so many times before. It was pleasant to be together again and share their lives.

"I've been very busy working on V108 again," she murmured. "Some of the results that Dr. Kuan has reported don't make sense to me. He said he has a therapeutic for the virus, but he won't share his results. I'm afraid it may not work as well as he claims it does. Why else would he withhold the results?"

"Well, if he's anything like you, he may want to be sure his treatment is perfect before letting it out of the lab," Logan teased her. "But it's getting awfully late to still be working on it, isn't it?"

"Yes, it is." She sat up against the bed's headboard and let him put his arm around her as they talked. "The mainland negotiators, the PRC Communists, have come to the table after they started seeing massive numbers of cases and thousands of deaths from the next wave of the virus. I think they consider it a delaying tactic because, from what Dr. Wang told me, they don't seem to be taking the disease seriously. Apparently, they don't believe it's as bad as the ROC has said it will be."

"Why not? They can tell that it's a new strain, can't they? A final wave? And they can see how it works: asymptomatic, slow onset, then deadly."

"Yes, but I think they're trying to develop their own treatment and think they won't need our therapeutic. If they can develop something fast enough, then they don't need to make any concessions and can keep up the invasion."

"That sounds risky. They need time to test and distribute any treatment. And they need more than a billion doses."

"Well, they say they won't give up their claim to Taiwan, but maybe they will sign a treaty for fifty years and then take over." Kayla raised an eyebrow.

"Like they did for Hong Kong?" Logan laughed out loud. "They deliberately broke that treaty. No one will trust them again."

"As of last night, they walked out of the negotiations and said they would resume the invasion." She seemed distressed. "The longer they delay, the more people will die. I thought they would act like normal, responsible people and want to save as many lives as possible."

"Remember that Chairman Mao once said he had so many Chinese citizens that he could afford to lose a few million. China would still go on."

"And Chairman Zi seems to see himself as the reincarnation of Mao, so who knows what his logic is."

"Let's not talk about global problems anymore tonight. Let's go out to dinner and have some fun," Logan said.

"That sounds wonderful, but another wave troubles me," she said with concern.

***

Six days later, the day before Kayla was to return home, she received news that the Communists had returned to the bargaining table and were ready to resume the talks if the ROC gave them the treatment to use on key members of the CCP. A few members of the Central Committee had come down with the disease, and they obviously thought that they were not among the expendable Chinese citizens that Zi believed he could lose.

"They probably just want a free sample to use in reverse-engineering a treatment," Logan grumbled. "They do that all the time for chemicals they pretend they invented but have really copied. Their whole economy seems to be based on copying and stealing."

"Well, they aren't all like that. I've met some very smart people on the mainland over the years."

"How about other infections? Is there any data on how widespread the disease is?"

Kayla lifted her cell phone and clicked several buttons. "Here's the data that Dr. Wang sent me yesterday. They have had over a million deaths ... This can't be right! He says they had over a million deaths this week alone. The deaths are spread out across the whole country, mostly in large cities, but there have been no reports of foreign deaths." She stopped and read the text in detail. "You know what's odd? They have noticed that only Han Chinese have been infected and not any of the minorities. That's really strange."

"Oh, why's that?"

"Well, I expected that all people would be affected in the same way. You know that over ninety percent of the Chinese population is Han Chinese, right? The ethnic group can be traced all the way back to the Han Dynasty some four hundred years ago. Another nine-plus percent of the population is made up of about fifty-five other minorities. Of course, they are widely intermarried, although some Hans have made it a point to keep their race pure and only marry other Hans. Nearly all the higher-ups in the Communist party are Han."

Logan was also checking messages on his phone. He read one from Cotes to her: "Chinese invading again. They have plan of attack that negates Stinger missiles. Landing more troops and munitions on Taiwan. Negotiating at same time they invade. Situation unstable."

Kayla said, "I'd better contact Dr. Wang and see what's going on. His message is a day old. He may have more recent news." She began to write a text message to Wang while Logan poured a glass of water into the flowerpot. The geranium was growing bigger every week, and he had transplanted it in a larger pot.

Logan frowned and checked his watch. "Hey, listen, why don't we go for a walk in the park while we can and then have lunch at the little café by the zoo?" He smiled at her and walked over to stand next to her by the window. "We can talk about the world's problems later."

She finished her text and looked up with a grin. "Sounds great to me. Let's go."

They left the hotel on foot and crossed over into Lincoln Park. It was a sunny day but chilly; they had to wear jackets and hats to ward off the cool breeze. The wind was steady from the west, forming small whitecaps on the lake surface, which suggested a storm was heading their way. They strolled arm in arm and talked pleasantly about the little things around them—squirrels, dogs, happy people, and colorful trees—anything to take their minds off what was happening in the rest of the world.

After a half hour of walking, they reached the café and sat down inside for lunch. They both ordered bowls of hearty, vegetable beef soup and hot tea. It seemed surreal to be sitting in a café in a park, behaving normally, while people were dying by the thousands from disease and war on the other side of the globe. It was just as surreal that people were dying all over America from disease, starvation, and gang warfare while they ate their simple meal.

"What happened to the last of the Antifa guys you captured? I heard they fought to the last man and only a few surrendered," Kayla asked between spoonfuls of soup.

"You're right," he said. "Thirty-six surrendered, and only twenty-three of those lived after we got them to the hospital. We have a team interrogating them to find out what happened at the end. You see, so few survived that we don't understand the inner workings of their group. Most of the leaders died, and few left any kind of legacy documents. It's like a tribe that has largely vanished into history."

"Amazing to die like that. I suppose they didn't know that the whole world wasn't so dedicated to self-destruction."

"Well, if you're an anarchist, maybe it's the consistent way to go." He chuckled. "What a waste, though. And all the destruction and killing they did was so meaningless. And for what?"

"What about the Caliphate? When will the CNF begin to deal with them?"

"We aren't ready for that yet." He was disturbed by the idea. "They are too strong and seem to be getting help from outside sources. We have to stop that before we can do anything. So we're planning to intercept their supply route soon."

Kayla's phone chirped, and she stared at the screen. "Oh, look. It's Dr. Wang." She smiled as she punched the Talk button and held the phone so that Logan could also hear. "Hello, Dr. Wang. How are you?"

"I am as well as I can be under the circumstances, Dr. Grimley," Wang said. "I hope you're well also. Are you on a secure line?"

" . . . Oh no. I don't have a secure phone with me. Let me call you back shortly on a different line." She hung up and stared at Logan. "I wonder what's happening."

"Let's go back to the hotel, where we have some privacy, and you can call back on my coded phone. OK?"

They hustled back to their room. They didn't say much. Logan worried that something catastrophic had happened. They sat at the coffee table with the secure phone in front of them. Kayla keyed in Wang's number and punched the Speaker function.

When Wang answered, Kayla said, "OK. I'm secure now. We can talk. The commander is on the line too. What's the matter?"

"We have had a catastrophic setback here. We have learned some things that I didn't know until an hour ago."

"What happened?" she asked with concern in her voice.

"How should I begin? You know that Dr. Chin worked with the virus you brought us to make it more useful. He weaponized it in a certain way to make it more easily deliverable to the population so his agents could distribute it on the mainland."

"Yes, and I was very concerned about that. You assured me that the illness could be contained by the therapeutic if it had to be. Otherwise, it could be extremely virulent."

"Yes. But what I didn't tell you, or anyone else, was that Chin attached a component to the virus that would only attack people with a certain gene in their system. We call it the Han gene—one exclusive to the Han ethnic group." He paused. "It was actually added as a safety precaution so that only people with the Han gene would be infected. In that way, it couldn't spread beyond China, which would prevent a worldwide pandemic of the type that had led to the COVID crisis."

"Wait a minute! How could he do that? Most of the people on Taiwan and in China are of the Han race. It would be lethal to all of them."

"But we have the vaccine here in Taiwan, and it seems to work well to protect all our people," Wang said cautiously. "Even if it did spread back here, we are largely immune. And all our allies would be largely immune too. Besides, we expected to have the therapeutic ready in case some people did become infected."

"Wait, Doctor," Logan said. "You said you expected to have the treatment. Don't you have that yet?"

"Alas, no. I only found out today that there is no therapeutic. None at all. Dr. Kuan has betrayed us. He did not develop what he had promised."

"Oh no!" Kayla cried. "I thought there might be a problem with his work. He was too secretive about his results. What happened?"

Wang seemed very distressed. "We had a meeting with him today to demand that he explain why it was taking so long to finalize the treatment. What he said was outrageous!" he shouted into the phone.

"What did he say?" Kayla asked in suspense.

"He said he never even started to make a real therapeutic. He had his lab technicians working on related topics, but they didn't realize how he had deceived them. He falsified the data he showed his review team. He never intended to be able to treat the disease!" Wang shouted. Then he paused and sounded like he was coughing uncontrollably. Finally, he returned to the conversation.

"You see, we learned that Dr. Kuan is not only of the Manchu ethnic group, but Chairman Mao treated his family especially badly after the revolution. His family had been prominent in Manchuria, and the Communists killed his grandfather and ruined the family. Drove them into abject poverty. His family has resented the Communists, and especially its leaders, for three generations. He finally saw an opportunity to avenge his family's humiliation."

"That's ridiculous," Logan said. "Why destroy a whole race for the misdeeds of a few power-hungry men?"

"The Communists have done much worse, Commander. Kuan's final words were: 'This is finally the end of the Han Dynasty.' And then he killed himself with a handgun right in front of us."

All three of them sat in silence for nearly a minute. Logan looked at Kayla to gauge her reaction. She shook her head in disbelief, and tears formed in the corners of her eyes.

"The Communists have come back to the table and promised to stop the invasion," Wang continued, "even as they continue to land forces on our island. They want the therapeutic. They think we have it and won't give it to them. They said they will now invade and seize it. But we have nothing to give them."

"How lethal is the virus, Doctor?" Logan asked, incredulous.

"They said that half a million people died in the last day alone. The streets are littered with bodies—so we hear from our sources on the mainland." Wang waited a second and added, "The soldiers they are dispatching are dying almost as fast as they arrive. It is like the apocalypse."

"Oh my God!" Kayla blurted out. "This is all my fault!"

"No, no, my dear," Wang said soothingly. "You developed the mutation of the virus, but we are the ones who misused it. We have failed to control it. We are to blame here in my lab. I'm to blame for trusting Kuan with such an important assignment."

Kayla was overwrought with emotion. "But what can we do now? Half the people in China will die in the next few weeks if there is no treatment." Kayla's face was slack and as white as a sheet, her mouth open in shock.

"That is why I called you, Dr. Grimley," Wang said. "I know I have no right to ask such a favor, but we need your help to find a treatment. You may be one of the few people in the world who can find a way to control this dragon that we have unleashed."

"But how?" she screamed into the phone as she swept one arm in front of her in disgust. "We can't do this quickly. It will be difficult to do at all, but especially with a gun to our head and no time to develop it properly." She paused and stared out the window as tears rolled down her cheeks. "My God! What have we done?"

"I'm afraid we have done a monstrous thing," Wang said so softly that it emerged as a whisper. "We have opened the

Pandora's box of death and must now lock our invention back in the box again."

"I will try," Kayla said. "Maybe we *can* find a treatment. I know of one weakness in the virus. Maybe we can use that to control it." She looked at Logan and reached across the table to take his hand. "But I will need help and resources. And someone I can trust by my side."

"I think we will need the services of the admiral and the commander again to get a sample of the modified virus to you to work with. Can you help me, Commander?" Wang sounded desperate.

"Yes. I can help you with your dragon," Logan said. "But let the two of us talk about it and call you back with a plan. We need to discuss the situation with others too."

"Of course. I can only say that I'm sorry, my friends." Wang ended the call.

Logan and Kayla leaned together and held each other tightly. *What a nightmare,* he thought. *How will we get through this?*

They stared at each other and saw each other's sorrow. They were stunned. Logan had not expected another apocalypse when they had awoken this morning. They clutched each other as they both dealt with the sudden news.

"We can do this. We make a good team, you and I," he said quietly.

They hugged like that for several minutes, staring out the window. As they gazed at the beautiful day outside, they had to acknowledge the grim reality occurring on the other side of the world. The red geranium on the windowsill remained a bright spot in the otherwise overwhelming day.

"It's a strange, new world," Logan said, stunned. "Everything, everywhere seems to be falling apart."

"We can survive," she murmured stoically. "And, one day, it will be better."

The blue surface of the lake ran far out into the distance and merged with the pristine azure of the sky. To the south, dark storm clouds formed, a harbinger of what might still come.

About the Author

F‌red G. Baker is a hydrologist, historian, and writer living in Colorado. He is the author of *Einstein's Raven, ZONA: The Forbidden Land, The Black Freighter*, the *Modern Pirate* series of short and long stories, and the *Detective Sanchez/Father Montero Mysteries* series. He is also the author of nonfiction works such as *Growing Up Wisconsin: The Life and Times of Con James Baker of Des Moines, Chicago and Wisconsin* and *The Light from a Thousand Campfires: Improving Your Hiking, Backpacking and Camping Skills* (with Hannah Pavlik).

***

Request for Reviews

T‌hank you for reading my book. If you enjoyed it, I invite you to write a review on Amazon.com. Reviews are important to help authors get the word out about their work, and I would appreciate your taking the time to write one.

Please look for my other books on Amazon and Kindle Books. Just type in my name to see other titles that may be of interest to you. You can also check out my website at www.othervoicespress.com.